# TIGER THE LURP DOG

## KENN MILLER

BALLANTINE BOOKS • NEW YORK

*This book is dedicated to all those who fought or*
*suffered in the Vietnam War, but especially to the*
*men of the following units:*

"A" Troop, 2/17 Cavalry
Brigade L.R.R.P., 1st Brigade, 101st Airborne
  Division
"F" Company (L.R.P.), 58th Infantry
"L" Company, 75th Ranger Infantry

# CHAPTER 1

**T**IGER THE LURP DOG SCURRIED AWAY FROM THE TENT
and ducked behind the trash barrel as his main man,
Mopar, stormed past smelling of adrenaline and anger. Mopar was trying to contain his anger, but the
nose never lies, and Tiger knew enough to get out of
his way.

Cursing under his breath about his eleven months
in the field going unrewarded, Mopar shouldered his
way into the tent and strode over to his cot. He
kicked at his rucksack and missed, then, deflated,
sat down on his footlocker and shook his fist in the
direction of the operations bunker, where the lieutenant and Pappy Stagg were processing the new
man into the platoon. There was no one else in the
tent but Marvel Kim. Marvel could tell that Mopar

1

was angry, but he refused to be impressed by his anger.

"What's got you so teed off?" he asked, looking up placidly from the M-79 grenade launcher he was cleaning. Marvel was strong and stocky. He had a chubby Buddha face and an Airborne haircut so short that it was little more than a dark shadow on top of his head. He was Mopar's best friend, but the normal things that upset Mopar rarely got a rise out of him.

"It's not good for you to get so pissed," he said. "All this anger is dangerous. Everybody knows that hotheads die young. Now, what's wrong this time?"

Mopar scowled. "It's Pappy Stagg and the lieutenant—a couple of real backstabbers! Here it is, not a week after I sign my extension papers—not two days after they say we're gonna get sergeant's stripes—and what do they do? They bring in a lifer E-6 and tell me he's gonna be our new team leader! Can you believe this shit?"

Marvel Kim shrugged and ran an oily rag through the barrel of the grenade launcher. He had no trouble believing that shit. That was the way the Army went about its business, and unpleasant as it could be, there was no use crying about it. The only thing to do was to wait with an open mind, and see what sort of luck the new staff sergeant brought with him. But Marvel knew better than to try to persuade Mopar of this. Poor Mopar had had his heart set on wearing sergeant's stripes home on his extension leave and bragging to that girlfriend of his, that Sybill Street, about his duties as a recon team leader. And while Marvel figured he owed him a sympathetic shrug, he couldn't see much good in helping him bitch about something that should have been expected.

Mopar was beginning to come down from his first

flush of anger and disappointment, but he was still sore.

"A new lifer!" He frowned and slapped his thigh. "From the way they were carrying on about old times, he's another one of Pappy's Special Forces protégés. That's all we need—another ex-Green Beanie running around telling us how soft we have it, not having to go in the field with gooks!"

Marvel Kim let the word "gook" float past without comment. It was the one Korean word he knew of that had found its way into the military vocabulary, and it would have been impossible to object every time he heard it without sounding like some kind of softheaded peacecreep. He even used it himself from time to time, although he much preferred "dink" or "zip" or one of the other words that had been coined in reference to the Vietnamese.

Marvel sighed, then looked up at the doorway of the tent. "Can it, Mopar," he whispered. "Looks like we got a visitor."

Mopar turned around just as the staff sergeant he'd seen in the operations bunker stepped into the tent. There was a moment of uncomfortable silence as he and Marvel looked first at the new lifer, then at each other, then back at the new man, who was standing there with his hands on his hips, seeming to fill the doorway of the tent.

Marvel smiled and waved an invitation. "Come on in, Sarge!" he said, and the new lifer stepped out of the gloom into the middle of the tent with the light streaming in behind him.

If anything, he looked tougher and meaner than he had when Mopar first saw him in the operations bunker. He'd been standing next to the gaunt and towering Pappy Stagg then, and he hadn't looked as tall as he did now. He had thick shoulders and the neck of a wrestler, but he stood light on his feet—light and alert, and yet relaxed.

He wore a teal blue Special Forces combat patch on his right shoulder, master parachute wings and a Combat Infantry Badge over his left breast pocket, and on the pocket itself there was a subdued, olive-drab Pathfinder patch with wings and torch of black thread. On the other pocket, beneath a barely legible nametag, was an arrowhead Recondo patch. There were Vietnamese jump wings sewn above the nametag, but no wings on the new lifer's green baseball cap, and the cap itself looked like it had just come out of a box in supply. The new man's face was dark from the sun and seemed somehow too long and thin for his neck and shoulders. He smiled, and a network of tiny white scars wrinkled his upper lip, turning his smile into a leer.

"My name," he announced with the faint drawl of a professional NCO, "is Staff Sergeant E-6 Wolverine. But being as how I don't stand on ceremony, you can just call me Wolverine."

He nodded in Marvel's direction.

"You must be Spec Four Kim. Pappy tells me you're a halfway decent radio man, and about the best M-79 gunner in the Army." He smiled again, a little more warmly this time. "But tell me, where in the hell did your mother come up with a name like 'Marvel'—outa a comic book?"

Marvel smiled politely. He'd heard the same line in Jump School and then again from Pappy Stagg when he'd first come into the Lurp platoon, so it wasn't unexpected.

"And you . . . ." The new man looked over at Mopar and tried not to frown. Mopar was a wiry young troop, gray-eyed and thin of face, with a head of light hair too short to comb, yet long enough to stand up in clumps and cowlicks. His uniform seemed to be in order, but there was a thin gold earring in his left ear, and a knotted bodycount rope of green parachute cord around his neck.

4

"You must be Spec Four Mopar. I hear you're going to be my assistant team leader."

Mopar shrugged. He'd been Farley's ATL when he was alive, and before that he'd been J. D.'s number two man on a few missions, and he wasn't exactly bowled over by the honor.

Staff Sergeant Wolverine hadn't had much authority as an E-6 in Special Forces—at least not over American troops—and he tried to remember how to sound commanding but fair as he looked around the tent.

It was a regulation U.S. Army General Purpose Medium tent, with room for ten cots. There were four of the tents in the Lurp compound, three for the troops, and one for the team leaders, Pappy Stagg, and the lieutenant. This tent was the closest to the operations bunker, but by far the shabbiest. Instead of tent poles it was supported on a large wooden frame that allowed for a screen door in front, but the canvas was old and patched, and there were puddles on the ground to show where it leaked. Even so, the bunks were even and well spaced; each man had a footlocker and hooks on which to hang his gear, and for a nice homey touch a few of the bunks were partitioned off from their neighbors by sheets of plywood on which were taped pictures of cars and monsters and naked women.

Sergeant Wolverine pointed to one of the pictures and grinned.

"Now that's what I call a bloodflushin' rodraiser of a *huliding*," he said, throwing in the Vietnamese for "fox spirit," just for the cameras, just to show a little class. He pointed again, with his chin this time. "That one there—with the red hair and the shaved bush and those bouncy little pigsnout tits. Let me tell you troops, I'd eat a mile of commo wire just to hear her fart over a field phone!"

He grinned and ran the tip of his tongue over the

5

little white scars on his upper lip. "Just whose bunk is that? The man has got some excellent taste!"

"Used to be Jessup's," Marvel answered. "He's dead, but we kept the picture. The guy who sleeps there now is on R&R."

Sergeant Wolverine took this in with a judicious nod, then decided to change the subject. "Now these footlockers," he said with a wave of his hand, "I want them moved off to the side of the bunks. We start taking rockets, everybody'll be scrambling for the bunkers, and I don't want nobody tripping over the footlockers. Get them back out of the way."

Wolverine wasn't sure he should have said that. It wasn't a good idea to come into a new unit and start changing things around. But now that he'd committed himself, he knew he had to go on. He pointed to the candle on Marvel's footlocker and frowned.

"Them candles got to go. They're a fire hazzard. Why don't you have electricity in this tent?"

Now Mopar spoke up. "I been asking the same thing myself. They got lights in the team leaders' tent, which is a damn sight further from the generator. I guess we just don't rate."

Wolverine decided to ignore the sarcasm. "Well you rate now," he said. "If I have to kiss ass all the way up the chain of command to LBJ himself, I'm gonna see that you have lights in this tent. I don't take no stumbling dicksteppers out on my team. You're gonna need lights, because before you load up on any insertion ship with me, you *will* have your maps and codebooks memorized. Got that?"

Marvel nodded like a good soldier, but Mopar had had enough of this new lifer and he didn't care who knew it. "Got what? Got enough of you coming in here throwing your weight around, Sarge? Sure, I got enough of that! Got enough sense to study our maps and codebooks? Yeah? Well we got that too, dammit! You can't come in here treating us like a bunch of goddamn Basic Trainees!"

Marvel was trying desperately to shut Mopar up before it was too late, grimacing, shaking his head, rolling his eyes, and tapping his lips with his finger, but Mopar ignored him and went on.

"I've had just about all I'm gonna take of this shit. I don't care who you are, or what you've done—you can't come in treating us like we don't know our job! We don't fuck up—we don't half-step, and that's why we're still alive!"

Marvel thought that Mopar was fucking up pretty seriously, but he sure wasn't half-stepping. He was going all the way, and from the look on the new staff sergeant's face, Mopar was talking his way into either an ass-kicking or an Article 15 and bust back down to slick-sleeve Private E-2. But suddenly the little scars above Sergeant Wolverine's mouth tightened and pulled his lip up into another leering smile. Wolverine held up his right hand and shook his head, still smiling.

"All right, all right. I've heard enough. Pappy said you'd be a might touchy, and I can see the old buzzard was right. He also said you're a good man, and maybe he's right about that, too." Wolverine paused and tugged on the bill of his baseball cap, then sighed and shook his head once more.

"Now, I'm gonna let you slide this time, Spec Four Mopar—just to show how big my heart is. So let's have no more of this contentious bullshit, and we'll get along fine." He glanced over at Marvel, then turned back to Mopar and nodded. "Now, I want you to round up the rest of the team. I'm gonna go stow my gear, and I want everyone here when I return. I don't care what sort of detail they're on—pull them off it and get them back here. You got that?"

Mopar nodded unhappily. He got it all right, but he wasn't going to say so out loud.

Wolverine turned and started for the door, then stopped and turned back around.

"One more thing," he said, suddenly worried that he'd come on a tad too strong and was getting off on the wrong foot with the troops. "I told you my name and I expect you to use it. Let's have no more of this 'Sarge' bullshit. You just call me 'Wolverine' or 'Sergeant Wolverine' and we'll get along fine. Got that?"

Marvel nodded, but Mopar waited until the new staff sergeant was gone before answering.

"Got it Sarge." He hefted an imaginary foot-long penis in his hand and shook it at the doorway of the tent. "Got it *dangling,* you fuckin' Lifer Pig!"

He turned on Marvel Kim, who was grinning that goofy grin of his, and appeared to be on the verge of giggling.

"You think this is funny, don't you, you silly gook? All your talk about luck and omens and figuring the odds, and you can't spot bad luck and trouble when it comes walking into the tent. Always looking to the future, huh? You think he's got two, maybe three tours? Shit, Marvel! You're looking so far down the line you miss out on the bad luck that's at your feet. If that prick hadn't come into the platoon we'd both be making sergeant, and I'd be a Team Leader! That's bad luck. Marvel—bad luck in the here and now!"

Mopar swung his boots up on his cot and stretched out with his hands clasped behind his head.

"Giggle away, you goofy dork!" he said, breaking into a smile now, in spite of himself. "And while you're at it, you better step outside and police up Tiger. He was avoiding me the last time I saw him."

Wolverine shook his head and sat down on one of the footlockers. They were still in the aisle, still blocking the way to the bunker, but he decided not to say anything about that now. He wasn't feeling as much like a hard-driving leader of men as he had ten minutes before. He took off his baseball cap and scratched the top of his head, and even Mopar, who was still reluctant to give him the benefit of the doubt, had to admit that he looked a good deal less formidable than he had on his first visit to the tent.

"This is the whole team? Two Spec Fours and a raggedy-ass little brown and black dog?"

He glanced over at Tiger, who was curled up on a pile of dirty fatigues, chewing contentedly on an old green field sock. With his dirty brown coat and black stripe markings, Tiger looked like he'd been born in a camouflage suit. He was a medium-small dog, lazy and self-indulgent, yet alert and shifty—a true recon dog. He looked up at Wolverine and wagged his tail in casual greeting.

"What's he do? Carry the support radio?"

Marvel Kim looked over at Mopar and saw that he wasn't in the mood to answer, so he answered for him.

"Tiger's the sneakiest little thief and coward in the world," he said. It was exactly what Mopar would have said, but Marvel didn't say it quite as well. "Mostly he sleeps and eats and pisses on things. But when we come in from the field he's always there on the berm above the chopper pad, wagging his tail to welcome us back. It's good to see him there, even if he won't come down off the berm until the pilots kill their engines."

This wasn't the answer Mopar would have given, but it was much closer to the truth. Mopar credited Tiger with all sorts of unlikely wisdom and insight, and it was just as well that he hadn't bothered to speak up, even though Wolverine had directed the question to him in the first place.

"So this is it? This is Team Two-Four of the Long-Range Reconnaissance Patrol?" Wolverine sighed and put his cap back on his head. "Where the hell is the rest of the team, for chrissake?"

Now Mopar spoke up.

"Two of them's dead. Gonzales is on R&R, and Ketchum got out of the Army. We've been floating—filling in on the other teams and pulling more than our fair share of radio relay."

Mopar hated radio relay. While Marvel Kim thought it was deceptively dangerous duty, sitting on a fire base with nothing but straightleg artillery for security, Mopar just hated the boredom and frustration of following the teams on the map and missing out on all the fun they were having out there in the mountains.

"Well, you can forget about that." Wolverine was pleased to note the impatient scorn with which Mopar had mentioned radio relay. "I'm the ranking team leader in this platoon, and I'll go tooth and nail to get us missions. If you guys are as good as that old buzzard Stagg says you are, I'll see that we spend ninety percent of our time in the field."

It was an extravagant promise. There was no way any reconnaissance unit could get that much field time. But Wolverine was determined to spend as much time as possible out in the field, even if it meant volunteering the team for rinky-dink security patrols or even point work for the infantry. Just about anything was better than sitting on radio relay or filling sandbags in the rear.

"All right," Wolverine stood up and stretched. "Now that we got that out of the way, I think I'll take me a little stroll around the compound—get in some terrain familiarization. Anyone want to show me around?"

He addressed the invitation to both of them, but since Marvel Kim had finished cleaning his M-79 and was now working on his rifle magazines, it was up to Mopar to accept. He got to his feet slowly and took his time putting on his floppy Lurp hat. He pulled on the brim and styled it until his eyes were lost in shadow, then reached down and snatched the sock away from Tiger.

"Come on, you mutt!" he said, smiling slightly now that he was done with his snit. "Let's show this cherry E-6 around the Lurp compound."

Tiger sprang to his feet, snapping at the sock and wagging his tail happily.

Mopar had no idea how much better he smelled with his anger blown away.

# CHAPTER 2

NESTLED BETWEEN THE CHOPPER PADS OF THE 23RD AIR Cav on the north and the muddy brown warehouse tents and dark green conex containers of the 7077th Support and Supply Battalion on the south, the Lurp compound was not in the most distinguished company. To the east of the compound, separated from the sleeping tents by a couple of rolls of concertina wire and a shallow trench, was the neatly sand-bagged Cav mess hall and a corner of the sprawling Cav motor pool, with its sheds and oil drums and trucks and burned-out helicopter hulks. Directly across the road from the Cav mess—the Slop Shop—was the fenced-in compound of Brigade S-2 Intelligence—the Two Shop.

Although neither of these institutions contributed

much to the tone of the neighborhood, they were important even so. When the Lurps weren't in the field, when they tired of their own freeze-dried Long-Range Patrol rations, they were always welcome in the Cav mess, even though they pointedly ignored the Cav's uniform code and insisted on dining in their grubbiest "tiger-stripe" camouflage fatigues.

The Lurps—all of them except the lieutenant, Pappy Stagg, and the commo chief, Sergeant Johnson—were much less welcome in the Two Shop than they were in the Slop Shop. The Lurp platoon was normally under operational control of Brigade S-2 Intelligence, and the results of their patrols supplied most of the information that the Two Shop wizards processed and analyzed and turned into what passed for intelligence. But the Lurps were boisterous, loudmouthed, and far too curious to be welcome in the Two Shop, and a great deal of hostility existed between the enlisted men of the two detachments.

To the west of the compound, beyond the concertina wire at the far edge of the Lurp chopper pad, was the bunker line, and beyond that the perimeter of the base camp. Abandoned rice fields stretched a few miles from the perimeter into the foothills. Some of these foothills had only a few years' growth on the paddy terraces that had once gleamed like jade stairways on the slopes and in the draws. Even now, from the air, the terraces looked like steps, but mossy steps, treacherous steps that led into the dark and foggy mountains behind them.

While Tiger sniffed the guylines and lifted his leg against the antennas on top of the operations bunker, Mopar and Wolverine paused on the high ground between the bunker and the tent, and looked out at the mountains.

"There must be a million gooks out there," Mopar said, shaking his head in awe at the thought of there being that many gooks in the whole world. There was an odd, wistful tone to his voice that Wolverine noted with approval. A good recon man was, above all, curious, and Wolverine was glad that his new ATL could look out at the mountains and get to wondering what-all was waiting out there for him.

They jumped off the bank onto the muddy compound driveway and trudged down to the gate. It wasn't really much of a gate—just a barricade of steel and barbed wire that could be moved across the drive, a plywood sign announcing that this was the compound of the Headquarters & Headquarters Company Long-Range Reconnaissance Patrol Platoon, and another, smaller sign warning all visitors to report to Brigade S-2 for entry clearance—but everybody called it the gate for lack of anything better.

"Don't pay no attention to that sign," Mopar said. "We don't get many visitors. But anyone who wants to can just walk on the compound. We only pull the barricade across at night. But hell, we know it ain't enough to keep anyone out. The only thing to challenge any unauthorized visitor would be Tiger's barking—and he's the quietest dog I ever saw."

There had been plans to put up a real gate and a real sign, an arch with jump wings and Ranger tabs hanging from it, but Pappy Stagg had vetoed that idea. Pappy felt that it'd be a waste of time and money, and anyway, he already had his hands full trying to get the Lurps to keep a low profile, and a gaudy compound sign wouldn't help things at all.

"We don't really need a gate," Mopar explained. "None of these rear-echelon Legs ever come poking around. They figure the least we'd do if we catch them nosing around would be to laugh at them, and the most we'd probably make them play catch with a baseball grenade. They don't come around, so we don't need a gate."

Whenever he came out of a snit Mopar became garrulous and friendly, as if in compensation for having been a sulky prick while the snit was still on.

"Now down the slope there's the chopper pad," Mopar said with a wave of his hand. "You know; ropes and rope ladders and McQuire rigs—we even have a bunch of parachutes we'll probably never get to use."

Mopar wondered if Wolverine had ever infiltrated into a real-life target area by parachute, or if all of his jumps had just been training. He started to ask him what he'd been doing in Special Forces, then thought better of it. If he'd been doing anything interesting, Mopar realized, he probably would not be willing to talk about it right off with someone he hardly knew.

"Over there—hell, you can smell it from here— that's the shithouse."

Mopar waved at Team Two-Two's pointman, Bill Kemp, who was pulling the shitcans out the back of the latrine so that he could burn off yesterday's accumulation of shit with diesel fuel.

"It's a three-holer, and Pappy scrounged up some real toilet seats, so we don't get splinters in the ass every time we sit down to relax."

They paused next to the rigging shed while Tiger sprayed the skids of the helicopters on the pad, then moved on past the supply tent and commo shed for the ammo bunker and the sandbagged firing pit where the men tested their weapons before each mission.

"We got to turn in all of our demo and grenades and special weapons when we come back from a mission," Mopar said when they passed the ammo bunker. "Seems chickenshit to me, but Pappy runs a tight ship when it comes to some things."

Wolverine wiped the sweat from his forehead with the back of his hand and lit a cigarette with a survival-pack lighter.

"What about smoke grenades?" he asked. "You don't turn those in, do you?"

Mopar nodded. "Smokes, frags, gas, det cord, Claymores—everything but our ammo. Pappy says he don't want us getting ourselves blown away back in the rear. Says it's unfair to the poor gooks who got to live out there with the leeches and snakes for us to kill our own selves off and keep them from getting a fair shot at us."

Mopar paused and looked over at the jeep that was coming through the gate.

"Did you know Pappy Stagg before coming to the platoon?"

Wolverine nodded but didn't volunteer any specifics.

"Well then you know how he is," Mopar said. "He's the best Top in the whole fucking Army. But he does have his ways."

The jeep had pulled up on the drive beneath the operations bunker, and Pappy Stagg was down there next to it, joking with the driver, who was off-loading two red nylon mailbags.

"I gotta go, Sarge," Mopar said. "I'm expecting a letter from this girl. And I want to beat Marvel to the newspapers." He waited for Wolverine to nod in dismissal, then raced off for the bunker with Tiger bounding along beside him.

Wolverine watched them for a few seconds, then threw down his cigarette and ground it under his heel.

"Sweet Jesus," he said under his breath, "don't let them catch up with me here!"

# CHAPTER 3

Wolverine was not named Wolverine when he first joined the army. He'd been only seventeen then, and he'd enlisted under his original name, over the forged signature of his father, the Reverend Doctor Matthew Wolverton of the Living Message of God Full Gospel Church.

The recruiting law was very specific: No one under the age of eighteen could be enlisted without parental consent; and there was no way that the Reverend Doctor would have given his consent if it had been sought. He had already secured a clerical scholarship for his son, and if Three Rivers Bible College had been good enough for him, than it was good enough for the boy. The Reverend Doctor Wolverton had always struggled to do the best he could for his

17

only begotten son, and it was his God-given responsibility to guide him along the paths of righteousness and Christian living, and having preached the Gospel at revival meetings outside military bases from Alabama to Washington State, he knew that soldiers were a sinful lot, given to the evils of strong drink, foul language, and immoral women. There was no way he would have signed, and so Wolverine was forced to sign for him. The recruiter was behind on his quota for the third month, so was forced to overlook the obvious forgery and send the young recruit on his way with a few words of advice: "Keep your mouth shut and your ears open, and you'll do all right."

All through Basic Training and Advanced Infantry Training, Wolverine strove to follow this advice. When the drill instructors spoke, he listened and tried to memorize everything they said. At night during his stint of firewatch in the barracks, he would pace up and down between the racks of sleeping men, practicing his drawl, repeating memorable phrases, and checking his posture from time to time in the reflection of the barrack's window.

When the other trainees sat around talking about women and cars and home, Wolverine always stayed on the edge of the conversation. He nodded when the others nodded and laughed when they laughed, but he tried to keep his mouth shut and his ears open, just as the recruiter had suggested. It wasn't until he got on the bus that would take him to Fort Benning to qualify as a paratrooper that he felt confident enough to join in laughing and shouting and bad-mouthing back and forth with the other guys. He had purged the last vestiges of evangelistic hyperbole from his speech, he no longer had to worry about sounding like a preacher's kid, and he was determined to leave his Full Gospel past behind him.

It wasn't until the morning of his fifth parachute

jump that the past caught up with him for the first time. He was "S"-rolling his parachute on the Drop Zone, and feeling high and happy and excited to have that last, qualifying, jump behind him, when a tall, bald chaplain, a major, drove up in a jeep and checked the roster number on his helmet against a list on the top of his clipboard.

"Excuse me, son, are you Private Wolverton?" the chaplain asked, his voice genial with Christian fellowship and the assurance of rank.

There was no use in lying, so Wolverine just nodded, mumbled an unhappy "Yessir," and finished rolling his chute.

"And is your father the Reverend Doctor Matthew Wolverton of the Living Message of God Full Gospel Church's Roving Outreach Mission Bus?"

Again there was nothing to do but nod and mumble another "Yessir."

The chaplain opened his zippered notebook and took out a sheet of orders.

"I'm afraid I have some bad news, son," the chaplain said, and Wolverine—worried that he was about to be thrown out of the Army for illegal enlistment on the very day he qualified as a paratrooper—turned away to hide the tears of frustration that had welled up so suddenly in his eyes.

"There's been an accident, son," the chaplain said, looking down solemnly at his clipboard and notebook. "A very bad accident. Both your parents are in the hospital in Washington State. Here, these are emergency leave orders. It took a while for us to track you down, but I had them cut as soon as I found you. Hop in, you can turn your chute in for a shakedown and I'll give you a lift back to the barracks."

Against his wishes, Wolverine got in the jeep and, after turning in his parachute, rode with the chaplain all the way back to the barracks, trying his damnedest not to smile, or whistle, or let on how he felt. The chaplain had said nothing about a discharge.

By six that evening Wolverine was on a plane bound for Seattle, and by noon the next day he was sitting in a chair by the window in his mother's hospital room, looking out at the green lawns and the mountains beyond. His father was in surgery, and his mother was busy praying. When she finished her prayers, she cleared her throat and reached over to touch the copy of *Peyton Place* on her nightstand. She pulled her hand back as if it had been burned, then turned her pale blue eyes on her son.

"Trash!" she hissed, unable to rail in her full church voice because of her broken ribs, but still capable of the righteous venom that had made her the ideal wife for the Reverend Doctor Wolverton.

"Pornography! Ungodliness! Unclean profanity!" She struggled until she was sitting half upright and could point at the paperback detective novel she'd thrown to the floor. Wolverine rather liked the blonde on the cover, but he didn't feel combative enough to say so.

"Crime!" she said. "Immorality!" She paused to gather her strength before flinging her hand toward the book on the chair next to the door.

"*The Ugly American!* I know what that's about! Treason! Godless Communism! Race-mixing! Oh! The things they print these days!"

"You read it, Ma?"

"Never! Praise the Lord!" She patted the Bible on the bed next to her pillow. "I have my book here. I have the Good Book, the Word of God!" Her eyes narrowed and she glanced suspiciously at the doorway.

"I'm watching these people here," she whispered. "I've got my eye on these doctors and nurses, and that woman—that shameless woman with the book cart. They can hide from each other, but I know, and the Lord knows, what—what obscurity they deal in!"

Wolverine sighed and turned his gaze back to the window. He'd learned years before that it was useless to correct her English. As long as he could remember, "obscure" had meant "obscene," "trivial" had meant "travail," and "fellowship" had been a verb—something that good, decent, God-fearing Christian people did when they got together over churchyard potluck suppers.

"The Christian people in this country ought to get together and put a stop to this sort of thing!" She patted her Bible again, closed her eyes while she recited a passage from the first letter of Paul to Timothy, and then after wheezing and coughing and sputtering into a Kleenex, she went back on the offensive.

"There has to be a way to find out who reads this sort of trash. We need an organization of Christian librarians to keep an eye on people for their own sake—for the sake of their souls."

Wolverine stood up to excuse himself.

"Listen, Ma, I got to go to the bathroom. I'll be right back."

"Sure—go on. Do whatever you want. Walk out on your mother, just like you did before. Go on. Your father—God preserve him!—is still in the operating room, but you can't sit still long enough to find out if he's dead or alive. You have to be on your way. Back to your disgraceful ways—sinning, and drinking strong drink, and Heaven knows what else! Someday—someday you'll wake with your internal soul lost forever, and you'll cry out to Jesus. But it'll be too late. Go on! Walk out on your dying mother—I'll pray the Lord to forgive you!"

"Ma! I only said I was going to the bathroom!" Wolverine had protested, but it did no good. His mother had opened her Bible and was reading to herself, her lips moving and her finger tracing the words, and she refused to acknowledge her prodigal son.

That was the last time Wolverine saw his mother. Six months later, a few weeks past his eighteenth birthday, with the help of his company commander and the Catholic battalion chaplain—both of whom were sick and tired of having to respond to postcard inquiries about the moral health of his companions—Wolverine petitioned the Judge Advocate General for a change of name. He got the name change he wanted and in the process won a twenty-dollar bet from his first sergeant, who had doubted the Army would approve a name like "Wolverine." From then on, Wolverine always said that he came from the logging country, where men were men, and sissies who couldn't take the work and ran off for the soft life of an Airborne soldier were unwelcome to return. It was a good lie, a classy lie. And since Wolverine always told it with a grin, for the most part people believed it.

But there was still no running away from the past, still no escaping the eye of the Lord and the undying concern of his vigilant Christian librarians.

"Sweet Jesus, let's make us a deal," Wolverine said as he sat down on his bunk in the team leaders' tent and lit another cigarette with his survival-pack lighter.

"You keep your propaganda out of my mail call, and I'll promise that if I die with a weapon in my hand I won't blindside you when I get to Heaven!"

# CHAPTER 4

**W**OLVERINE WAS NOT THE LEAST BIT EMBARRASSED the next day, when he came thundering into the team tent, hollering for Mopar and Marvel to get their gear together and meet him down by the chopper pad in an hour, ready to pull a five-day radio relay on Firebase Alexine. Only the day before, he'd promised to kiss ass all the way up the chain of command to LBJ himself—if that's what it would take to get them out in the field where they belonged. But with Gonzales still on R&R and the team already understrength to begin with, Pappy Stagg was as high up as he had to go, and another dull stint of radio relay was the best mission he could get his new team.

Mopar and Marvel grumbled and bitched as they

23

got their gear together and trooped on down to the chopper pad, but by the time they climbed aboard the helicopter that would take them to Alexine, their attitudes had improved considerably, and they seemed glad to get away from the compound for a while—even if they were only going to dull and muddy Firebase Alexine.

"I know what you're both thinking—I promised you better than this," Wolverine allowed when they were finally set up in the radio bunker on Alexine and could lay back, drinking C-ration coffee and waiting for first light, when Team Two-One's mission—and their own in support of it—was scheduled to begin. "I know it must rag your asses to hear the way those chumps on Two-One were carrying on about their mission—all that bragging about how 'J. D.'s Rangers' gonna do this, 'J. D.'s Rangers' gonna find that, and so on. But that's just tough shit. As soon as your man Gonzales gets back, soon as we have a full team, we'll get our chance to show that crazy nigger J. D. and his band of red-neck cutthroats the proper way to run a Long-Range Recon Patrol. I know I promised you more field time and an end to this radio relay bullshit. But this is the Army, not some pie-in-the-sky Sunday school, and you're gonna have to get used to the fact that promises don't count—not even when someone as upright and honest as your new team leader makes them."

Wolverine smiled, and stretched, and farted contentedly. He and Two-One's team leader, J. D., went way back. When Wolverine had first come across J. D., they were both young privates fresh out of Jump School, newly assigned to the 82nd Airborne Division and determined to make names for themselves. J. D. had always had more flair than foresight, and back then he'd always been the first to volunteer for anything exciting, difficult, or dangerous. He was the first of their group of new paratroopers to jump

24

number two man, behind the stick leader, where he could see out the door beforehand—which had then seemed a daring and prestigious thing to do. J. D. was the first to make PFC and Spec Four, the first to smart off to their terrifying bear of a platoon sergeant—and the first to be busted back down to Private E-1. J. D. was always the first to wade into any beerhall brawl, the first to drain his mug in chugalug contests—and, of course, he was always the first to tell the world of his exploits.

Wolverine and J. D. had started off together in the same platoon, and then they'd gone their separate ways—J. D. off to Ranger School, first as a student and then an instructor, and Wolverine off to Special Forces. Now, at last, they were in the same unit again, and Wolverine was looking forward to this stint of radio relay as a chance to find out whether J. D. was half as good as he said he was.

"There's a lot of interesting missions coming up," Wolverine promised. "And you can count on us getting our share of the fun. Old Stagg might have stretched things a bit to con me into this platoon, but I know he didn't flat-ass lie. Still, my Mama—bless her holy little heart—she didn't raise no fool. I don't take no dicksteppers on my team. If you want to stay with me and come out of this tour alive, you gotta be smart and you gotta be hard. Do you got that?"

"Got it, Sarge."

"Fine. By first light tomorrow—before Two-One goes in—I'm gonna quiz you both on the codebook. If you don't have it memorized, you're gonna be in a heap of trouble. Is that clear?"

"Clear, Sarge," Mopar mumbled unhappily.

"All right, now. If you got that down, we'll get along fine." Wolverine dug a pack of cigarettes out of his rucksack and lit up with his survival-pack lighter. He looked up at the sandbagged bunker ceiling and blew a lazy series of smoke rings. He was taking his time, but he wasn't through talking just yet.

"Enough of all that," he said. "We'll get our missions. But in the meantime, we got us a job of radio relay to perform, and we're gonna do the best damn kick-ass job of it that this platoon has ever seen. I expect you to practice strict commo discipline, you hear me? No talking over the horn—I want to hear nothing but whispers. You got that?"

Mopar and Marvel nodded glumly, unhappy at being told how to do their job.

"Now, the commo log will be perfect. No breezy bullshit—but I want every damn crackle of static recorded. The maps will be kept up to the minute and the overlays kept dry. You two got that?"

It was Marvel's turn to respond. "Got it, Sarge!"

"Fine." Wolverine nodded. "Now, one more thing we best get straight right now: When there's no officers around, you don't have to be so damn polite. I told you before, lay off this 'Sarge' bullshit, O.K.? I had to make my own name for myself, and I like it. So just call me 'Wolverine' and we'll get along fine. But don't go forgetting that my namesake's the meanest motherfucker in the whole North Woods— and I'm three times his size and four times as mean as he ever thought of being. You two bandits got that down clear in your minds?"

"Got it, Sarge," said Mopar, "we've got it coming out of our ears!" As long as Wolverine insisted on talking like a lifer, Mopar was determined to keep on calling him Sarge.

"Very good," said Wolverine with a smile. "I think we're gonna get along just fine."

They did get along just fine, cramped together, all snug and cozy, in the leaky radio bunker on Firebase Alexine. And the field team, J. D.'s Rangers, got along just fine, out in the rain and wind and misty darkness on the rim of the Aloe Valley, for J. D. had grown himself a crop of good sense in the years since Wolverine had last served with him. Or at least it seemed that way, for he had stuck to the high ground, monitoring the trails that led over the ridges from the valley, and even when a twenty-man supply column struggled past his position, slipping and cursing in the rain, J. D. had resisted the urge to open up on them, choosing to sit tight instead, to report them but let them pass by, unaware that they'd been observed.

At the end of the mission, when word came over the horn that J. D.'s team was safely aboard the helicopter and flying home to the Lurp compound, Wolverine put down his canteen cup and lit a cigarette—his first that morning—out of sympathy with the men on the field team, who were certainly all lighting up now in the extraction ship, for such seemed to be the custom on every recon team in the Army.

"Not bad," he admitted with an embarrassed grin and a fond shake of his head. "Not bad at all. Here I was all worried that crazy nigger would do something brave and stupid, but he kept his cool right nicely. That's the way to run a recon mission—all sneaky and cool. It's not that hard, you know. But if you don't get wise, you don't survive—and by the time I'm through with you, we're gonna have the wisest and sneakiest Lurp team this man's Army has ever seen. That's an ironclad promise I'm giving you now, troops. An ironclad promise."

# CHAPTER 5

T HE MAJOR IN CHARGE OF THE TWO SHOP WAS RATHER
fond of the Lurps. Sure, they tried hard to live up to
their reputation as troublemakers and mavericks,
but they were unquestionably the elite of the Brigade, and without them the Two Shop would have to
depend on the notoriously unreliable Red Agent reports of indigenous spies and the murky conjecture
of the Aerial Photo Examination Section in order to
prepare intelligence summaries for the general.
Without the Lurps there would even be a paucity of
Electronically Derived Intelligence, for who else was
there to plant the Black Boxes and other sensing devices along suspected enemy infiltration routes?

The Lurps were the only combat element of Brigade Headquarters, and without them the major

would be just another staff officer, like all the other majors in the Brigade. But with the Lurps under operational command of the Two Shop, the major was at least in nominal command of American combat troops, and that would surely improve his chances of an early promotion to lieutenant colonel.

The major was so fond of the Lurps that he worried about their safety. It didn't bother him to lose an occasional man, or even an occasional team in the field—that young maverick lieutenant of theirs wrote all the letters to the next of kin. But the major was determined not to lose anybody, whether a Lurp or an intelligence analyst, to an enemy rocket. He hated to think what would happen if a 122-millimeter rocket should impact on the chopper pad while the Lurps were waiting for insertion or practicing their rappelling. So he directed the lieutenant to have his men build a bunker alongside the rigging shed by their chopper pad.

Because Team Two-Four was still understrength and unable to go to the field, the task of filling the first batch of sandbags for the bunker fell to Mopar and Marvel and Gonzales, and the supervision of the detail was assigned to Staff Sergeant Wolverine. But because Wolverine had spent too many years in the egalitarian camaraderie of Special Forces to allow himself to stand idly by as his men did all the work, the overall supervision of the sandbag detail fell to that lazy little mutt, Tiger the Lurp Dog.

"Look at him, stretched out on top of the sandpile just as comfortable as can be while we're sweatin' our asses off, breakin' our backs to fill sandbags," Mopar said, shaking his head in admiration. "Tiger ain't done a lick of work in his life, and he's a damn sight happier than we'll ever be."

Tiger perked his ears forward at the mention of his name, but he didn't bother to move—not even when

Gonzales scooped a shovelful of sand from beneath his tail.

"It ain't that he can't dig—hell, I've seen him throw more dirt than a backhoe when he wants to bury a bone. But that was fun, and this is work. And Tiger, he don't never confuse the two."

Mopar tilted his shovel over the empty sandbag that Marvel was holding open for him, dumping the sand half in the bag and half over Marvel's hands.

"Next time around, I'm puttin' in to come back as a dog. They might not live as long as we do, but they have more fun, and I can see the advantages of a shorter tour of duty."

Marvel brushed the sand off his hands and wiped them on his pantlegs. He'd been in the Airborne Infantry for five months and in the Lurp platoon for five and a half now, but he was just getting to where he could listen to this talk about short tours without getting depressed, or pissed off and nervous. But he still wasn't to the point where he could hear too much of it and keep smiling. He was determined to live to be a hundred and six years old, topping his grandfather by twenty years to make up for his father's early death, and he would have felt a great deal safer if everyone on the team shared his lofty ambition. It was dangerous and foolish to talk about the advantages of a short tour of duty. But as he'd already pointed that out to Mopar at least a dozen times without effect, he contented himself with a frown and a grunt of disapproval. Mopar refused to admit that it was unlucky to make jokes about short tours and reincarnation, so there was nothing for Marvel to do but change the subject before it brought him down.

"Hey Sarge," he said, grinning over at Wolverine, who was holding sandbags for Gonzales, "I may be wrong, but it seems I remember you saying we'd spend ninety percent of our time in the field. Now, I can take an exaggeration as well as the next man, but here it's been two weeks and we haven't gone out yet. It isn't safe back here, and it's even less safe on radio relay—and while I think the field's generally pretty safe, I don't like going out on someone else's team."

Wolverine tied shut the sandbag Gonzales had just filled and tossed it onto the pile with one hand. He'd been trying to get two more men to fill out the team. He'd begged Pappy Stagg to break up one of the other teams—preferably J. D.'s team, because they all seemed to be good men—and he'd even offered to go recruit some new men into the platoon. But all Pappy ever did was say "Patience. You've got to have patience," and follow up with the suggestion that he use the dead time to train the men he already had.

Wolverine wiped his forehead with his sweat rag.

"We haven't been half-stepping these last few weeks, you know. We just about got our immediate action drills down, and as soon as I can convince you that slackmen aren't supposed to carry radios, we'll be ready for anything. I've run a four-man team before, and I can do it again."

Wolverine had tried to persuade Pappy Stagg to let him go with the team he had. Four men could move faster and quieter than six could, and Pappy Stagg knew it, but didn't want to admit that he did, citing the Table of Organization and Equipment of a Long-Range Reconnaissance Patrol team, which specified six men.

Marvel smiled. He tied the sandbag that Mopar had just filled and lifted it to the top of the pile. He wasn't as strong as Wolverine was and didn't want to risk a dislocated shoulder tossing sandbags around, so he used both hands. He had to suppress a giggle at the vigor with which Mopar jumped into the debate on his side.

"Bullshit! You can't put the blame on Marvel for walking slack with a radio and then turn around and say we can go as a four-man team!"

Wolverine hadn't intended to blame Marvel, and he couldn't imagine how Mopar had come to that conclusion, but he kept his mouth shut and let Mopar rave on, because it was best to let things come out. He didn't want Mopar to go off into a full-blown snit.

"I'm the ATL, right?" Mopar tapped his own chest with his index finger and favored Wolverine with a defiant stare so righteous and fierce Wolverine had to turn his face to keep from laughing.

"I'm the ATL, and I walk point, right? ATLs don't often walk point, but I don't hear you saying anything about that. Marvel might be a silly gook most of the time, but he's good in the field, and I don't want no one else walkin' my slack or carrying the radio! We got four men only because you can't round up anyone else, and unless you want me to strap a radio on Tiger and have him bark in our situation reports, you better just lay off Marvel. It ain't his fault we only got four men, but you sound like he's trying to hog things!"

Marvel giggled, Gonzales spat, and Wolverine shook his head but didn't bother to defend himself because he, too, was hot, and tired, and bored with sandbags, and didn't trust his own temper.

"You want to take Marvel's radio away, then you can give it to Tiger for all I care!"

Once again Tiger perked his ears, but this time it wasn't at the mention of his name. He lifted his head off his forepaws, glanced off in the direction of the operations bunker, and wagged his tail lazily. Pappy Stagg was coming down to the chopper pad with a clipboard and sealed manila envelope in his hands, and behind him, on the drive beneath the bunker, stood the Two Shop major's jeep, although the major himself was nowhere to be seen. Tiger stood up slowly, shook the sand off his coat, then trotted off to meet Pappy and escort him down to the chopper pad.

Pappy looked at the pile of sandbags and nodded his approval, then glanced at his clipboard and frowned.

"You hoodlums think you're ready for a mission?" he asked, and immediately everyone threw down his shovel or dropped his sandbag and turned expectantly to hear the good news.

Pappy Stagg had to smile. He knew he had a good crew in this platoon. Sure, they didn't care too much about shaving and breaking starch, but they were good field troops, and that's what really counted.

"Now this team leader of yours . . ." Pappy rolled his eyes in Wolverine's direction. ". . . He's been bugging me all week to get you bums out in the field—feeding me so much bullshit about how sharp you are I was goin' to have him arrested for false reporting. But the lieutenant wouldn't go along with me on that, so here we are."

He handed the manila envelope to Wolverine.

"Now the TO and E of a Long-Range Reconnaissance Patrol team is six men, and don't you bums go writin' home tellin' your mothers I'm sending you out understrength, 'cause it wasn't my idea. But Staff Sergeant Wolverine here assures me you can handle it, and the major wants a team, so it looks like you're going."

Pappy Stagg shrugged helplessly and shook his head.

"May the mothers of America forgive me!" he said, while Marvel giggled, Gonzales nodded, and Mopar rubbed his hands in anticipation.

"There's a map and some aerial photos in the envelope, and Sergeant Johnson will have your codebooks and commo information as soon as he gets back from the relay site. Now you better get a move-on—overflight is set for 1700 hours, and insertion is first light tomorrow, so get your shit in order."

He looked down at his wristwatch, and Tiger cocked his head and perked his ears and stood at full alert because he knew what it meant when Pappy Stagg glanced at his watch.

"All right, move on out!" Pappy Stagg barked, and Tiger took a frisky leap to the side and pawed the ground in delight. "I said a four-*man* team! The dog stays here!"

Mopar, Marvel, and Gonzales sprinted off to return the shovels and extra sandbags to supply, and Tiger the Lurp Dog bounded along behind them, then raced merrily on ahead, hoping someone would chase him.

# CHAPTER 6

WOLVERINE HAD WORKED THIS PART OF THE COUNtry before. He'd been running missions for the innocuously named Study and Observation Group then, he and an American lieutenant and a team of six Nung Chinese. He had no trouble now following the river to the Recon Zone without even glancing at his map. When the helicopter approached the RZ, he unfolded his map and studied it carefully, relating the contour lines to the ridges and mountains below him. But as soon as the ship moved on past the western boundary of the RZ, he folded his map and stuffed it back in his thigh pocket.

There was a waterfall out there somewhere, a waterfall that didn't appear on any map, and he was determined to find it if he could. He'd seen it before, on

35

other overflights, and once he'd caught a glimpse of it through a curtain of rain when riding back from a mission across the border. It was a beautiful waterfall—tall and thin, wispy as Ho Chi Minh's beard, yet as graceful as something from an old Chinese landscape painting. But he hadn't been able to find it on a map, and every time he'd ever seen it, he was either too nervous about insertion, too relieved at being extracted safely, or too involved in some upcoming mission to get a good fix on its location. He did know that it wasn't on any of the map sheets for this entire area because he'd checked them all, and he'd never been able to find anyone else who had seen it.

Still, he knew it was there. He'd seen it more than once, and he was certain that he'd seen the same thing each time. It was a waterfall all right, and not a rainbow, not a wispy cloud, and certainly not an optical illusion. Of course, he knew that there was no way for there to be a stream high enough in the mountains to produce a waterfall—the water flowed through the lowlands here—but he knew he'd seen it, and he knew it wasn't a seasonal feature brought on by the monsoon rains, because he'd seen it in the summer, in the winter, and again in the early autumn.

But those sightings had been spread out over a period of two years, and there was a chance—just the slightest chance—that he had seen a different plume of water each time. It wasn't on the maps; it had never been reported as a map correction; and as far as Wolverine knew, no one else had ever seen it. He took the binoculars from Pappy Stagg and leaned out the door of the helicopter to scan the distant mountains.

"Hey, Sarge," Mopar nudged him with his elbow and leaned close to holler over the roar of the rotors, the engine, and the wind, "our RZ is back there.

What're you looking for? You see smoke or something?"

Wolverine shrugged and lowered the binoculars. "No," he said. "I don't see no smoke. Just taking a look, that's all."

Mopar nodded. "If you see a waterfall, let me know. That crazy gook Marvel says there's one out there, but I think he's fulla shit. He ain't never seen it himself, but he says he can feel it, and it's got some luck to it."

Wolverine turned away from the door and handed the binoculars back to Pappy Stagg. "Did he say whether it was good luck or bad?"

Mopar shrugged. "Even Marvel can't figure that out until he sees the damn thing, and you and I know it ain't there."

Wolverine smiled and nodded. "If it's not on the map," he said, "it ain't out there. Water isn't gonna flow uphill just to make a waterfall. Any fool knows that. What's wrong with your buddy Marvel, anyway? All this talk about luck, and whatnot."

Mopar shrugged. "Just his personality."

"Personality? Shit!" Wolverine hollered over the noise of the engine and the rotors. "The Army won't let you have one of those until you make E-7!"

The helicopter looped back off another pass over the RZ and then headed on back to the base camp. Wolverine rode all the way home with his eyes on his map and his right hand tight around the pistol grip of his CAR-15. There was a waterfall out there somewhere, but now that he wasn't the only one who knew about it, he no longer wanted to find it.

# CHAPTER 7

Mopar could never get to sleep the night before a mission. There was always too much to do, too many things to prepare, and too much to worry about. There were maps and codebooks to memorize, map overlays showing proposed and alternate routes of march, Escape and Evasion routes, and rally points to be prepared. Equipment had to be drawn from supply, and grenades, Claymore mines, and demolitions checked out of the ammo bunker. Weapons had to be test-fired, radios checked, morphine and pill kits signed for and distributed. A helicopter overflight of the Recon Zone had to be made, and then after working through late chow, a premission briefback had to be presented to the pilots and representatives of the Two Shop.

By the time all this was accomplished it was usually late at night, and the final hours before trooping down to the chopper pad to wait for first light were usually given over to the preparation of individual gear—spraying boots and pant legs with DDT to keep off the leeches, taping down anything that could rattle, filling canteens, selecting rations, and packing and unpacking rucksacks and moving things around until the weight rode easy on the straps, and everything that might have to be reached instantly fell easily to hand.

Mopar always had time to worry the night before a mission. Once he was on the ground in a Recon Zone he never had any trouble relaxing, but the night before insertion his stomach always ached so badly he was forced to make hourly trips to the shithouse, and no matter how warm the night air might be, he always felt a chill.

Tonight he was more nervous than usual. On the overflight he had argued with Wolverine about his choice of a primary insertion Landing Zone. There was a stream running through the valley in the northwest corner of the Recon Zone, and Mopar had wanted to go in there, on a sandbar where the stream bent to the southeast. But Wolverine had vetoed that suggestion with what Mopar felt was undue and arrogant haste. Wolverine had found an LZ in the south, a long swath of open ground halfway up a ridge. He wouldn't even consider Mopar's sandbar LZ as an alternate, although he had been willing to grant that it should go on the overlays as a possible emergency extraction LZ, in case the team had to get out in a hurry and couldn't make it anyplace better.

"Jesus H. Christ, Mopar!" Wolverine had exploded when the subject came up for the last time, just before the briefback. "I don't have time to argue with you about this. We already have an LZ—*my* LZ—marked down on the overlays. The pilot that flew that overflight is inserting us tomorrow, and he likes it. And, goddamn it, I'm sure I know more about LZ selection than any Spec Four in this man's army! So why don't you just shut the fuck up and act like a soldier?"

When Marvel tried to come to Mopar's defense by pointing out that Sergeant Farley, the last team leader, used to insert on sandbars all the time, Wolverine cut him off with a fierce look and a disparaging comment about Farley being so stupid he got himself blown away on one of his wonderful low-ground LZs.

This was the first time any of them had seen Wolverine lose his temper, and Mopar—although still angry himself and convinced that his sandbar was an ideal insertion LZ—wisely decided to shut up about it. Marvel and Gonzales had not gone on the overflight and hadn't seen any of the potential Landing Zones, but they were clearly on Wolverine's side. Marvel had only been trying to explain why Mopar liked the sandbar, but he made it clear that he didn't want to go in on it. So Mopar, realizing that he was completely outranked and outvoted, allowed as how he had nothing against a fast, high LZ like Wolverine had chosen and had only been playing the devil's advocate with his sandbar LZ.

Later that night, however, as he sat on top of the operations bunker brushing burrs from Tiger's coat, Mopar gave voice to his misgivings. "High ground . . ." he muttered, pinning Tiger down with his elbow so he wouldn't be able to squirm away from the brush. "Every gook for three ridgelines is gonna be watching the high ground as soon as they hear the ships." Tiger wiggled and squirmed and yipped when the brush caught a tangle of hair in his tail, but Mopar held him down and kept brushing.

"We could come in skimmin' low over the river and unass over that sandbar without slowing down—

but no. Wolverine's got to have his fuckin' high ground!"

Mopar knew that Special Forces reconnaissance teams usually inserted at last light, when most of the enemy troops were likely to be concentrated in the draws and valleys close to the water. But the Lurps went in after first light, usually long enough after first light for the fog to have lifted and the enemy to have moved away from the rivers and streams, back into the high ground. That, at least, was the rationale Sergeant Farley had used for going in along stream beds and on sandbars—that plus the fact that such insertions did not require any slow and highly visible descent of the insertion helicopter—and even if Farley had gotten himself killed on an LZ, it hadn't been close to water, and it was an extraction, not an insertion LZ.

Wolverine's chosen LZ was just too visible from the next ridgeline for Mopar's peace of mind, and if nobody else was willing to listen to him, he could at least blow a little steam Tiger's way without having to worry about sounding like some sort of malcontent pussy. Tiger had never ridden in a helicopter, and he had no opinion one way or the other regarding insertion LZs. All he cared about at the moment was escaping the brush, but Mopar held him tight and wouldn't let him go. Marvel Kim had persuaded Mopar that it was good luck for him to groom Tiger the night before a mission, and while Mopar still had a few doubts, Marvel did know a lot about luck and rituals. He had been right about some strange things in the past, so Mopar always made a point of brushing Tiger before a mission—just in case.

"Someday," Mopar said, putting down the brush and stroking Tiger's back with his hand, "I'm gonna have to take you out with us and let you smell all those good nasty smells out there in the jungle."

Now that Mopar had put away the brush, Tiger relaxed. He licked Mopar's hand and rolled over on his back to have his belly rubbed.

"It's a good thing you don't bark much, but you'll have to get over this fear of helicopters if you want to go with us."

It was total fantasy. Mopar knew that he'd be worried to distraction having to keep track of Tiger in the field. But it was fun to think about, and Tiger seemed to enjoy hearing it, because he sighed, and closed his eyes, and stretched contentedly as Mopar talked.

"That whole place, the jungle is rotting and stinks to high heaven—you'll love it! Maybe we can train you to sniff out trails and caches. You'd like it. I know you would."

Tiger sneezed, then twisted and rolled and scrambled to his feet, his ears back, his ruff bristling, and his nose twitching nervously. He could smell cigar smoke and sweat, and he could hear someone coming up the ramp out of the bunker. It was J. D., Mopar's first team leader and since Farley's death one of the two soul brothers remaining in the Lurp platoon. Tiger, unredeemable bigot that he was, lowered his head and backed off suspiciously.

"Tiger, the Ku Klux Lurp Dog! What's going on, Tiger? You and Mister Mopar here having a nice chat?"

J. D. laughed and stepped out of the darkness at the bunker entrance. He was wearing mirror sunglasses, even though it had been dark for hours. With the tip of his cigar glowing like the red boomlight of a helicopter, he gestured toward the gloomy sea of clouds rolling up on the stars to the west of the perimeter.

"Them's muddy skies, Mister Mopar," he said. "By the first light tomorrow, your whole Recon Zone gonna be sewed up tighter'n a dyke's cunt," he smiled. "But I be out there in *my* RZ, just kickin' ass and takin' names. I be pickin' pockets and icing dinks while you Two-Four clowns be back here burning shit and filling sandbags." He took a puff on his cigar and blew the smoke at Tiger. Tiger sneezed again, then snorted indignantly, and would have jumped off the bunker and disappeared into the shadows if Mopar hadn't grabbed him and held him there.

"Mister Mopar . . . Mister Mopar . . ." J. D. sighed wistfully and shook his head. "You shouldn't never have let that crazy dead nigger Farley talk you onto his team. Now let's examine, what do you have? You have some kind of Wolverine be your team leader, and you find yourself much worse off than before. You'll see in the morning. That fog be setting on your RZ, and you don't be gettin' in. But J. D.'s Rangers—we be out there sneakin', and peekin', and havin' us a high old time." He glanced up at the sky. "One look. That's all it takes and I *know* what kind of weather we be having tomorrow!"

Mopar chuckled. "Where the fuck did you learn about the weather? Trenton? They don't have any weather in Trenton! You're outa your mind, J. D. That soup is movin' in your direction, sure as shit. It might blow over, but it's moving for your area, not ours."

Mopar knew that J. D.'s Recon Zone was half a map-sheet to the north of his own, and judging from the Two Shop briefing they'd sat through together, the place was swarming with NVA.

"You might have to kick a little ass if you can't keep your bums from stumblin' around and snoring," Mopar said. "But you won't have time to stick around taking names."

Mopar was a little jealous of J. D.'s Recon Zone because his own promised to be relatively tame—even if, as he feared, somebody on the next ridgeline was watching the LZ.

J. D. danced off a way and flipped his cigar into a puddle. "Now think on this, Mister Mopar: My Recon Zone be so far back in the NVA rear that they got an R&R center there. You think we're the only ones be gettin' R&R in this war, Mister Mopar? Shee-it! Them NVA got theirselves an R&R center put us to shame. They got them some Chinese bargirls and the best Russian vodka—and it all be waiting for me up there in RZ Zulme. You be stuck back here burning shit down to the shithouse and trying to keep that no-pride Tiger from running off with the used toilet paper, while we be out there capturing some of them sweet Chicom bargirls. Think about the golden opportunity you let slip by! You shoulda stayed on my team, Mister Mopar. Did J. D. ever lie? Baby, you know when I be telling the truth! Chicom bargirls, and you didn't want none!"

He'd thrown away his cigar, but now he lit a Kool, took a long drag, then opened his mouth to let the smoke tumble out, gray, and lazy, and uninhaled.

"Shee-it," he said, all of his bravado gone. "Truth is, I ain't gonna be fucking around doing something crazy this time. I aim to go in nice and quiet and sneakylike, find me the thickest bush I can, and lay dog for three days. We'll be moving just enough to keep Pappy Stagg and the Two Shop happy, but we won't be trying anything bold this time. I leave all that bold bullshit to you Two-Four chumps, on your four-man team. Who do you got for four men, Mister Mopar? You got a Special Forces madman for a TL. Have one crazy gook commo man walkin' slack with an M-79, and a pointman who talks to dogs, then end it off with a Cuban tailgunner who don't know how to talk at all. You be the ones havin' an interesting mission, Mister Mopar. Not us."

Mopar relaxed his grip on Tiger and watched him jump off the bunker and zip off around the back of the tent after a rat or a toad or something.

"That isn't the way Marvel has it blocked out. He's been charting everybody's future, ever since Wolverine came into the platoon. I don't know what's in store for your team, but I do know that Marvel says Two-Four's gonna have a very boring mission."

"Marvel!" J. D. slapped the top of the bunker and cackled with delight. "That boy Marvel's my favorite zip! That boy Marvel's my favorite radioman and my favorite on an M-79. But that boy Marvel's more full of shit than a cholera submarine. That boy Marvel's more superstitious than an Alabama swamp witch. Always be assblowing about luck, and he ain't even been on J. D.'s Rangers! Marvel? What the fuck does Marvel know about RZ Zulme? There ain't no waterfall there!"

The pilots of the insertion and escort ships were down in the operations bunker huddled around the radio, sipping coffee, and waiting for a weather report, and the crew chiefs and doorgunners were pulling last-minute maintenance by flashlight, when Two-Four filed down to the chopper pad. It was still dark—darker in fact than it had been when Mopar and J. D. were watching the clouds roll in the night before—and it wasn't until Gonzales passed around an unfiltered penlight so that the men could check their camouflage face-paint in their signal mirrors that Mopar noticed the gap where Wolverine's front teeth had been. Wolverine caught his stare and grinned to show that he still had the rest of his teeth.

"Never wear my falsies in the field," he explained. "Too shiny." He nudged Marvel Kim to get his attention, then shone the light on his own face and grinned again. "How's it look, Kim? You're the expert on what's lucky and what ain't—you got anything against me leaving my teeth in my foot-locker?"

Marvel knew no more about Wolverine's false front teeth than Mopar did, but he didn't seem the least surprised. He was, however, somewhat puzzled by Wolverine's question.

"No, of course not. Nobody ever said false teeth aren't lucky—but if you feel better without them, then fine. No teeth and false teeth have the same luck. Old men have gaps and false teeth, and that makes them lucky."

Anything having to do with old men was lucky to Marvel Kim.

Two-One, J. D.'s team, was coming down the berm now. They never got down to the chopper pad first because J. D. was fond of the grand entrance.

Gonzales snatched the penlight from Wolverine's hands and shone it on J. D. He was dressed in tiger fatigues, like the other men on his team, and like them he carried a stubby black CAR-15 "Commando" version of the M-16. He carried the same sort of canvas rucksack as the other men, and like them he'd taped down all the snaps and clasps and buckles on his web gear. He wore unpolished jungle boots, like the others, and he'd toned down the highlights of his face with green camouflage paint. From the eyebrows down he looked every bit the standard-version reconnaissance commando—but from the eyebrows up he looked like a pimp. Instead of a floppy Lurp hat, or subdued beret, or a knit watch-cap, or a pirate scarf of camouflage-patterned parachute silk, J. D. was sporting an elegant, pearl gray, skinny-brim Homburg with a black silk hatband and a little green feather.

"Holy shit!"

Wolverine leaped to his feet, laughing and wheezing through the gap in his teeth, and before J. D. could defend himself, Wolverine snatched his hat.

"Hey you toothless ol' Wolverine! Be cool! Give me back my pickpocket hat!" J. D. sounded on the verge of indignant tears, but Wolverine danced away with the hat behind his back.

"Hey, baby, be cool!" J. D. pleaded. "You can't be rippin' off a man's pickpocket hat!"

Wolverine wadded the hat into a ball and tossed it to Marvel, who tossed it to Gonzales, who passed it on to Mopar.

"Sorry, J. D." Wolverine tried to sound sympathetic but it didn't come out that way. "Unauthorized headgear is a major no-no in the Long-Range Reconnaissance Patrol."

J. D. didn't know whether to shit or go blind, or lock and load his CAR-15 to show he meant business and wanted his pickpocket hat returned immediately. Mopar was already on his feet with the hat tucked under his arm like a football, running a zigzag pattern up the berm toward Tiger.

"Mopar! Damn your white ass!" J. D. shouted, but it was too late. Mopar had already passed the hat on to Tiger, and Tiger was tossing his head and growling fiercely as he raced off for the operations bunker with the hat in his teeth.

J. D. started up the berm, determined to recover his pickpocket hat even if it meant chasing Tiger into the bunker. But before he had gone more than a few meters he stopped. The pilots were coming out of the bunker now, and behind them came Pappy Stagg.

"The soup's lifting!" Pappy yelled, swinging his big black head-breaking club of a flashlight over his head. "Crank 'em up! Saddle up, and get your asses on those ships! There's a war on, and if you keep half-stepping and grabassing you're gonna miss out on all the fun!"

J. D. stood still for a second or two, trying to decide whether to chase down Tiger and recover his hat or give it up and join his team on the helicopter. He glanced over his shoulder at his team clambering aboard the insertion ship, and when he turned back around Tiger and the hat were gone.

"Fuck it." He shrugged and started back for the chopper pad. "My bottom lady always did say I was too flamboyant to wear gray."

# CHAPTER 8

Despite Mopar's misgivings, it was a beautiful insertion. The troopship carrying Team Two-Four flew almost due west from the compound, staying high above the fog-shrouded draws and rugged mountains, then circled well to the south of the Recon Zone until word came over the radio that J. D.'s team was safely on the ground. The pilot brought the ship down in a lazy spiral to within a few hundred feet of the jungle canopy, cranked on the airspeed, banked north, then feigned landings on three separate hilltops to the west of the Recon Zone before coming in fast and low over the LZ Wolverine had chosen. As soon as the grassy space where the team was to insert came into view, the pilot dropped suddenly, broke pitch, and flared slightly, ten feet off the ground, while the Lurps jumped out and ran for the woodline. When the last man had unassed, the insertion ship climbed so that its skids could clear the treetops at the end of the LZ, then climbed some more and continued to fly straight and fast and low until well clear of the Recon Zone.

From the time the ship broke pitch over the LZ until the Lurps were safely in the woodline at the end of their Landing Zone only six seconds had elapsed, and the lieutenant, watching through binoculars from the Command and Control ship a thousand meters off to the north, grinned and flashed the thumbs-up sign to the crew chief, for it had been a fast and beautiful insertion, and the air crews deserved some thanks.

A hundred meters into the woods, satisfied that the undergrowth on all sides was now thick enough to hamper flank movement and provide some concealment, Mopar found a relatively open patch of ground and called a halt. Silently the other men moved in and stood back to back with their rucksacks touching to listen for a few seconds to the jungle around them. There was no sound of movement, no crashing in the bush or rattling branches; only the occasional buzzing of an insect or the distant cry of a bird in the far reaches of the canopy and the steady, barely audible dribble-drip-drip of condensed water filtering through the leaves. On a signal from Wolverine the team sat down.

They sat with their backs together like the hub of a wheel, their legs extended in front of them like spokes, each man with his weapon in hand. Marvel Kim and Wolverine exchanged glances, then with a bashful and reluctant half-smile, Marvel handed Wolverine the headset to his radio. Wolverine had allowed Marvel to carry the support radio and take care of air-ground coordination and any artillery fire the team might need to order. Farley had let Marvel make all the routine reports usually without even bothering to check to see whether their maps jibed, and Marvel figured that by the end of the mission Wolverine would be wanting to trade radios just for the sake of convenience. Then, if it became necessary to bring some fixed-wing aircraft or gunships on station or order some artillery fire, Marvel planned to simply go ahead and do his job on the support radio the same way he was prepared to work the command net. There was really nothing all that difficult to any job in the Army, if you kept a cool head and used your mind to figure the odds and techniques involved.

Wolverine took the headset from Marvel and muffled it with his Lurp hat. He eased his left arm out of his rucksack strap, unbuttoned the top of his tiger shirt, and put the headset inside, nestling it in the hollow between his clavicle and his deltoid muscle. Then he reached back and pulled a green sweat towel from his rucksack, draped it over his head and shoulder, and hunkered down to make his transmission.

All Marvel could hear was the squelch breaking whenever Wolverine squeezed the handle to transmit, but even that was so faint a sound he wondered if Mopar, who was sitting with his ears cocked away from the radio, could hear it.

When Wolverine finished his transmission he handed the headset back to Marvel, got a commo check on the radio he was carrying—the support radio—then fished his notebook and ballpoint pen out of his shirt pocket and bent over to write. He hadn't used his pen and pad, nor even a compass, protractor, or map to figure the team's position before his report, but now he was scribbling away with such diligent concentration that Marvel and Gonzales naturally increased the width of the sections of the security wheel they were covering to make up for his absorption. Neither one of them had seen any signal from Wolverine that they were to take over his area of security, but they were good in the field and didn't need a signal.

Gonzales was sure that Wolverine was testing him, trying to trip him up and catch him half-stepping, so he made a point of sweeping his rifle into Wolverine's section of the security wheel where he would be sure to see it. Marvel, on the other hand, assumed that Wolverine had enough confidence in him to expect such consideration, so he only swept with his eyes, keeping his rifle in his own zone and refusing to make a show of it.

Wolverine took out his map, removed it from the acetate, and spread it out on his lap. Marvel had never seen anyone unfold a map completely while laying dog off the LZ after insertion. He wondered if it had been folded incorrectly back in the compound, but it seemed hardly likely that Wolverine would make a mistake like that. Marvel peeked over Wolverine's shoulder and watched him trace along a river that ran through an almost solid maze of wavy contour lines in the northwest corner of the map-sheet, thousands of meters from their own position, way up in J. D.'s Recon Zone.

Wolverine glanced at Marvel and shook his head. He shot a couple of compass azimuths, scribbled some figures on the cardboard back of his pad, and then after studying them for a few seconds and looking back at his map, he crossed out the figures and flipped his pad over to write on the top page. When he had finished writing he ripped off the top page and passed it to Marvel.

"J. D. on high-speed trail . . ." the note began. There was no attempt to write entirely in acronyms and abbreviations—when Wolverine wrote a field note he wanted it to be clear. Marvel read on:

". . . At least 300 NVA/new uniforms/batta boots/

softhats/est. 200 AK, 50 SKS . . ." Marvel smiled to find that abbreviated "est." He read on: "1 confirmed RPK/ many stretchers/heavy packs. Moving W/NW from trail to stream." Marvel could only guess an azimuth or even J. D.'s position without taking out his own map, but he knew that the river that ran through J. D.'s Recon Zone also flowed only a few hundred meters from Firebase Culculine, where the relay team and the artillery support were based. Wolverine—or maybe it had been J. D.—had come to the same conclusion Marvel had: ". . . NVA headed for our R/R." Radio relay; that was hardly an abbreviation to Marvel anymore.

"Six—" This was printed out, and Marvel wondered if Wolverine was such a lifer he felt it disrespectful to let a numeral stand for the lieutenant, "wants us to lay dog here until NVA past J. D. Pass along."

Hoping Mopar would notice that Wolverine was still using a white-paged field pad even though they were now available from supply in discreet shades of light brown and pea green, Marvel passed the note around.

Culculine was sure becoming a bad-luck firebase. Marvel had always felt that it was safer to stay deep in the field, on a real Lurp mission, than to stick around a place like Culculine. The last time the NVA blew a gap in the wire, the leg infantry and the cannoncockers put up a pisspoor fight and wouldn't have been able to keep the gooks out if they hadn't had gunships on call.

When Mopar had read the note and passed it along to Gonzales, Marvel took out his own pad—a green one—and without looking away from his zone of security for more than a few seconds, he scribbled his own note and passed it on to Mopar.

"What did I tell you?" he wrote. "R/R not safe. Don't pass it on."

Mopar nodded, wadded the note up, and stuffed it into his right thigh pocket, under a freeze-dried Lurp ration, where it wouldn't be likely to work out and fall in the jungle to leave trace of their passage.

If Farley were still alive and leading the team, there would have been whispering all around.

For two hours Two-Four lay dog in their first halt position, alternating back and forth as first one man, then another, stood up and took a careful step away from the hub of the wheel to piss away the premission coffee. After piss call it was time to eat. Again each man waited his turn before resting his weapon on his thighs and turning away from his security zone to dig a ration and collapsible canteen out of his rucksack.

Marvel couldn't help thinking about Farley. If he were still alive and felt the wind was blowing enough to diffuse the smell among the trees, he would have passed around a cigarette, or maybe kept one after another going in a chain, because the leeches had wasted no time zeroing in on the Lurps' body heat and needed to be burned off. But Wolverine had made it clear that he tolerated no tobacco in the field, even though he smoked a pack a day in the rear. So the leeches were kept at bay with bug juice, and Marvel had to nibble on a cornflake bar instead of puffing on a cigarette.

It was no big thing. Even Farley had forbidden cigarettes when the air wasn't up to filtering the smoke or when there was no sign of enemy in an area—and on the last few missions before he got killed, that had been most of the time.

While Marvel was nibbling on a cornflake bar and thinking about Farley, Mopar was getting impatient to be moving on. There was a trail just another fifty meters or so uphill, right along the crest of the ridge. Or at least there had seemed to be a trail there on the overflight the afternoon before. Mopar was hot to get on up there and check it out. Wolverine had said it was just an animal path, and there was a five-dollar bet riding on what it really turned out to be. Mopar tried not to fidget, but it was getting harder and harder to sit still. His right leg ached from being straight too long, and he had a charleyhorse in his left leg, even though he'd bent and flexed it every few seconds to keep the blood moving. He was just about to take out his pad and write a note of his own, suggesting a point recon to the crest of the ridge, when he heard the radio break squelch, two long and one short.

Marvel handed the headset to Wolverine, and word came that J. D.'s team was moving away from its first position near the trail and edging out, off the right flank of an NVA column, hoping to follow it down to the low ground near the water. Wolverine passed around another, shorter, note, huddled over his map and compass with Mopar for a second, then scratching his palm and holding up five fingers to remind him of the bet, he stepped back and motioned for Mopar to lead out on point.

Easing sideway through the narrow, vine-snarled gaps between the tree trunks, and pausing every few paces to let Marvel step up and lift away any vines or branches that may have hung up on his rucksack, Mopar led the team due west a hundred very slow meters along the contour of the ridge until the vegetation thinned and he found a place where enough sun penetrated the canopy to put a little grass on the slope. He'd been hoping to find a natural stairway of exposed tree roots, but anything—except a trail—was better than slipping and sliding on the slick and treacherous slope farther back.

Ten meters from the crest of the ridge Mopar froze. Almost immediately the men behind him halted. Mopar stuck out his tongue to test for wind direction, but the air was stagnant and close and so hot he had to dab the bridge of his nose with the back of his pointman's glove to keep the mixture of sweat and bug juice and dissolving camouflage paint from trickling into his eyes. A little breeze would have helped his hearing, but as it was he could hear nothing but his own pulse and the slow, deep, even breathing of the men behind him. It would take a nose and ears like Tiger's to tell if there was anything on the trail in this dead air.

Mopar glanced over his shoulder at Marvel, then looked back to the front. He shrugged to shift the weight of his rucksack, took a couple of quick, shallow breaths to calm his stomach, then started out again, even more slowly and cautiously than before, now that the crest of the ridge was so close. It was a good ridge for a high-speed trail, and as he looked up to check the canopy for the rend through which he'd spotted the trail from the air, Mopar regretted not having bet a little more—at least enough for a blowjob at Missy Li's.

He had a leave coming up in a month, so he was saving his money and staying away from the whorehouse, but bet money was found money, and it was all right to waste found money on fleeting pleasures.

Bent over at the waist, and stepping carefully to avoid making noise in the undergrowth, Mopar edged closer to the place where the trail ought to have been. He eased his rifle off safe and primed himself to part the leaves on the crest and peer out at a platoon of NVA taking an early lunch on the trail. Even though there were no sounds of rattling mess kits or of chopsticks clicking against rice bowls—even though there was not a trace of the pungent scent of Nouc Mam sauce, or anything else suspicious in the air—Mopar was hot to sneak a peek at an enemy meal, or failing that, a good, hard-surfaced, high-speed trail. But there was nothing—nothing under the break in the canopy except dead branches, and dead leaves, and thousands of little green grass shoots that had just sprung forth from the soil displaced by the stray artillery round that had rent the canopy. There was nothing else of interest on the entire crest of the ridge; no enemy troops on chow break, no high-speed trails—not even an animal path. But it wasn't until the team had zigzagged back and forth on the crest for ninety minutes without turning up the slightest sign of passage that Mopar was willing to concede defeat. At the first rest after moving back down the slope on the far side of the ridge Wolverine passed him a note of consolation: "Aerial recon unreliable. Need Lurps on the ground."

Mopar had no interest in counting abbreviations, but he found it strange that Wolverine insisted on passing notes when it was becoming obvious, just from the stale feel of the air, that there wasn't an enemy troop within earshot, and there probably wouldn't be any in the whole Recon Zone, even down next to the stream.

Farley had been a lot more reasonable about whispering in the field, and if the pilots flying the day he got killed had had the balls to come in on the secondary LZ as requested, instead of hovering out over the scrub to drop a ladder, Farley would still be running Two-Four with an almost pristine field notebook in his breast pocket, and Wolverine would probably still be back in Special Forces, or sitting around the operations bunker swapping lies with Pappy Stagg. It was silly to pass notes and use hand signs where there was obviously no one in the area, and cupping his hand next to Wolverine's ear, Mopar said so.

The hard look he got in reply to his whispered opinion was enough to stiffen the hairs on his neck and send him teetering on the brink of another sullen snit, but he was too proud of his field discipline to let his resentment simmer very long, and after a second or two he merely nodded and told himself that Wolverine would have to be broken in slowly. Sooner or later, even a hotshot lifer E-6 with three tours in Special Forces behind him would have to come around and start doing things the way everybody else did.

Following the proposed route of march they'd decided on when preparing their map overlays, the team moved down the slope and into the dank, dripping, leech-infested jungle that filled the draw between the ridge they had just inspected and the ridge to the south. It was a difficult descent. The ground was slippery, and it was sometimes necessary to grab a vine or a low sapling to keep from sliding, bumpity-crash-bump, feet first and ass down, into the trees. Marvel Kim was worried about losing commo in the draw. Twice during the descent he signaled for Mopar to halt while he got commo checks, first with the whip antenna he'd used on the ridge, then, two-thirds of the way down, off the pole antenna he carried broken down and folded in his rucksack.

It was hard to move in the jungle with pole antennas. They weren't flexible and they snagged on the vegetation. So before setting off on the last leg of the descent, Marvel took down the pole and ran out a wire antenna. He slung the wire over a tree branch and got another commo check, and without waiting for Wolverine's permission or to check the coordinates with him, he also reported the team's position and situation. From now on until they regained the high ground there would be no instantaneous communication with the radio relay. As he pulled down the wire antenna and coiled it on top of his radio, Marvel smiled and giggled at the absurdity of going willingly into what could be the valley of the shadow of death with only the spottiest commo. Mopar always claimed he liked being entirely on his own, out of reach of the relay team and the rear, cut off from the rest of the world, but Marvel didn't believe him. Nobody liked being without commo. And anyway, reporting back to the rear was the most important part of a Lurp's job, even if it did seem silly to run out a wire and risk giving the team's position away just to send in a negative situation report.

There was a stream in the draw. It was only a little pisstrickle that fed into the larger stream where Mopar had wanted to insert, but the vegetation around it was close and heavy and wet, and there were leeches everywhere. The leeches inched along the leaves and rose up like charmed cobras on the jungle floor as they zeroed in on the Lurps' body heat and the smell of their sweat and blood. The leeches were hungry, and Marvel took that as another sign that there was no enemy presence in the area. He ran out the wire and got a commo check with the relay team, then doused his collar and boots with bug juice while Wolverine pointed east and motioned for Mopar to move toward the larger stream.

It was impossible for the men to sit down in their security wheel here in the thick and tangled jungle. Every time they paused to listen for movement they stayed on their feet in order of march, sweating and silently cursing the leeches, until Wolverine signaled for them to move out again. As they moved closer and closer to the main stream, the vegetation grew thicker and thicker. It was impossible to move silently now. The trees were much lower than they were on the ridge, and they were much closer together. Between the trees were tangles of hanging vines and curtains of wet leaves. Every few steps Mopar was forced to stop and allow Marvel to come up behind and free him from the vines and branches that snagged his rucksack. Gonzales, on rear security, simply gave up and stopped trying to straighten bent branches and replace the leaves the other men had knocked aside in their passing. The growth was just too thick, and there was no way to avoid leaving a trail.

If there was no way for Gonzales to sanitize their trail, there was even less way for Mopar to avoid the leeches that crawled up his boots and attached to his face and neck and hands as he brushed the leaves on which they waited in ambush. He felt one leech inching along the back of his ear, moving toward the warmth and rhythm of the pulse of his neck, and for just a fleeting instant he had to fight down a surge of sympathy for the poor bastards on the other side who had to live in these jungles without benefit of American insect repellent. It wasn't the first time he found himself putting himself in the other guy's place, but he repressed his feelings more quickly than usual and went on with his job. A man had to stay on guard against getting soft.

Mopar found a trail parallel to the main stream. It was overgrown and snarled with thin, raspy vines and obviously hadn't seen any heavy traffic for at least a month. But it had to be reported all the same. Marvel Kim ran out his wire and called the trail in himself. Wolverine glanced impatiently at him and held a cautionary finger to his lip, when Marvel whispered too loudly into the headset, but he didn't interfere or have anything to add to Marvel's transmission.

Mopar wanted to get back to high ground. He talked a lot of brave bullshit about operating without commo, and a little bit of it was true. He knew the other guys—the gooks—didn't always have radios, and if they could get by without commo, then so could American Lurps. The leeches bothered him more than the lack of commo. He was sick of the leeches, sick of the stench of the stagnant pools and rotting vegetation along the stream, and sick of wasting time moving slow when there wasn't a gook in the whole damn Recon Zone.

But that lifer, Wolverine, insisted on following the trail and searching along the stream, and Mopar was determined to do a knock-up, top-notch job of it. He dodged the low branches and droopy, leafy boughs that overhung the trail and slipped sideway between the vines, keeping out of the elephant-ear plants that clogged the surface of the trail. Thirty meters on, he found an abandoned sleeping position a few meters off the trail.

Gonzales photographed the sleeping position, but it was old and filling up with new plant life, and Wolverine shook his head when Marvel offered to call it in. When Gonzales was finished photographing the site, Mopar led out again, wondering how in the hell the gooks would choose to sleep down here with the most voracious leeches. Ten meters on from the sleeping position, just off the trail and between it and the stream, Mopar found a patch of ground that showed signs of recent digging. He signaled a halt, and Wolverine came up to see what he'd found. It was a relatively recent cache.

Marvel tossed his wire over a branch and called in the cache's location while Mopar and Gonzales stepped back to provide security. When Marvel had finished his report Wolverine took the headset from him, muffled it with his towel and Lurp hat, appended the phrase "Beans on the fire" to Marvel's report, and handed the headset back to him with a mischievous smile.

There was nothing about beans in the codebook.

Marvel raised his eyebrows quizzically, and Wolverine motioned for him to leave the wire hung and step closer to the cache. After lowering his rucksack carefully to the jungle floor, Wolverine squatted next to the cache and began to dig with his knife and canteen cup. He made a pile of twigs and fallen leaves, then another pile of dark, moist soil. He dug for more than an hour. The sweat poured down his face and washed away the protective coat of camouflage paint and insect repellent that would have discouraged the mosquitoes that swarmed there along the stream. When he finally struck wood and turned to flash Marvel a toothless grin, his cheeks were streaked with green and gray, and his lips were puffy with insect bites.

For the first time on the mission, Wolverine relaxed his noise discipline.

"Give me a hand here, Kim," he whispered. "Help me clear off this lid and open it, and I'll show you a trick I learned in SOG."

Marvel almost ripped the wire from his radio in his rush to kneel next to Wolverine. Farley had never had any new tricks to teach—but then he'd never worked for MACV-SOG.

It took another ten minutes for Wolverine and Marvel to pry the lid off the wooden crate Wolverine had uncovered. Mopar and Gonzales were both getting bored, glancing over their shoulders from time to time to see what was going on. Finally Wolverine and Marvel got the crate open and stepped back to allow Mopar and Gonzales a look.

There were four AK-47 assault rifles in the case, plus two nine-mil pistols and four cardboard boxes of ammo for the AKs. The rifles were still packed in Cosmoline, and the pistols were wrapped in soft, oily cloths. Wolverine reported the contents of the cache, and once more said something about beans on the fire. He knelt down to rummage in his rucksack and came up with a jungle blanket, a couple of Lurp rations, and a collapsible canteen of water. He put these aside, then smiling broadly, reached in with both hands this time and came up with three ammo boxes that looked exactly like those in the cache.

"Bolo beans," he whispered. He held one of the

boxes up for everybody to see. "They've got a triple charge. Charley busts one of these caps, he's gonna get the bolt of his own weapon blown back through his chest."

Sometimes it was better to break noise discipline than to write on the pad. The very existence of bolo beans was highly classified, and Wolverine didn't want to risk carrying a written explanation around with him. It was one thing to get killed with a few boxes of enemy ammo in his rucksack—the gooks searching his body would probably not be too suspicious of that. But it was another thing altogether to carry a written explanation of one of SOG's sneakier tricks around in his pocket. He didn't plan to die on this mission, but that was no reason to get careless. Wolverine wouldn't even have been able to get hold of the bolo beans without Pappy Stagg's connections—not now, now that he was out of SOG. They were hardly an item to be signed for in supply, not even in the Lurp platoon. Wolverine replaced three of the ammo boxes in the cache with booby-trapped rounds, then fitted the lid back on the crate and pressed it tight.

Mopar was impressed. He kept his eye on his security zone, but he couldn't resist peeking over his shoulder at Wolverine.

"Maybe after this next extension is over I can extend for SOG," he thought. "If Pappy Stagg and Wolverine put in a word with the right people it shouldn't be too hard." It was almost impossible, he knew, to get on a Special Forces "A" Team without going through the Special Warfare School at Fort Bragg. But with the right clearance, the right experience, and the right references, it shouldn't be too hard to get in one of the really off-the-wall projects where a man didn't have to know too much about training indigenous troops, as long as he knew how to patrol and keep his mouth shut. Mopar didn't know too much about SOG, but from what he heard, it sounded like they had a lot of fun when they were in the rear and didn't have any superstitious awe of international borders when they went into the field.

He turned back to his zone of security and watched the stream flow past fast and gloomy, a few meters away through the bush. He hoped that Wolverine would decide to monitor the cache to see if anyone came along to uncover it, even if that meant putting up with the leeches and working off a wire antennae. But Wolverine had other things in mind. After the cache was reburied and the ground had been covered with leaves and the fresh soil scattered, he made another transmission on Marvel's radio, took down the wire, then motioned for Mopar to move out on point as soon as Marvel had his wire coiled and put away.

Mopar shrugged to shift the weight of his ruck-sack, then, when everyone behind him was ready, he moved out along the trail, looking for a narrow place to ford the stream. When he found one he crossed first, then covered the other men as, one by one, they darted across the stream and into the jungle on the other side.

After another hour of looking for trails, caches, sleeping positions, and other signs of enemy activity—all with negative results—the team moved up to the high ground on the opposite side of the stream from the cache and found a bramble thicket where no one could approach them without making enough noise to betray his presence. After Marvel had made a commo check on the whip antenna, the men put out their Claymores and set up, back to back and legs out like spokes, to wait for the night to filter down through the jungle canopy.

Gonzales took the first watch. He was still upset over the discovery that the exploding Communist weapons the American Forces Radio Network constantly warned the troops not to fire were not, as he'd happily assumed, explosive merely because they were products of inferior Marxist industry. He glowered and mumbled in Spanish, and Wolverine and Marvel stayed up to console him with their presence as the shadows blended into an impenetrable darkness broken only by the weird glow of rotting vegetation, scattered like shattered radium watch dials on the jungle floor.

Walking point always kicked his ass the first day in the field, so Mopar went to sleep as soon as he received permission from Wolverine to do so. When Marvel woke him for third watch, hours later, there was already a little moonlight breaking through the canopy and dripping like molten silver on the branches of the trees, dappling the bramble bushes and the sleeping Lurps.

# CHAPTER 9

Aᴛᴇʀ ɢʟᴀɴᴄɪɴɢ ᴏᴠᴇʀ ᴛᴏ ᴍᴀᴋᴇ ꜱᴜʀᴇ Wᴏʟᴠᴇʀɪɴᴇ was still asleep, Mopar took the headset from Marvel. Cupping his hand around a whisper, he asked Marvel how much of J. D.'s situation report he'd been able to hear. Marvel tilted his head back and looked up into the shadows and the moonlight. He smiled, his teeth flashing in the moonlight coming through the canopy, then stared at the trees as he answered.

"Movement all around. J. D.'s set up between two trails, and he's got heavy traffic on both of them at the same time. He's got motorcycle traffic on the lower trail."

Mopar couldn't decide if Marvel sounded like he was trying to be blasé, or if he was talking through his dreams. At any rate, he sounded goofy with all this talk of motorcycles on the lower trail. But Mopar let him go on without interruption.

"There's no way to say 'motorcycle' in CAR code, you know, so J. D. reported a run of Hell's Angels—right out in the open: 'Hell's Angels, Sonny Barger's boys'—just like that, as plain as day to us, but incomprehensible to any gooks listening on the push. J. D.'s got a real gift for exclusionary thinking."

Marvel giggled and slid over a little closer to Mopar so he could whisper up next to his ear and not have to worry about waking Wolverine. By now, he too was certain that there were no enemy troops in the vicinity—they were all in J. D.'s Recon Zone or hustling down the streams and trails to link up with the main force under cover of darkness. There were no streams or trails anywhere near the bramble thicket, but even if there had been a platoon of NVA encamped fifty meters away, they wouldn't have been able to hear his whispers through such thick jungle.

"Now get this, Mopar—this is out of sight! Not only can the relay team hear motorcycles almost every time J. D. transmits, but we can hear them too sometimes, when J. D. holds his headset next to the trail and just squeezes the transmit button! I tell you, Mopar, J. D.'s the type of guy who can make his own luck in this life."

Mopar shrugged. He wondered what in the fuck had gotten into Marvel to make him start gushing over J. D. with all this weirdo nonsense about "exclusionary thinking" and making his own luck. Marvel got to gushing over people sometimes when they acted the way he expected them to act, but he'd never had much good to say about J. D. before now. Mopar just couldn't imagine why Marvel was so impressed. It was only good sense for J. D. to transmit when the motorcycles were going past his position. That way he wouldn't have to worry about the gooks hearing him transmit—not over the noise a motorcycle could kick up, sliding and spinning on one of these muddy trails! And even more important, nobody hearing the engine sounds that came over the horn could doubt he was telling the truth. J. D. was very touchy about his credibility.

Mopar hoped that if he ever found himself in J. D.'s situation he'd have enough sense to sit tight and lay dog, quiet and still as humanly possible, all night and all the next day if necessary, until the gooks were gone or until the gunships came on station.

"What about calling in an air strike or some artillery? Has he made any requests?"

Marvel shook his head. "Requested? Yeah—but just for gunships to circle off station. It was denied. Not by our Six, but by that major from the Two Shop."

Mopar sighed unhappily. J. D. was too impatient. He was nowhere near as reluctant to swap lead as a good recon man should be, and that was why Mopar had left his team for Farley's. But even though Mopar wouldn't have trusted J. D. to keep the gunships circling off station until they were really needed, he was outraged that the major had denied support to a team in a potentially tight spot.

"I know what you're thinking," Marvel said. "This major isn't playing by the rules. But there isn't anything J. D. can do about that, and even less we can do. And anyway, old J. D., he didn't seem too unhappy about the situation, even after the major cheated him out of the guns. It can be good, or it can be bad, but a guy like the major—a guy like J. D.— can make his own luck in this life."

Mopar had had enough of Marvel's horseshit. It was bad enough for him to be gushing over that do-rag jigaboo madman J. D. when he'd never really been able to appreciate him before. But Mopar was outraged that Marvel would gush over the major, who may not have been a non-Airborne Leg but was the next thing to one, with his false-hearted, good leader, ho-ho ways and his staff of snotty wizards. Now the major was breaking all the rules of the game, refusing a team fire support as requested.

"You're talkin' out your ass again. Go on, crash. I'm on top of things now and don't need your bullshit to keep me awake. If we keep whispering we're gonna wake up Wolverine!"

Marvel sighed and rubbed his eyes. He was tempted to stay up and try to explain what he meant about a man making his own luck to Mopar. Sometimes he suspected that Mopar understood luck almost as well as he did, but just refused to admit that there was such a thing as luck at all. Luck wasn't something a man could bully and push around, so Mopar wasn't interested. But Marvel was too tired to waste sleeptime talking. He stretched his legs, careful not to rattle the brambles, then rested his head on his rucksack, pulled his half of the jungle blanket up to his chest, and went to sleep hugging his rifle.

For the first hour of his watch Mopar sat with his back against his rucksack and his rucksack against Wolverine's, and every time there was traffic on the radio Wolverine seemed to stir and tense up, as if listening to the radio through his sleep. During the second hour of Mopar's watch, Wolverine slept like an old lion, never stirring, but threatening at any point to break out with a sudden sawstroke of snore and wake up half the jungle. Mopar didn't nudge him, even when he started to exhale with a wet hiss, even when he snorted and smacked his lips in his sleep. There was nobody but the Lurps to hear Wolverine, even if he took to snoring like a sawmill. But out in RZ Zulme, things were getting even tighter. J. D. was only breaking squelch, and didn't dare risk a whisper into the headset now that the motorcycles were past and the traffic on the trails was thinning out.

Mopar could hear the relay team breaking squelch to acknowledge J. D.'s squelch breaks, and he could hear the traffic between the relay team on Culculine and Pappy Stagg back in the rear. But he couldn't hear J. D., and he was too late to hear the motorcycles, so he sat with the headset next to his ear and his rifle across his lap and wondered just what in the hell was really going on out there in J. D.'s Recon Zone.

If the gooks really had been going by with motorcycles loaded down with cargo slipping and falling and getting stuck in the mud—running headlights no less, and making no effort at noise discipline—then why hadn't J. D. figured out what those motorcycles were hauling? If the gooks were as close as J. D. said they were, it shouldn't be too hard to get a good look or two from the shadows under the bushes—at the very least get some detail into the reports. But J. D. didn't seem concerned enough about detail. Wilkinson—J. D.'s rear security, his tailgunner—never went on a mission without one of those mini-Starlight scopes. Why wasn't he using it now to find out what the bikes were hauling and what the gooks were humping on their backs?

Mopar ran a list of twenty things through his mind and still couldn't figure out what the gooks were carrying. But it was easy to guess what sort of things they had on the bikes: Rockets and recoilless rifles and mortars and rice. There'd even be coffins, perhaps, to boost their gook morale. J. D. should never have let the bikes get past without a positive ID or two, Mopar thought with growing irritation. The least they could do is guess.

Mopar made a situation report without asking the relay team about J. D., even though the temptation to do so was hard to resist and the punishment would be no more than an ass-chewing from Pappy Stagg after the mission. It just wasn't a professional thing to do, wasting air time when another team had movement.

He took out a canteen, unwrapped a cornflake bar, and relaxed as he waited for the relay team to pass his sit-rep and J. D.'s on to Pappy Stagg in the rear. He didn't know how Marvel's watch had gone, but it couldn't have crept by like this. Marvel at least had had the chance to listen to some of J. D.'s better situation reports. But all Mopar was getting was squelch breaks, and he could hear only the relay's half of those. Life might be a butt-puckering, pulse-thundering thrill in J. D.'s Recon Zone, but here among the brambles on a totally cold ridge in a very dead RZ, Mopar was losing his patience and dying to know what the motorcycles had been hauling.

There had been nothing said during his watch so far—no questions about specifics relayed from the rear, no updates from J. D. himself, and Mopar wondered how much had been covered in previous traffic but wasn't exciting enough for Marvel to pass on to him.

He bent down and shook Marvel awake. "Listen," he whispered, "I've been monitoring the radio all this time without any idea what's on those bikes. What did J. D. say during your watch?"

Marvel rubbed his eyes and sat up slowly. He looked around at the darkness and the scattered phosphorescence and the other men sleeping half in shadow and half in dappled moonlight. He yawned. He'd been dreaming about finding a large yellow balloon drifting down a slow jungle river beneath an arch of overhanging branches, and he wondered if he could pick up where he'd left off if he went to sleep without answering Mopar's stupid question. It had been an oddly pleasant dream, and Marvel was certain that it meant something.

"Come on, you silly gook—what did J. D. report during your watch? I want it all, in detail."

Marvel stretched and yawned again. He took his time answering. J. D. hadn't been able to see much, he explained, and all he'd said about the cargo of the motorcycles was that it seemed to be made up mostly of rectangular crates of some kind, and long cylindrical objects—rockets or bangalore torpedoes.

"Where do you think they're going? Culculine?" Mopar asked.

Marvel shrugged and doused some bug juice on a leech that had just fastened to his cheek. He brushed the dying leech off his face and shivered with disgust.

"Fucking leeches—they aren't even part of the food chain. What do they live on when the Lurps are back in the rear? I don't even think they exist until we come along, and then they just sort of generate out of all the rot and decay on the ground and come feeling for our heat. I hate the fuckers, I really do."

Mopar frowned impatiently. He hated leeches as much as the next man, but he hadn't shaken Marvel awake to discuss them.

"Come on, you dork! What do you think they're up to?"

"Who? J. D.? He'll probably get his ass in a sling opening fire on somebody, and they'll have to give him his gunships. He'll kill about a million zips, give Pappy Stagg a few more gray hairs, then bring his team out alive and well in the morning and get himself a medal and an asschewing. J. D.'s too flashy, and that's his bad luck."

"You know I wasn't asking about J. D., damnit Marvel, you dipshit!" Any louder and Mopar wouldn't have been whispering anymore. Gonzales rolled over in his sleep, and Wolverine's breath caught for a second in a half snore, then evened out as slow and regular as before.

"What about the gooks? What do they have in mind?"

The combination of Marvel's Korean blood, Hawaiian upbringing, and his visits to the fortune teller in the Louc Ma marketplace when everyone else was in the whorehouse had made him an expert on indigenous psychology, and Mopar trusted his judgement in all matters related to the gook mind.

"There's only one place they can be headed," Marvel said. He looked toward the north, the direction of both J. D.'s Recon Zone and the radio relay team on Firebase Culculine. "Poor Culculine . . ." Marvel shook his head sadly. "They're going to wipe her off her mountain. I told you radio relay was dangerous. I broke it down and laid it out and labeled the parts, but you wouldn't listen to me. Radio relay was too boring to be dangerous. It was chickenshit and boring and degrading. But it wasn't dangerous. That's what you said . . ."

Marvel paused, embarrassed and aware that he'd spoken too long and with too harsh a whisper. Wolverine and Gonzales were both stirring now, but neither of them was awake yet, so he went on and finished what he'd started out to say.

"You just wouldn't admit I was onto something. If you'd admitted I was right, maybe it would have changed the luck of the thing. Maybe if you hadn't tempted fate laughing when I said radio relay was dangerous, those poor fuckers on Culculine wouldn't have to get hit to prove I was right!"

Wolverine was awake now. He sat up and held a finger to his lips and scowled fiercely. Then, with a cold, malevolent smile, he took his finger from his lips and drew it across his throat. Mopar and Marvel held their breath to prove their sudden devotion to noise discipline, and satisfied that he'd made his point, Wolverine nodded politely and went back to sleep.

73

Gonzales was awake now, although he didn't change position or even alter the timbre of his breathing enough to give that fact away. He was thinking about home, wondering if those Sierra Maestre Oriente mountains back home resembled these gook mountains of Vietnam. He'd never been in the Cuban mountains, but he planned to go there someday with an army of his own. He'd have only good men in his army—nobody like Mopar and Marvel, who were given to squabbling in the field, where victory depended on keeping a united front against the *comunistas*. They were good men, but they didn't understand the *comunistas* and they weren't motivated by thoughts of victory. Gonzales spent most of his guard watch on slow nights thinking about victory. But it wasn't yet time for his watch, and after a few minutes, he too drifted back to sleep, leaving Mopar and Marvel to man the radio for updates on J. D.'s situation and keep alert eyes on the shadows and speckles of filtered moonlight and the faint, diffused green glow of vegetable matter rotting back into the soil with a pale, cold fire.

J. D. failed to make his midnight situation report, and the next scheduled sit-rep after that. With a growing, fascinated horror, Mopar and Marvel passed the headset back and forth, but all they could hear was the radio relay whispering ever more desperately into the air waves: "Tacky Blinker Two-One, Tacky Blinker Two-One . . . This is Tacky Blinker Six Alpha, over . . ." and "Two-One, this is Six Alpha. If you hear me break squelch by code."

Again and again the radio relay tried to raise J. D. on the horn, but there was no answer, and after an hour Mopar decided it was time to wake Wolverine. He bent down to touch him on the shoulder, but Marvel stopped him.

"Let him sleep. There's nothing any of us can do now but keep our ears next to the radio in case J. D.'s all right and we can pick him up. Maybe we should start figuring out what we're going to do when they overrun Culculine tomorrow and we lose our radio relay—but there's no sense in waking Wolverine. Nothing even he can do for J. D. now."

"I told you J. D. was too flashy to ever see his grandchildren. And I told you that radio relay was more dangerous than going to the field. Maybe now you'll listen to me and start planning for your old age."

Mopar put a finger to his lips and frowned, but he didn't wake Wolverine, and he didn't tell Marvel to shut up with his bullshit about grandchildren and old age.

"Twenty-one," he thought silently, "just let me live to be old enough to buy a beer in the supermarket and I'll be satisfied."

All the next day the team stayed in its night halt position with a wire antenna slung over a tree branch in hopes that by some fluke of the airwaves they'd be able to pick up a message from J. D. that the radio relay and the Birddog spotter plane that was now flying over his Recon Zone might miss. It was a slow and funereal day, gloomy with fog until well after noon and made chill and unpleasant by intermittent rains once the fog was gone, and everyone except Gonzales was certain that J. D. and his whole team had been killed.

Once, just after returning to station after refueling, the spotter plane picked up a signal that it took to be J. D.'s ultrahigh frequency emergency radio. But before the pilot could fix on it the transmission stopped, and only Gonzales, bullheaded in his belief that the *comunistas*—any *comunistas*—were no match for a crafty dude like J. D., had any faith that J. D. would come back on the airwaves, alive and all right. The other men were already beginning to wonder why the Birddog didn't give up on raising J. D., go back to the airbase, and come back with a couple of jets to lay a little napalm along the riverbank, where, judging from J. D.'s last transmissions, there must have been at least a thousand NVA hiding under the canopy. If J. D. were dead—and it was becoming more and more certain that he was—there was nothing to do but avenge him.

But the lieutenant, or the major in the Two Shop, or whoever was making the decisions, did not see things with such a clear eye. And so the Birddog stayed over J. D.'s Recon Zone, while the gooks rested and cleaned their weapons and rehearsed their assault on Firebase Culculine.

Shortly before dusk Wolverine had Mopar move the team to the crest of the ridge and fifty meters northeast, to the very edge of their Recon Zone. Here, in the thickest bush they could find, they sat up for their second night in the field.

Commo was excellent. Marvel could get the relay team easily with the whip antenna, and Pappy Stagg answered his first commo check on the pole antenna without going through the relay. But Wolverine insisted that he run out the wire—just on the long shot that they might be able to pick up J. D. when no one else could. The Birddog had already returned to the airbase, the clouds were heavy and low, and J. D.—if he was still alive and trying to transmit—would need every ear that could be spared.

Once again Mopar was the first man to go to sleep. He rested his head on his rucksack, cradled his weapon in the crook of his left arm, covered his face with his jungle blanket, and dreamed that he and Tiger were in the field together on a point recon and walked through a space/time warp that took them to the porch outside Sybill Street's apartment. It was an old dream of Mopar's and he'd had it many times before, usually when napping back in the rear. But this time he and Tiger actually got inside Sybill's apartment and Tiger had a chance to lift his leg against Sybill's kitchen table before the dream clouded up and dissolved into something different and unpleasant and impossible to remember on waking.

A soft rain was falling on the upper reaches of the canopy and dripping through the branches and leaves when Marvel Kim shook Mopar awake. Mopar shivered, pulled his jungle blanket tight around his shoulders, and sat up, stiff and cramped and miserable and wet. He peeled back the knit band he wore to cover the radium dial of his watch and checked the time. It was still an hour until his scheduled turn at watch, so he knew immediately that something was up. He shrugged off his jungle blanket and reached for the charging handle of his Claymore with one hand and the pistol grip of his rifle with the other. Everybody was up and alert, but with a glance Mopar could tell that none of them was preparing for action. Wolverine was holding the headset of his radio—the support radio—against his ear, and Gonzales was listening to Marvel's headset.

"They're hitting Culculine," Marvel whispered. "Listen . . . you can hear the mortars."

Mopar dropped the charging handle of his Claymore and cupped his hand behind his ear. At first he couldn't hear anything but the rain in the treetops, but after his ears adjusted to the sound, he could make out the faint crumpling of mortars, far away to the northeast. It was hard to believe that people might be dying to that sound, it sounded so soft and innocuous at this distance.

Gonzales and Wolverine exchanged glances, and then a second or two later Mopar and Marvel could hear the sudden ripping sound of small-arms fire—sounding much closer than the mortars had, although that was to be expected because small-arms fire always sounded closer than it was when heard at night. There was one burst, then another, then a long drawn-out rattle of machine-gun fire, followed by an ominous silence. The mortars had stopped, and now, apparently, so had the small-arms fire.

"Legs . . ." Mopar muttered disdainfully. The troops guarding the Culculine perimeter were Legs and didn't have enough sense to hold their fire and wait for a target. Paratroopers would never have opened up in panic like that, Mopar thought, suddenly worried about the guys on radio relay having to depend on a bunch of Legs for perimeter security. He could just imagine the Legs crawling out of their bunkers at the first letup in the mortar barrage and shooting wildly at shadows while their officers shouted and blustered and tried to get them under control.

The mortars began to sound again, and far off to the east Mopar thought he heard a bugle, but he wasn't sure that it wasn't just his imagination. Now, even before the mortar barrage ceased, there came again the sound of small-arms fire.

Wolverine took his headset away from his ear and leaned over to whisper in Mopar's ear and then Marvel's.

"They blew a gap in the wire," he said, trying his damndest to sound laconic and objective about it, even though he knew that the relay team was now in danger. "Artillery's depressing a couple of guns for direct fire, Those poor jerks are jumping through their apexes—listen."

He handed the headset around so that Mopar and Marvel could hear the panic in the fire direction center. The poor bastards were screaming orders into the radio, even though their own people were operating on a different push and couldn't hear what was being yelled over the external net.

"Disgraceful!" Wolverine said, shaking his head

sadly. "If it weren't for the relay team, I'd be rooting for the gooks."

Mopar's jaw dropped. He stared first at Wolverine, then at Marvel. What was this treasonous peace-creep bullshit? What the fuck had happened to the hardnose lifer who'd insisted on using a field pad and hand signals, even when it was obvious that they were in a cold Recon Zone? Were two days in the field—one of them spent laying dog in a night halt position—enough to turn a three-tour Special Forces veteran into a babbling peacecreep? Mopar was disgusted.

By now there were gunships circling over Culculine, and Gonzales, who was keeping on top of things by monitoring the Lurp command net, acknowledged a message from the rear and turned to whisper in Wolverine's ear that the helicopters that had been waiting on the Lurp chopper pad were now being diverted to provide emergency medevac for the wounded on Culculine. Wolverine nodded and passed the word on without comment.

"No support," thought Marvel, forcing himself to smile his sappiest smile so Mopar wouldn't think he was upset at the news. "No arty on call. No gunships, no medevac, no extraction ships, and pretty soon—if things keep up this way—no radio relay. From here on out everything is going to depend on luck."

"No support," Mopar thought with a satisfaction that allowed him to stop worrying momentarily about the guys on relay. "Now we can show our stuff!" He hoped that in the morning Wolverine would decide to go back by the stream, to keep an eye out for gooks coming back from the attack along the trail they'd found. "If the relay gets knocked out or extracted," he reasoned, "Pappy Stagg will be able to pick us up off a whip antenna, even from the low ground with an air relay."

Gonzales pressed the headset of the command radio against his ear for a second, then passed it to Wolverine.

"The gooks are inside the wire," Wolverine whispered after acknowledging the relay team's last transmission. "McKinney and Smith are going out to give the Legs a hand, and Davis is staying on the horn as long as he can."

Marvel was right. Radio relay was dangerous duty after all.

# CHAPTER 10

TIGER THE LURP DOG YAWNED AND STRETCHED OUT on the sandbags atop the operations bunker. Below him, on the chopper pad, the whole platoon was drawn up into a neat formation in front of a make-shift speaker's podium and a folding table on which stood seven pairs of spit-shined jungle boots. Tiger had been curious about the podium and table earlier, when Mopar and Marvel Kim were setting them up. He'd listened with sympathetic interest but no real comprehension when Mopar explained the signifi-cance of the boots. It was an old paratroop custom, he'd said. The boots represented the dead paratroop-ers for whom the service was being held, and Mopar made it clear that Tiger was not to spray them. It had all been most confusing, and Tiger had finally retreated to his customary observation post, to watch the goings-on at a safe and dignified distance.

The lieutenant and the major from the Two Shop came out of the bunker and walked past Tiger without even nodding. Behind them, smelling of aftershave and spray deodorant, and sucking on a wintergreen Lifesaver, came the overweight chaplain from Brigade Headquarters. This was his first visit to the Lurp compound, and already the lieutenant's insistence that he include in his service six men who weren't yet officially dead had put him ill at ease. He, too, walked past Tiger without acknowledging his presence and followed the other two officers down to the chopper pad. Tiger thumped his tail lazily against the sandbags when he heard Pappy Stagg call the formation to attention, but then with a snappy salute Pappy turned the formation over to the chaplain, and Tiger turned away, suddenly bored and disappointed, distracted by a light breeze coming down the hill from the Cav mess hall.

"Paradise rest! At ease!" the chaplain barked in his best drillfield voice, and there was a rustling and mumbling in the ranks.

"The Lord giveth and the Lord taketh away," the chaplain said, the wintergreen Lifesaver lodged between his right lower molars and his cheek.

"We are gathered here to mark the passage of our beloved comrades to their eternal reward." The chaplain lowered his eyes sadly and peeked at a slip of paper he had cupped in his hand.

"Robert McKinney. John L. Wilkinson. Thomas P. Fisher. James Dunlap Dwight." Here there was a titter in the ranks that almost made the chaplain lose his composure. He had no way of knowing it, but J. D. had always claimed that his full name was Jahmal Diddley Dwight. "James Dunlap Dwight," the chaplain said again before finding his place on the list. "George Roberts. Louis Haggins. And

William Murphy Clark. These seven brave young American soldiers were your friends. You knew them well, and knew what sort of men they were. Clean-cut, patriotic American boys who gave their all and paid the ultimate price in defense of their God, their Country, and our American Way of Life."

Here, the chaplain paused just long enough to hear the word "shit" come drifting, slowly and distinctly, from somewhere in the back ranks. The major and the lieutenant swept the formation with fierce eyes, but the chaplain went on as if he hadn't heard.

"Right now, as we stand gathered here in sacred fellowship to memorialize our departed comrades, they, these seven brave American boys, are in a much better place, filling out forms in that great gold and ivory replacement depot in Heaven."

The chaplain pressed his palms together and beamed at this reassuring thought. He looked out at the men assembled in front of him and was suddenly overwhelmed by a feeling of fellowship that he hadn't expected to feel for the Lurps after all the stories he'd heard about them. They were all dressed very neatly in regulation olive-drab American fatigues, with rank on their sleeves, patches on their shoulders, and nametags and cloth paratroop wings sewn over their breast pockets. They wore black baseball caps with the recondo arrowhead appliqué instead of the disreputable camouflage boonie hats they normally wore around the base camp and, the chaplain assumed, in the field. If he looked closely at the front rank, at Mopar, say, he could see an earring or two, but he was feeling expansive and tolerant, and wasn't too offended by this unmilitary display. He was tempted for a second to step out from behind the podium, plant his feet wide like he'd seen the general do when addressing troops, and maybe put a little mild profanity into his sermon just to show that he wasn't a prissy old goody-goody after all. But he remembered that this was a funeral service, and it was his duty to keep things serious and godly.

"I didn't come here to read the Bible to you men. You all know where the chapel is, and anytime you're in need of spiritual advice you can find me there. My door is always open, and I've got a case of New Testaments with me, here on my jeep, for any of you that need one after the formation."

Smiling a cold smile from the middle of the formation, Wolverine tried to stare the chaplain down, but the chaplain avoided his eyes.

"While we are gathered here on this helicopter pad, far from the comfort and safety of home, each of us must remember never to forget our comrades who are not here with us today. We must never forget. But by the same token, we must each look to the future and think what may be in store. These seven brave young American boys—each had a loving family at home, and friends, just as we have. Just like each of us, they knew they were facing danger in this distant, inhospitable place. And yet . . . and yet each of these men went to his reward bravely, never a second thought, because they knew they were doing it in defense of the families and friends they left, so far away, at home."

"No second thoughts at all," Sergeant Johnson muttered and the men around him smiled. Nobody knew if any of them had had time for second thoughts, but there was no doubt that, given the time, all of the men, even J. D. and that crazy McKinney who'd died helping the Legs defend the firebase, would certainly have had them at the very end.

The chaplain didn't hear Sergeant Johnson, but he saw the smiles and misunderstood them. He thought that the men around Sergeant Johnson were smiling in fond remembrance of their departed comrades, and so, encouraged, he went on.

"The Lord keeps a special place in Heaven for young men who have died for their country in just battle. And the Lord knows our battle is just."

"Your battle? You fat-faced sissy!" Wolverine thought scornfully. "This puffy wimp couldn't hold a congregation of old ladies back home. No doubt that's why he came in the Army, the chairborne, straightleg cunt."

"The Lord has a special place for our dear departed comrades." The chaplain glanced again at the paper in his hand, abandoning discretion this time. He read the names once more, then paused for dramatic effect.

"They are with the Lord now, sitting at His feet in that great, high-vaulted cathedral of Heaven. They are feasting at His table, strolling in His gardens, part of the serenity and holiness of Heaven."

In spite of himself, Wolverine was impressed. In all of his years traveling the revival circuit on the Full Gospel Bus, he'd never heard a preacher dwell so long on Heaven without mentioning Hell. Sergeant Johnson, on the other hand, was far from impressed. In his mother's church, Heaven was described in much greater detail and with much greater enthusiasm than this pastyleg could muster. Sergeant Johnson nudged Wolverine with his elbow and smirked.

"That sounds like a load of bullshit to me," he said out loud. "J. D. damn sure ain't strumming no harp in no heavenly palace."

There was an instant of stunned silence. The lieutenant looked crestfallen and angry, and the major looked embarrassed. The chaplain shook his head and smiled weakly.

"Let us pray," he said, and folded his hands.

Every man in the formation looked down at the

ground except Wolverine. Wolverine hadn't prayed for two years now, not since that night in the mortar pit of a besieged Special Forces camp when he'd said a prayer—just for the cameras, just in case. He'd begged then to live until dawn. The next morning, trying to bend the stiffened arm of the new commo man so it would fit into a body bag, he swore never to say another prayer. He refused now to lower his eyes to be polite.

"I ain't gonna pray to no bloodthirsty prick like Jehovah," he said, just loud enough for Marvel Kim and maybe Sergeant Johnson to hear. "I ain't even gonna vote for the fucker next time he runs!"

He looked up at Tiger, sunning himself like a lion on top of the operations bunker, and imagined him nodding in agreement. There wasn't any more space in Jehovah's Heaven for Tiger the Lurp Dog than there was for a bullheaded, fed-up, backsliding heathen Wolverine.

# CHAPTER 11

Mopar, Marvel, Wolverine, and Gonzales all hoped the Two Shop would send them into J. D.'s last Recon Zone. Mopar didn't want to spend his upcoming leave thinking about J. D. and the others out there dead and unrecovered in the jungle, and Marvel Kim was hot to pull a flawless, uncompromised mission in J. D.'s last Recon Zone in order to shake off the unlucky gloom before it grew into a fatal dread. To an extent, he believed that luck could be made and controlled. And it was time to make some good luck. And Gonzales was gnawing his traces to get out there and call in a couple hundred tons of death and misery and napalm on the *comunistas* who had wasted his only real buddy—that crafty dude, that crazy nigger, J. D.

Wolverine took a more practical tack. He went to Pappy Stagg and pleaded for a mission. He pounded on the commo desk to bolster his argument and threw in a little bogus reasoning for good measure.

"For Chrissake, Pappy—those Legs in Casualty Resolution won't list our boys as KIA until we come up with some bodies. Figure it out: There's at least sixty thousand dollars' worth of insurance at stake! Tell that sorry-ass major we're gonna commandeer a slick and insert ourselves—without support, if we have to! Tell him anything. But tell him we want those families to get their insurance money. And the only way to get it is to come up with some body parts or equipment. Ain't a major in the Army who doesn't care about insurance. And if you play up the good old family bit—hell's bells, Top! That's enough to scare the shit out of any major!"

Pappy Stagg frowned and looked over his shoulder to make sure the lieutenant was gone. He'd already run Mopar and Marvel and Gonzales out of the operations bunker, and now he and Wolverine were alone and could talk freely.

"You got some evidence all hocked up for this? Is that it? You've already got their ID cards out of their footlockers, thrown together some torn up web gear and tiger pants, and maybe smeared them all up with beef blood or something, and now you're all set to go out and make a find—is that it, Sergeant Wolverine? A find—a needle outa a hostile haystack— maybe snatch a prisoner or two while you're there . . . show 'em what you can do, eh?"

Wolverine started to protest, started to say something more about insurance money and the Legs in Casualty Resolution, but he dropped it all in midsentence and fessed up with a grin and a shrug, because he knew that Pappy Stagg saw through his bullshit about duty and honor and insurance.

"Sure, Top! There *is* a war on, isn't there? So why not fight it with a little enthusiasm?"

Pappy Stagg stood up and stretched. He threw his long, ropey arms back and took a deep breath, then brought his hands forward slowly and exhaled, cleaning his pipes and clearing his head. He was wearing tiger pants and a black Ranger tee-shirt, and when he brought his hands forward, Wolverine could see the top of the parachute canopy he'd had tattooed on his chest many years before. Pappy Stagg had a famous tattoo. His entire pectoral area was decorated with an enormous set of parachute wings, and the joke around Fort Bragg's Smoke Bomb Hill when Wolverine had first run across him was that Pappy Stagg was going to update the wings on his chest and bring them to par with the Master Parachutist wings he'd earned since getting the tattoo. The star and wreath on top of the parachute canopy of a set of masterblaster wings would have nestled neatly just beneath the hollow of his throat, but surely would've hurt like hell to have done, so it was probably a good thing that he hadn't ever gotten around to updating his tattoo. Still, Wolverine couldn't help thinking how much more impressive he'd look with a star and wreath showing over his tee-shirt.

"It's a war, Sergeant Wolverine, not a vendetta. And not a fucking talent show. We follow orders and go where we're told. I don't know what's got into you. You're a professional soldier, a Staff Sergeant E-6 in the United States Army, not some goddamn prima donna. So start acting the part. Is that clear?"

Wolverine played with his coffee cup, sloshing the dark coffee back and forth, seeing how close to the rim he could get without spilling any.

"Clear, Top." He put down his coffee cup and looked up at Pappy Stagg with a determined gleam in his eyes and a cynical half-smile on his lips.

"But you gotta admit one thing, Top, and that's this: Out there where J. D. went under, anything less than a Mike Force company, and anything more than a four-man recon team, is the wrong force for the job. Four men, Top—you know how quiet four men can move."

Pappy Stagg sighed and massaged his forehead with the heels of his hands.

"Wolverine, Wolverine," he said, making a great show of his sorely tried patience and sounding every one of his forty-seven hard years, "when are you going to face the fact that you're not in SOG anymore? I know, I know . . ." He put up his hand to wave away any protests on Wolverine's part. "These Lurps are good in the field. They're all volunteers, three or four times over, and they could probably put a jack-o'-lantern on Ho Chi Minh's pillow if someone gave them the mission. But they're still a bunch of kids—Mopar, Marvel, the only reason they're running recon for Lurps instead of Project Delta is that they're too damn young to get in Group." The minimum age for a Special Forces assignment was twenty, and both Mopar and Marvel were still months short of that. "They're just kids, Sergeant Wolverine. How do you think the mothers of America gonna react if they find out some nasty old master sergeant's been begging Higher to send their nineteen-year-old darlings out on four-man recon teams, when the established Tactical Organization and Equipment schedule for a Lurp team calls for six men? I couldn't do it if I wanted to—you've been in the Army long enough to know that! What do you think? Do you think I can just tell that major what I think we oughta do in the way of missions and he'll lock his heels, give me that good old 'Clear, Sergeant! Airborne!', and bend to the paperwork? Come on, Wolverine. Start thinking like a staff sergeant and not a Spec Four!"

"Yeah, Top, but it sounds kinda chickenshit to me. These guys are Airborne Ranger Long-Range Recon men, not a bunch of goddamn Girl Scouts, for chrissake! They're good! All they need is a mission worth their while. And you know I'm right about a four-man team."

Pappy Stagg shrugged and poured himself a cup of coffee. It was going to be a long night, what with Two-Two out in the Aloe Valley and Two-Three on an ambush in the Game Preserve.

"Right?" He washed the word out of his mouth with a long slug of coffee. "What the fuck are you using that kind of terminology around here for? Being right and being ten feet tall might get you on the basketball team, Sergeant Wolverine. But just being right ain't gonna get you nowhere. So I don't want to hear no more about it. Is that clear?"

Wolverine swallowed hard, ashamed of himself for talking like a preacher's kid, pulling words like "right" out of his hand and slapping them down on the table for Pappy Stagg to mock.

"Clear, Top." He drained his cup of coffee and got up for a refill. "All we can do is hope the major comes to his senses before the bodies disappear and the gooks move on."

Pappy Stagg smiled and reached for his pipe. "Hope in one hand and shit in the other," he said, "then come back and tell me which hand fills up first."

Three days after the memorial service, Two-Four and two men from commo section who wanted a little field time to stave off those radio relay auxiliary blues went out to find a radio site—an enemy radio relay—that according to Red Agent reports had recently moved to a hilltop in the southeast corner of the Aloe Valley map-sheet. All of the men, particularly the two from commo section, who hadn't been on a mission for more than a month, were stocked up and ready to bust a few caps, to ice a few gooks, and capture an impressive collection of Russian radios and NVA codebooks. But they weren't so lucky. They walked the ridges and climbed the mountains and combed every bit of high ground in the whole Recon Zone without finding a radio site, a radio, or a living soul that hadn't inserted as part of the team. Mopar found a long-abandoned thatch and bamboo hootch, and then, not far away, he found a chipped rice bowl and part of a human spine. But there was no sign of recent habitation, or even recent passage, and the mission turned out to be another disappointing bearfuck. Shortly after the team was extracted at the end of five fruitless days, a wall of stormy clouds moved in and settled low over J. D.'s last Recon Zone, so that even if the major had ordered up the mission Lurp Team Two-Four really wanted, there would have been no way to insert them and no way to maintain commo, because the whole works was socked in and souped over, and lay under a thick wet blanket of clouds.

Before the clouds over J. D.'s last Recon Zone lifted, before Pappy Stagg could present Wolverine's case to the major, it was time for Mopar to go on his extension leave and Marvel to go to Fifth Special Forces Group Headquarters in Nha Trang for Recondo School.

"Well, that's that," said Wolverine. "Looks like J. D. and Wilkinson and the boys'll have to stay officially undead a month or so longer, and then we can see about finding their bones for the insurance companies."

Mopar was extremely unhappy with this state of affairs. The thought that J. D. and Wilkinson and the other guys were out there next to one of those trails, their body parts scattered by animals, their legs and torsos rotting into the plants and feeding the worms and glowing at night like so many bleached creatures of the dark, deep sea—just the thought of this was enough to put a crimp in the good mood he should have felt about his leave.

It was a definite bummer, going home with this pall of unresolved horror hanging like burnt shit and diesel smoke over the platoon, and the night before he was supposed to go back to the Administrative Rear to process for leave, Mopar felt so lowdown, antisocial, and contemptuous of all tradition that he got drunk on Wolverine's Jack Daniels, smoked three bowls of Project Delta Red all by himself, and neglected to brush and groom that shifty little scoundrel, Tiger the Lurp Dog. This last was a most fortunate oversight on Mopar's part, for if he had gone looking for Tiger—brush in hand, cooing his kind intentions—he would have been sorely disappointed.

There had been no peppery tang of bug spray to alert him, no trace of nervous sweat in the air to clue him in that someone was leaving in the morning, so Tiger had taken out on his own shortly after sundown to patrol the base-camp dump and see what his nose could turn up in that incredible wealth of refuse.

# CHAPTER 12

T HE NEXT MORNING, WHILE MARVEL KIM SAT IMPA-
tiently gunning the engine of the jeep, Mopar went
off to search for Tiger. He looked in all the tents and
down in the operations bunker. He peeked into the
other bunkers, the protective bunkers that only
Tiger ever bothered to crawl into, but again—Tiger
wasn't to be found. Mopar checked down by the chopper pad and called over the fence toward the Cav
mess, but there was no answer from Tiger.

"Come on, hurry up!" Marvel Kim called from his
seat in the jeep. "If you keep fucking around you're
going to miss your plane!" Marvel Kim was always
punctual, and his normal benign patience always deserted him when there was a plane to catch or some
other deadline hanging over his head. "If you hadn't

been sulking last night, you would have brushed Tiger and clued him in that he should stick around to say goodbye in the morning. Come on! That little bitch Fifi down at the personnel tent is probably in heat and Tiger took off to get a piece of ass. Are you coming, or do you want to miss your fucking plane?"

Mopar climbed reluctantly into the jeep.

"That mutt!" he sighed. "He's like the rest of us— gets a chance at a piece of tail and forgets all about his buddies. That Tiger," he said with an affectionate shake of his head, "he's one cockhound of a Lurp Dog if I ever did see one!"

Marvel Kim put the jeep in gear and drove out of the compound. Almost immediately Mopar's dark mood returned.

"I tell you one thing," he said, "if I get hassled by any peacecreeps, I'm gonna try and reason with them for about three and a half seconds. And then I'm gonna start kicking ass."

He glanced right and left, just in case a wandering peacecreep had come over for a firsthand look and had managed to sneak onto the base camp. It hadn't happened yet, but Mopar didn't want to get caught half-stepping if a peacecreep did show up.

"I'll stomp them into the pavement. Smash!"

He brought his boot down on the floor of the jeep.

"One for J. D.! Smash!" He brought his other boot down, even harder than the first. "One for Wilkinson! Smash!"

Marvel Kim hoped he wouldn't keep smashing all the way to the airstrip. Mopar knew enough dead guys to get him at least as far as the access road, but Marvel wasn't sure the floorboard of the jeep could take that much punishment.

"What are you going to do if you get back and discover that your Sybill Street has become a peacecreep? You going to smash her too?"

Mopar was horrified at the idea of smashing Sybill

Street. The thought of her having become a peace-creep was almost as horrible, but not quite.

"Sybill Street a peacecreep?" Mopar pondered for a second, then shook his head. "Nah, that's impossible. She's too much of a snob to ever become one of them demonstrators. She's got a lot of self-respect—for a woman." He shifted in his seat and reached for the pack of Marlboros on the transmission hump, shook out a cigarette, and lit it with his engraved Airborne Ranger LRRP Zippo lighter.

"Anyway, it don't really matter that much. Women are always full of contrary bullshit. But it don't take much for a man to turn them around to some basic good sense."

Marvel Kim sniggered. He admired Mopar's spirit, but he'd seen a few of Sybill Street's letters, and they were full of rot and nonsense about the Geneva Accords and Senator Fulbright. It was hard to imagine Mopar trying to put the moves on a girl who let Senator Fulbright creep into her letters, but then Mopar was full of that drive-on Airborne spirit, and he didn't scare easily.

"Anyway," Mopar went on, "she can talk all the peacecreep bullshit she wants—I won't hear a thing 'cause her thighs'll be covering my ears!" Mopar stuck out his tongue. "Slurping, Marvel. Can you dig it? I'll be rocking that little boy in her boat. I'll familiarize myself with every fold and crevice and curl, and drive that girl insane with love and my tongue! I'm gonna be one slurping Lurp!"

"Brave words," Marvel Kim said with a laugh. He glanced over at the rice paddies to the left of the road. Here and there, a thin mist seemed to rise like smoke or steam from the water, and the winter rice shoots shone green as cheap jade in the morning sun. A young boy, lazing on the back of an enormous gray water buffalo, looked up and waved as the jeep went past, and Marvel Kim waved back wondering what the boy thought about all the foreign military traffic going past his field every day.

Mopar knew what the boy thought of them. "Little fucker'd put a lot more shoulder into that wave if he hadn't left his hand grenades at home," he said. All this waving to the kids and tossing them candy might have worked for those old farts back in World War Two, but it didn't seem to do much good in Vietnam.

"Well, you're almost home now," Marvel Kim said when he pulled up between the Tri-Service AATCO manifest shed and the airstrip. There was nobody in the manifest shed, but the C-130 out on the runway was already feathering its props, and the loadmaster was standing by the open tailgate with a clipboard. When he saw Mopar get out of the jeep and pick up his rucksack, he began to wave his arms in the air. "Get the lead out!" he hollered through cupped hands. "We ain't gonna wait for you!"

"Looks like I gotta run." Mopar was suddenly reluctant to go. "When you get back to the compound, tell Tiger goodbye for me. And keep your own ass outa trouble. Don't go winning that dagger in Recondo School, you crazy gook. You're the one that says it's jinxed. And if you say it, it's true."

"Moving out!" the loadmaster hollered. The tailgate of the C-130 was still open, but the engines were beginning to whine now, and the loadmaster was checking to make sure the jump doors were secure.

Marvel Kim grinned his goofiest grin and leaned across the shotgun seat of the jeep to slap Mopar's shoulder. He didn't know what to say, so he just kept grinning.

"Be cool, Marvel," Mopar said. "Keep your ass down, and don't go winning that dagger!"

It was certain death to win the Recondo School honor grad's dagger, and Mopar trusted Marvel Kim to avoid it like an ulcerated pudendum. But it was necessary to warn him once more, just for form's sake, just for the cameras.

Marvel Kim giggled nervously and turned away for just a second, embarrassed and surprised at how final this parting seemed. He'd never had to say goodbye to J. D. and Wilkinson, or any of the others, and even though he knew Mopar would be coming back in a month, knowing and feeling were two different things now. When he turned back, Mopar was already sprinting across the tarmac for his plane. Determined to get in the last word and at the same time chase away the sudden foreboding that had come over him, he held up the amulet bag he wore on a parachute cord around his neck and yelled for Mopar to remember to bring back some of Sybill Street's pubic curls, as he'd promised.

The C-130's engines were making too much noise now, and Mopar was running too hard to hear, but Marvel Kim was sure he wouldn't forget.

They'd worked this one through together one night on radio relay, and they both agreed: There was nothing in the world more magic than a brown pubic curl from a good-looking white girl.

By the time Marvel Kim got back to the Lurp compound, the last clouds had blown away into the mountains and Tiger was sunning himself on top of the operations bunker. His stomach was swollen with rancid pork chops from the dump, his tongue lolled out of his mouth, and there was an expression of drunken contentment on his face. He opened one eye when he heard the jeep, and when Marvel Kim came by, he rolled over on his back, wagged his tail lazily, and stretched out for a belly rub.

"Holy shit, Tiger!" Marvel whistled appreciatively and reached down to scratch the dog's belly. "What'd you do? Fuck that little Fifi to death and eat her?"

Tiger's tail sped up, his back leg jerked spasmodically, and he closed his eyes and sighed with a satisfaction so complete that Marvel Kim couldn't help wondering if maybe Mopar was right, that a dog's life was better than a man's, and the short, fast tour was more rewarding than the long, slow climb into old age and peaceful memories.

# CHAPTER 13

T HAT NIGHT TIGER HUNG AROUND THE LURP COMPOUND until well after midnight. He took a nap on a pile of dirty laundry beneath Gonzales's cot, then after Gonzales returned from the shithouse and chased him away, he wandered down to the team leaders' tent and begged a taste of Lurp-ration chili from Sergeant Johnson, who, with Farley gone, was now the only soul brother he trusted. After sampling the chili and losing interest in it, he went off to walk his regular rounds. He scent-marked the corners of the tents and bunkers, sniffed around the guywires and antennas of the operations bunker, lifted his leg against the compound gate and the skids of the ships on the chopper pad, and poked his nose here and there, just to check things out.

He could hear Pappy Stagg's voice coming from the depths of the operations bunker, and when he stood in the entrance he could smell Pappy's pipe smoke and Wolverine's Pall Malls. There was nothing unusual in that—when he wasn't in the field, Wolverine often stayed up with Pappy in the operations bunker—so there was no need to go down for a firsthand inspection. Still, Tiger had a vague, uneasy feeling that something was wrong.

He wandered back to the sleeping tent and let Marvel scratch his ears. But the uneasy feeling wouldn't go away. After only a minute or two, he stood up, shook himself, and left before Marvel had a chance to switch ears and finish the job. Something was wrong, but Tiger had no idea what it was.

Out in front of the tent he paused by the trash barrel and lifted his nose to the breeze. There was rain in the air, but none of it was falling yet. There was a faint taste of marijuana smoke mixed in with the other night smells, but it wasn't as sharp and exciting as the aroma of Project Delta Red, and it was coming from someplace outside the Lurp compound, and therefore wasn't worth investigating.

After sniffing around the operations bunker and the compound gate to make sure no other dog was laying claim to his territory, Tiger ambled back to the team leaders' tent. He normally didn't like to spend too much time there, but tonight he felt drawn to the electric lights, and he knew that Sergeant Johnson always had food. He nudged the screen open with his nose and stuck his head inside to check things out. Sergeant Johnson saw him and invited him in.

His tail at half-mast, ready to wag if necessary but not really primed for it, Tiger strolled over to Sergeant Johnson's cot to sniff his boots and nuzzle his hand for a treat. Although his tail hadn't fallen any from its half-mast position, his ears hung lamentably, and when he discovered no treat in Sergeant Johnson's hand and looked up to rebuke him, his eyes were big and dark and pitiful.

Sergeant Johnson reached down with his big strong hands to stroke Tiger's head. "Poor dog, Tiger. Poor boy missin' somebody for sure," he cooed. Tiger settled down with a sigh and rolled over on his back to have his belly rubbed.

The lieutenant was lying on his bunk reading Sergeant Johnson's latest copy of *Jet*. He put the magazine down and turned around with a sigh of his own when he heard Sergeant Johnson ask Tiger if he knew who it was he was missing. The lieutenant had still not completely forgiven Sergeant Johnson for saying "Bullshit!" during the chaplain's speech, and he was now paying attention to everything he said, just in hope of starting an argument that he could finish with a first-class asschewing. It wasn't easy for a lieutenant to chew a senior staff sergeant's ass, and he'd been glad to let Pappy handle Wolverine and Johnson after the chaplain went home to his chapel. But now he regretted not getting in a few licks of his own.

"What the fuck do you mean Tiger's missin' someone? You know as well as I do that he hated J. D. And he wasn't any too close with Wilkinson and McKinney and the others either. He doesn't know they're dead, and if he did, he probably wouldn't care, as long as someone's left here to feed his shiftless ass."

Tiger cringed a little at the lieutenant's tone of voice, but Sergeant Johnson kept scratching his belly.

"Wasn't thinkin' of them, sir. It's Mopar he's missing. Him and Mopar's tight as spoons, sir."

"Shit." The lieutenant wasn't in a sentimental mood. "That little camp follower doesn't know one of us from the others. All he knows is how to get a free meal and how to piss on a tent peg."

Sergeant Johnson always laughed at officers' jokes. He chuckled and slapped his knee. But Tiger was sensitive to tone of voice, and he was not amused. He flipped back over on his belly, gathered his legs beneath him, and stood up haughtily. He shook himself to get the blood moving, stretched his forelegs, and favored both the lieutenant and Sergeant Johnson with a bored yawn, then sauntered back into the night with such a fine show of offended dignity that even the lieutenant had to chuckle.

Marvel Kim was cleaning magazines by candle-light when Tiger came nosing into the tent for the third or fourth time since sunset. Before him, on a towel spread over his footlocker, was a neat row of ten magazine springs, and in front of the springs, in a corresponding row, were ten empty magazine shells. The Lurp hat on his bunk was full of ball ammo, and there was another, much smaller, pile of tracer rounds on his neatly folded jungle blanket. When he saw Tiger, Marvel whistled softly and called him, but Tiger didn't come. Instead, he sniffed the legs of Mopar's empty cot, paced a tight circle, then collapsed with a resigned sigh on the ground, rested his head on his forepaws, and looked up at Marvel with big, sad eyes.

"Look at Tiger," Marvel said. "He's been fucked up all night, and now he's figured out why. He misses Mopar."

Tiger's ears perked alertly at the mention of Mopar's name and his own. He lifted his head and cocked it slightly in Marvel's direction, his eyes gleaming and his tail tense and ready, but it was Gonzales who spoke next.

"He don't miss nobody. That dog is drunk. You saw how he was this morning. He's still drunk, man."

"Drunk?" Marvel remembered Tiger's swollen

belly, but that wasn't unusual at all. Tiger was a dedicated glutton, and he was known to overeat. "You're out of your mind, Gonzales! You remember the time we gave him some beer in a canteen cup? It fizzed in his nose and he wouldn't touch it after that, right? How do you figure he's drunk?"

Gonzales cracked his knuckles and smiled one of his rare, sly smiles. Tiger lowered his head and closed his eyes. His ears twitched expectantly, then drooped with disappointment and boredom when he realized that Gonzales was no longer talking about him.

"In Cuba, just after the *comunistas* come, I see it all the time. Drunk dogs everywhere then, man. The *comunistas* kill so many people. Everywhere you look, man, they got dead bodies. And before everybody get so hungry they eat the dogs, the dogs got so hungry they eat the bodies. That's how dogs get drunk."

"Human bodies?" Marvel remembered asking Tiger if he'd fucked Fifi to death and eaten her body, but he'd been joking. And anyway, Fifi was just a Pekinese and could hardly even be considered a dog.

"Sure. How else a dog going to get drunk?"

It had been at least a week since Marvel had heard Gonzales say anything about Cuba, and even though that last time he'd also managed to work the *comunistas* into the conversation, he hadn't said anything quite this outrageous.

"What the fuck are you talking about? Are you trying to tell me Tiger's been out feeding on corpses?" Marvel didn't know whether to laugh or stay indignant.

Gonzales shrugged. Tiger might not have seemed so drunk now, all forlorn and lonely, curled up under Mopar's cot, his ears down, his tail tight against his body, and his nose between his forepaws, but he'd damn sure been drunk in the morning. And even well into the afternoon, he'd been staggering around with a bloated belly and a strange, dopey look in his eyes, just like he was drunk.

"You the one said he don't drink beer, and we know how he looks when somebody been blowing pot his way. I see it before in Cuba, man, before we get out. That dog was drunk today. When you get the *comunistas* killing people in Hawaii you'll see a lot of drunk dogs. I see it before, man, and it don't bother me a bit."

It bothered Marvel, though, and he refused to buy a word of it.

"He misses Mopar, that's all," he said, not even trying to grin or giggle or act like the idea of Tiger feasting on a corpse didn't make his scalp crawl with revulsion.

"Okay, man." Gonzales was getting tired of talking in English with someone who refused to admit that the *comunistas* could cause such perverse and unnatural changes to come over a friendly dog like Tiger. "You'll see. If not here, then when the *comunistas* come to Hawaii. Be a lot of drunk dogs then, you'll see."

And with that he blew out his candle, dropped his mosquito net around him, and went to sleep.

After another hour or so of watching Marvel clean and reload his magazines, Tiger's head began to swim with the terrible smell of cleaning solvent. He rose and sneezed and left the tent in an indignant huff. Once out in the fresh air, he felt better. He stretched and yawned, made one more round of the compound—pissing in all the appropriate places—then headed off for the bunker line and the perimeter.

The moon was hidden behind a thick shroud of clouds, and while Tiger had no trouble picking his way through the concertina and trip wires, the darkness hid him from the troops passing their watch on the closest bunker. After crawling on his belly to the tall grass, Tiger stood up and stretched contentedly, then trotted off in hopes of flushing a rabbit or panicking a family of mice.

The grass and scrub outside the perimeter was littered with flare parachutes, burnt-out flare casings, expended brass, and soggy scraps of paper. Crickets chirped in the bushes, frogs croaked and splashed in the flooded craters of forgotten fire missions, and an occasional snake slithered away in the grass, but Tiger flushed no rabbits and panicked no mice. Suddenly the frogs and crickets fell silent. Tiger eased down on his belly, sniffing, and switching his ears to keep them in the wind. He could hear two men— gooks, from the scent of them and the sound of their voices. They were moving parallel to the perimeter, just a short distance from Tiger's front, and though he bristled and wrinkled his lip, ready to attack the first ankle to come within reach, the men passed on, unaware that he was there.

When the men were gone, Tiger got up and followed their scent trail to the south and east, through a patch of well-tended gardens and across the rutted, muddy Louc Ma Road to a broad and hard-packed rice-paddy dike. After only a little way, the scent trail led off the dike into the paddy water, but Tiger didn't bother to follow it, for he wasn't fond of flooded rice paddies. Instead he followed his nose down a thousand meters of paddy dike and up a grassy embankment into a dark and sleeping hamlet.

Padding soundlessly on his light, well-cushioned feet, Tiger invesitgated every water barrel, wicker basket, and doorway in the hamlet before moving on to size up the henhouse. The henhouse was an old and rickety affair of bamboo, dried mud, and chicken wire, with a roof made from a sheet of flattened beer cans that had been salvaged from the base-camp dump. Tiger had no trouble sniffing out a hollow under the wire that was large enough for him to squeeze through. After finding the hollow he backed off to lay dog for a moment in the shadows, then, when he was sure the hens were all asleep on their beds of wet straw, he crawled forward, eased on under the wire, and came up silently inside the henhouse.

Stiff-legged and bristling with anticipation, he tiptoed across the carpet of chickenshit and feathers, paused for a second or two to choose his prey, then sprang forward and sank his teeth into the feathery back of a fat young brood hen. The hen woke with a terrified screech, but it was too late to do her any good. Tiger locked his teeth and crushed her spine, then tossing his head for good measure, he retraced his steps to the hollow and backed out tail first.

The hen in his mouth was now too dead to struggle, but the henhouse behind him seemed to explode with clucking, cackling, flapping, and panic as the other hens woke to see Tiger's eyes flashing gold and green as he struggled to pull the dead hen under the wire behind him. For just an instant, Tiger hesitated, tempted to crawl back inside and run wild, killing the stupid hens. But then he heard someone shouting and cursing in a nearby house, and he bolted so fast he left one wing of his brood hen hanging, in feathers and shreds, on the bottom of the chicken wire. Barely managing to keep his head up against the weight of the chicken in his mouth, Tiger fled down the back trail, around a bamboo fence, and away from the henhouse and the shouting, cursing farmer.

Hiding in a safe place among the bushes next to the trail, Tiger ripped the brood hen open, gulped down her sweet, wet intestines, and gnawed his way up through her stomach, her heart, and her lungs. But before he had time to peel back the feathers and skin to her flesh, he was forced to abandon his meal and flee once more, for the farmer was on his trail, brandishing a flashlight and a hoe, and smelling of rage.

Tiger left the hen with little regret—he had already eaten the best parts. He escaped the farmer with little trouble by doubling back to lay dog in the shadows and watch him recover what was left of his chicken. Then, when the farmer was gone, he rose and stretched, and started back for the base camp by a different path and different dike than he'd traveled coming in.

Somewhere off to the west, a helicopter gunship fired into a dark hillside, but Tiger ignored the distant swoosh and crump of rockets as he padded down the trail that led over the dike. The paddy water on either side of the dike was dark and still, the wind had died, and the moon was still hidden, high up in the sky. Tiger sat down to gnaw at a leech on his foreleg, then rose and continued on his way. The wind had picked up again now, but Tiger kept his nose to the trail and hurried along, interested only in the path ahead of him.

Suddenly he stopped and cocked his head. A few paces down the trail, a thin, invisible trip wire was humming, ever so faintly, in the wind. Tiger leaned forward to investigate with his nose, then without more than a second's hesitation hopped down into the water and splashed across the paddy to the next dike, where he scrambled back up to dry ground. Something was snuffling along the paddy dike he'd just abandoned, snuffling along on his scent trail. Tiger, ever curious, shook the water from his coat, then stretched out on his belly to watch in comfort.

Tiger knew what to expect. He had picked up the scent as soon as he lifted his head from the trail and cocked it to hear the vibrating trip wire. He was not at all surprised when at last he saw a big, dark, monkey-faced dog come sniffing and slobbering into view across the paddy. This was the same arrogant, sick-smelling dog that always stood by the side of the Louc Ma Road, barking and coughing with mad jealousy, whenever he rode past in the back of the jeep, and Tiger could not suppress the soft growl of loathing deep in his throat. But he was content to lay dog for the time being, confident that the other dog could not follow his scent trail through the paddy water.

The other dog was big, but thin and sick. His odor was strong on the wind now, strong with the stench of rotting teeth and disease. Tiger bristled his ruff and wrinkled his lips with hatred.

The big dog was striding along nicely now, sure of the scent, confident that his size more than made up for the fierce and healthy smell Tiger had left on the trail. He paused now to lift his head and sniff all around, but with his squashed-in-monkey snout, he could not smell Tiger, downwind and a paddy away. The big dog's luck was no better than his sense of smell. When he turned to put his nose directly into the wind, he hit the trip wire with his tail, and before he had time to yip or feel the slightest pain, he disappeared in a flash and a boom, then came down in pieces, splattering water and trail like a thousand heavy raindrops.

Tiger waited until his ears stopped ringing from the explosion, then stood up. He shook some water and pieces of dog flesh from his coat, yawned and stretched, then headed back for the base camp and the Lurp compound.

By morning he was back on station atop the operations bunker, lying there with all the aloof and regal dignity of a wet and muddy lion.

"Look at him, sir," said Sergeant Johnson as he and the lieutenant strolled past on their way to the Cav mess for breakfast. "You can't tell me that poor dog don't miss Mopar, sir. Just look at him—he's probably been lying around all night, just waiting for Mopar to come home. I tell you, sir, you've got that poor dog all wrong."

# CHAPTER 14

GONZALES WAS A TERRIBLE DRIVER. AS A CHILD IN Havana his family had had a chauffeur, and then after fleeing the *comunistas* and taking refuge in Manhattan, he had depended on subways, buses, and taxicabs for transportation. It wasn't until he was in the Army, stationed at Fort Bragg with the 82nd Airborne, that he first sat behind the wheel of an automobile, and that had been a buddy's Pontiac GTO, not an army jeep.

"Slow down, goddamn it!" Marvel shouted. "This isn't Daytona Speedway! I want to get to Recondo School alive." He hugged his rucksack to his chest and bit his lip as Gonzales veered around a slow-moving Vietnamese armored personnel carrier. The Vietnamese soldiers sitting on top of the APC jeered and flashed the "V" sign, and Gonzales flipped them the bird.

"Fuckin' gooks drive like women," he growled. Once safely past the APC, he let off the gas and downshifted so suddenly Marvel Kim was forced to reach out and brace himself against the dash to keep from flying forward and smashing the windshield with his forehead. In the back of the jeep, Tiger the Lurp Dog stayed curled up on an old flak jacket, as comfortable, steady, and unconcerned as a bag of cached rice.

"When I said slow down, I didn't mean like that!" Marvel had not bothered to include traffic deaths in his figuring, and he doubted that his combat luck could carry him through firefights *and* jeep wrecks without cracking. "Do you want me to drive? You can pull over on the shoulder and change seats."

"What the fuck are you trying to say, man?" Most of his accent was blowing away on the wind, and Gonzales sounded surprisingly like Mopar. "You saying I can't drive?"

Marvel nodded silently.

"Well, I can drive good, man. Drive fast, like an Airborne Ranger—not slow like an old lady." He began to speed up again, and in one sweep passed an entire convoy of refrigerator trucks and their gun-jeep escorts. "Sure I can drive, man. I'm more American than *you!*"

Despite his nervousness, Marvel giggled. Whenever any of the guys got down on him for looking like a gook, or having a gook name, he tried to giggle or smile. Sometimes he could pull it off and sometimes he couldn't, but he always tried. But this was just too absurd, and he couldn't let it pass. "American my ass! You don't even speak the language without an accent."

Gonzales leaned on the horn and careened past an oxcart loaded with watermelons. Marvel hugged his

rucksack and stared straight ahead, but Gonzales
didn't slow down.

"What do you mean I'm not American, man?
Cuba's in America. Columbus been there, man!
Korea isn't America—neither is Hawaii."

"What do you mean Hawaii isn't America? Hawaii's a state. Your Cuba—what's it? Just a Communist country!"

Gonzales downshifted and the jeep shot past a family of four chugging along on an overburdened Honda motorcycle.

"North Korea," he sneered. "The worst *comunistas* in the whole world have half your country,
man, and you don't care."

"Fuck Korea," Marvel didn't giggle this time, but
he smiled a nice, sappy, airhead smile and braced
himself as Gonzales swerved to miss a chicken that
was wandering dazedly in the middle of the road.

"Gonzales," he said as the jeep slowed and turned
off the Louc Ma Road onto the airstrip access road, "I
hope you let Tiger do the driving on the way home.
He can damn sure do better than you."

Gonzales ran through the gears, then screeched to
a stop right at the edge of the runway tarmac.

"Tiger?" Gonzales glanced over his shoulder.
Tiger was standing up now, with his nose in the air
and his tail curled as high and proud as a battle flag.

"That dog likes speed, man. He's hardcore, eats
corpses. That's the trouble with you, man—you and
Mopar both too soft. Always baby that dog. He eat
bodies, man. That's one hardcore little dog, that
Tiger. He's not afraid of speed."

Tiger wagged his tail in affirmation. Marvel
reached back to give him a farewell pat, then slung
his rucksack over his shoulder and picked up his
weapon.

"You take care of things, Tiger. Don't let this
crazy Cuban get himself killed until I get back."

Tiger wagged his tail, wiggled his rear end, pawed the flak jacket he was standing on, and tossed his head playfully. But Marvel's plane was already loading and he had to be on his way.

"I've got to run now," he said. "You guys keep cool and stay lucky."

"And you," Gonzales yelled after him as he sprinted across the tarmac for his plane, "you win that Recondo dagger and you die alone, man. I don't believe no superstition!"

Marvel paused just long enough to give Gonzales the finger, then ran on to his plane. "Ain't no way!" he thought. "Ain't no way I'm going to win that bad-luck Recondo dagger!"

He was determined to live at least a hundred years, and he wanted nothing to do with the Recondo dagger and its deadly curse.

Marvel Kim flew to Nha Trang with two PFCs from the artillery battery on Firebase Culculine. They had survived the ground attack without being wounded only to be bitten by a rat while rebuilding a bunker that had been destroyed by a NVA satchel charge. Now they were on their way to Nha Trang to receive a series of rabies shots, and no matter what Marvel said, he couldn't shake their belief that they were in for an easy three weeks of rear-area ghost time.

"What's a shot, anyway?" the guy who had seen McKinney take a burst across the chest said in airy dismissal. "Once a day we take a pinprick—then bam! We're gone! Out to the beach. Down to the Air Force snack bar. Shit, we'll be high every night, and old Dewfuss here," he nudged his buddy in the ribs with his elbow, "old Dewfuss probably have to get a few more shots, 'cause he can get the clap just looking at a hole in the ground."

"Ghost time, baby, good ghost time." Old Dewfuss,

who could get the clap just looking at a hole in the ground, grunted in affirmation.

Marvel smiled politely and decided to let them go on believing they were headed for a vacation. They'd find out soon enough. Everyone always did.

Mopar's flight from Bien Hoa to California was much longer and should have been more comfortable than Marvel's flight to Nha Trang. He flew on a real airliner, with adjustable seats, stewardesses, hot meals, and cheap headphones full of music. And as he was going home, he should have been high and happy and deliciously excited. But he wasn't.

The most petite of the stewardesses was almost as tall as Pappy Stagg, and the youngest of them looked to be suffering from the first flashes of menopause and letting it piss her off. Mopar was horribly offended by the way they stalked the aisles, glowering like old-maid English teachers in a reform school, and he wished that Marvel was there to freak them out with his psychopathically goofy smile. There was no booze on the plane, at least none back where the enlisted men sat, so Mopar was forced to sneak off to the john every hour or so, to toke on one of the joints he'd bought in the replacement depot while waiting for his flight.

It was terrible dope. Despite their carefully cultivated image, none of the Lurps was really a stone pothead. They smoked only the occasional bowl of high-grade Project Delta Red between missions, an almost ceremonial thing—passing the pipe, talking about the war—and among themselves the Lurps took pride in the quality of their dope and scorned those who smoked great quantities of inferior weed. The Lurps were connoisseurs, and Mopar finally decided that it was beneath his dignity to sneak tokes on shitweed. Before the refueling stop in Anchorage, he flushed the last of his joints down the toilet and went back to his seat to look out the window as the dark and brooding Alaskan coastline came up under the plane.

He wondered if any Russian Lurp teams had ever inserted along that coast. The only way to avoid the Dew Line radar would be to come in by submarine and insert by rubber boats. But there didn't seem to be any sort of beach, and judging by the lines of white surf breaking against the foot of the seaside bluffs, they'd have to launch six teams in hopes of getting one safely landed. Mopar was glad he wasn't a Russian Lurp. They had good weapons, but their radios and compasses—at least those that they passed on to the NVA—were crude, unreliable, and heavy. According to Gonzales, who claimed to know such things, Russian reconnaissance codebooks did not contain the word "extraction."

At Anchorage all the troops deplaned and filed, shivering in their tropical uniforms, across the tarmac into the transit lounge. While everybody else crowded around the stuffed polar bear or the towering Christmas tree, or lined up at the souvenir counter to buy Eskimo carvings and walrus-skin coin purses, Mopar stood alone by the windows with his cheek against the cold glass, looking out at the mountains, the stars, and the snow piled up next to the runways.

He tried to sleep all the way from Anchorage to California, and only when the pilot came over the intercom to announce that they were now descending for Travis Air Force Base did he give up his effort to follow Marvel's advice and stop trying to dream a prophetic dream about Sybill Street.

The Leg Spec Five sitting on his right applauded the announcement, and when the plane touched down at Travis he cheered, put his hand over his heart, and said something about how good it was to be back in The World, but Mopar didn't feel much like celebrating.

Marvel, Wolverine, Gonzales, Pappy Stagg, and Tiger were a world away, and Mopar suddenly missed them more than he'd ever missed anyone before.

After removing his earring to avoid hassles, Mopar cleared customs at Travis and found a seat on the bus for Oakland Army Base. There were no grenade screens on the windows of the bus, and with the exception of a beat-up Russian SKS rifle that a captain from the 1st Infantry was taking home to prove he'd been in combat, there were no weapons either.

Mopar had a window seat. Unlike everybody else on the bus, he refused to be impressed by the houses covering the hills, the gas stations by the off-ramps, and the colorful abundance of cars speeding by, bumper to bumper, in the fast lane. All those people in the houses and gas stations and cars had it soft and easy. They were half-stepping through life, growing cancers, getting fat, and worrying about the phone bill, and the closest they got to the war was watching it on TV. For the life of him, Mopar couldn't understand why the other men were cheering and laughing and slapping each other on the back with joy at being back among all these dull and sluggish civilians. He hadn't been expecting any brass bands at the airport, but he also hadn't expected to see the other men from his plane—particularly those like the 1st Infantry captain, who'd seen some action—cheering the sorry lardasses who'd stayed at home.

For the first time since signing his extension papers, Mopar regretted his decision to go home on leave, like some no-class Leg draftee, rather than taking his thirty days in Bangkok or Taipei—someplace where the girls were cheap and sweet and pretty and knew how to treat a soldier like a man.

Before reporting to the warehouse building where returning soldiers were issued their green Class A uniforms, Mopar went off in search of a beer. There were free steak dinners available in the transit mess, but he wasn't hungry and didn't want any thin, greasy Army steak. He wanted a cold beer—a cold, foamy beer in a dripping aluminum can—and maybe a handful of pretzels to nibble on between sips. He found an NCO club, but there was a sign on the door barring all transient personnel under the E-6 pay grade from entering.

Mopar was prepared for this. He unclipped the Spec Four emblems from his fatigue collars and attached the staff sergeant's stripes he'd borrowed from Wolverine just in case something like this came up. He straightened his uniform and ran his hand along his chin to make sure he had a close, lifer shave, and then he opened the door and strutted into the club. Porter Waggoner, or one of the other hillbillies Wolverine liked so much, was singing something about Carrow County over the jukebox. Four or five truculent-looking redneck E-7s were sitting at the bar. Mopar ordered a shot of Wild Turkey with a beer chaser, just to be hardcore.

"You got any orders on you?" asked the bartender. He was in civilian clothes, but his haircut marked him as a lifer. "We don't have any of you hardass Airborne types stationed here, so I know you gotta be a transit. I can't serve no transits that don't show me their orders. You're about the youngest-looking E-6 I ever seen."

Mopar smiled and decided to brazen it out without losing his temper. The redneck E-7s were watching him now, and they looked like they'd be glad to stomp his ass first and call the MPs afterward if he got too uppity, so he smiled and said something about a lot of guys getting killed, a lot of blood stripes coming down the Lurp platoon.

"We got one guy, this pineapple gook from Hawaii, who's only eighteen, and he's an E-6 already. Staff Sergeant E-6, same as me."

The rednecks were guffawing now, and the bartender was unmoved.

"I gotta see some orders, bud. No orders, no drink. No drink, and you ain't got no business in our club."

"They're back in the barracks. I'll go get them and come back for that shot and beer, so don't go letting these dudes—" he nodded in the direction of the redneck E-7s, "go drinking up all the Wild Turkey. It's an Airborne drink, and I don't think these overweight Legs can handle it."

One of the E-7s rose half out of his chair at that, but his buddies pulled him back down and told him to let it go, and Mopar, whistling merrily, tipped his hat to them, picked up his AWOL bag, and strolled out of the club. The first thing a man learns when he gets into a reconnaissance unit is to hold his fire and avoid contact when the odds aren't on his side. Mopar was proud of his self-control—so proud that he whistled and hummed all the way to the uniform issue point.

He fell in line behind two Leg noncombatants who were bubbling over with gratitude for their steak dinners.

"That's the best chow I've had since comin' in the Army," the chubby soul brother with the Support Command's "leaning shithouse" patch on his shoulder declared.

"No shit!" his partner, a tall, chinless hillbilly, agreed enthusiastically. "I done ate so much they gonna have to charge me excess baggage to get on the plane home!"

Mopar smirked and thought of the Sunday steak and lobster dinners the Special Forces Mess Association in Nha Trang served. There was no way the cooks here could come up with anything that good, not cooking for people as dumb as these two.

Mopar moved up to the first window and drew socks and a tie. He had his own tee-shirt, a black Airborne tee-shirt, and he didn't bother to draw shorts because he was no longer in the habit of wearing them. Underwear was one of the major causes of jungle crotch rot, and nobody in the Lurp platoon wore shorts. He passed the next window without stopping. They were issuing shoes and belts and caps there, but Mopar already had his. He had his jump boots, and they were nicely spit-shined, he had his airborne cunt-cap with the gaudy red, white, and blue glider patch, and he had a tan NVA belt with a star on the buckle to wear under his jacket. He moved on to the next window and drew the rest of his uniform, then took out his stripes and patches and handed the whole mess to one of the tailors, with instructions to cut the pants for a blouse and have the LRRP tab sewn above the Airborne tab, above the unit patch. The uniform was ready when he got back from the showers.

Mopar dressed slowly and carefully. He pulled on his socks, stepped into his pants—one leg at a time, just like the officers—then wiggled his feet into his jump boots and laced them up tightly. He stepped in front of the mirror to check the way the blouse of his pants broke over the top of his boots, and while he was there, he flexed his biceps to make sure they still peaked up, lean and knotty, as they had before he lost all that weight humping the hills and living on cornflake bars and Lurp rations. Next he put on his black Airborne tee-shirt, and after a minute of debate decided to wear his bodycount rope with its twelve knots on the inside, where he could feel it next to his skin and never forget the men he'd killed. He stepped back in front of the mirror, replaced his earring in the lobe of his left ear, and tried to brush down his cowlick with his hand, but the hair wouldn't stay in place.

Whistling happily, he went back to the bench where he'd left his AWOL bag and the rest of his uniform and began to dress out his jacket. First he pinned his brass to the lapels. Then he fastened his jump wings and their cloth background to the flap of his left breast pocket. Above his jump wings he attached his ribbon bars, and above the ribbon bars his Combat Infantry Badge. There was a Presidential Unit Citation in his AWOL bag, but he decided not to wear it because it had been awarded to the entire brigade, rather than the Lurp platoon alone, and really didn't mean a damn thing, since almost every brigade-size unit in the war had been awarded one.

After a quick glance over his shoulder to make sure no one was watching, he put on his poplin shirt, tied his tie, and slipped into his jacket. He cocked his cunt-cap on his head and styled it with the edge of his hand as he stepped back in front of the mirror. There was no doubt about it, he was looking good.

He turned to the left and admired himself from that side, then turned to the right and admired himself some more. He straightened the knot of his tie, adjusted his cunt-cap so that the glider patch was low and jaunty over his eye, then flashed himself a cavalier smile and stepped away from the mirror. He picked up his AWOL bag and shrugged to get the blood flowing in his rucksack muscles, even though he had left his rucksack in the rear, ten thousand miles away.

"Well, this is it," he said aloud. And with a determined sigh he started out for his leave.

By the time he made the main gate where the taxis were waiting, his Airborne spirit was at a peak. He was striding and strutting and looking *Strac*, and he couldn't help breaking out with a verse or two of the Lurp song as he walked.

"Merry men are we, we're rough and wild and free—hey!

There's none so fair that they can compare—

To the Airborne L-R-P!"

He didn't care who heard him. He didn't even care when the taxi drivers gathered there to wait for fares snickered and looked over their shoulders at him like he was some sort of stoned-out weirdo. They were just taxi drivers, just a bunch of lardass civilian Legs, and what did they know of spirit?

# CHAPTER 15

THERE WAS NO CLERK IN THE LURP PLATOON. BEFORE
the Two Shop major wrested full operational control
away from the major in command of Headquarters
Company there had been a clerk assigned to the platoon, but he wasn't even a paratrooper, and since he
was a Leg, the Lurps treated him with such scornful
condescension that he put in a transfer for the infantry and got himself killed in a firefight.

Now, with the platoon under the Two Shop, the
Two Shop's clerks took care of most of the Lurp's
administrative paperwork, and Pappy Stagg, Sergeant Johnson, and the lieutenant saw to the rest.
Occasionally when there was typing to be done,
when the lieutenant had to write a letter to someone's next of kin or wanted to write someone up for a

123

medal, Marvel Kim helped out because he was the only man in the platoon who knew touch typing. But Pappy Stagg was a competent hunt-and-peck typist, and as he was familiar with most of the normal forms, he took care of the day-to-day paperwork.

Early one drizzly afternoon, a day or two after Marvel Kim left for Recondo School, Pappy Stagg was sitting at the operations desk in the bunker filling out combat equipment loss forms for the weapons and radios lost with J. D.'s team. It was tedious and boring work, full of small print and cramped lines, and Pappy was wearing his glasses while he double-checked the tiny serial numbers on the supply sheets. Suddenly Sergeant Johnson came running down the sandbagged ramp into the bunker, his face a dark mask of pent-up anger.

Pappy Stagg took off his glasses, slid them under one of the forms, and looked up from his desk.

"What's wrong, Johnson? You look upset about something."

"Upset?" Sergeant Johnson lit a Kool and pinched the match out between his thumb and forefinger. "Damn right I'm upset, Top. I just come back from trash run, and you ain't gonna believe what I saw at the dump. You remember that monkey they got over at the engineer company?"

Pappy Stagg nodded. He liked monkeys. When he was with 46th Special Forces Company in Thailand he'd had a monkey of his own.

"You know that little squash-faced dog down at personnel? Fifi?"

Again Pappy Stagg nodded. "Yeah. So what do they got to do with anything?"

"Nothing anymore, Top. They're dead. MPs grabbed them this morning and dragged them down to the dump and blew their brains out. They shot the Awards and Decorations Section's cat, and they'll be coming for Tiger as soon as they get the time. The general's got a fly up his ass about rabies. Losing too many manpower days to animals. So he wants them all shot—the chickenshit motherfucker!"

Pappy Stagg's calm expression turned into a frown. "All right, Johnson, can that stuff about the general. And don't ever let me hear you talk that way about a commissioned officer of the United States Army again." He stood up and walked over to the commo desk and began to adjust the frequency dial of one of the radios.

"Nobody's sent any orders down here about pets, so I think we can take care of this without breaking any orders. Or badmouthing the brigade commander."

Sergeant Johnson started to sit down, but Pappy Stagg held up his hand to stop him. "Don't you have to do some coordination for Two-Two's mission tomorrow?"

Sergeant Johnson nodded.

"All right then, get to it. And while you're at it, have Wolverine police up Tiger and get down here with him on the double."

Sergeant Johnson smiled. "Right, Top. I knew you'd come up with something."

Pappy Stagg groaned and picked up the headset to the radio he'd just adjusted. "One of these days," he thought, "these young staff sergeants are gonna have to learn how to get things done in this man's army. They ain't always gonna have old Stagg around to pull their nuts out of the fire."

From the road the perimeter of the Louc Ma Special Forces Camp looked downright deadly—and it was, in fact, every bit as deadly as it looked. Right next to the shoulder of the road there was a barbed-wire fence as high as a tall man's chest, and on every post was a rectangular wooden sign saying DANGER MINES in English, Vietnamese, Cambodian, and Chinese. Beyond the fence was a barren strip of ground that obviously concealed at least a few of these mines, and twenty meters from the road was the first of many lines of concertina wire on which were huge empty cans and trip flares. Between each line of concertina wire, the ground bristled with jagged steel stakes and sharpened bamboo punji sticks. Some of these were angled in toward the camp and some pointed straight up at the gray, overcast sky. But most of them were angled out so that anyone lucky enough to make it through the minefield, but clumsy enough to set off a trip flare or rattle a can, would have a choice of staying on his feet to be shot or throwing himself down to die slowly, impaled on the stakes.

Beyond the concertina wire was another barren strip of land—another minefield—and then an ankle-high grid of charged wire that crackled ominously in the moist air.

A few meters beyond this grid were at least a hundred Claymore mines. Some of them were set up at ground level, standing free. Some were backed against sandbags or mounds of hardpacked dirt, and yet others were mounted, gut high, on wooden posts. Behind the Claymores was another row of concertina and trip flares, then a thick rampart of solid earth reinforced with concrete. Beyond this was a stockade wall of logs and sandbags, topped with barbed wire and dotted with concrete firing positions.

At every corner of the perimeter there was a watchtower equipped with high-intensity floodlights, machine guns, and night-vision scopes. These watchtowers were manned twenty-four hours a day by Nung Chinese guards, each of whom dearly hoped to win a month's bonus pay for being the first to spot and kill any unauthorized intruder.

Pappy Stagg had Wolverine stop the jeep before turning onto the camp's access drive. "Now *that*," he declared, "is a real work of art. Old Nick Hogg designed it himself. Then, just as he was getting settled in as team sergeant here, he got promoted and they made him a battalion sergeant major in the 173rd Airborne." He held the squirming Tiger down with one hand and waved expansively with the other.

"Put yourself in the other guy's boots for a second and try to imagine breaking through a perimeter like that. Kinda makes you glad you was born an American, eh?"

Wolverine grunted noncommittally and turned onto the access drive. He drove slowly over the lump where a fougas bomb was buried and paused while one of the Nungs swung the gate open for them and stepped back to wave them on. Just inside the gate there was a thirty-caliber machine-gun position, and behind that a sign saying Remember the Alamo!

Wolverine took a left and drove past the Nung barracks and a mortar pit. There was another sign here: Remember the Maine!

They passed the dispensary and a short, dug-in firing range where an American in tiger fatigues and green beret was inspecting a platoon of Strikers before sending them out on patrol. There was another sign here, between the dispensary and firing range: Remember Termopoly!

Wolverine sighed and drove on past the ramshackle hootches where the Montagnards lived. He slowed the jeep and honked at some chickens pecking on the roadway, and although the chickens weren't impressed with his horn, a wizened old Montagnard woman with enormous ears and a broad, toothless witch's smile came running out of her shack to wave at the jeep as it crept by.

"Pull over there on the right," Pappy Stagg directed, and Wolverine brought the jeep to a halt next to a very small plywood sign that begged the visitor, Forget About Louc Ma A-566.

They'd had almost the same series of signs, running like an old-time Burma Shave ad, along the access drive to the last "A" Camp Wolverine had served in. But the signs there hadn't done any good. The damn place had almost been overrun, and Wolverine knew he'd never forget Thuan Dien, "A-517."

Wolverine got out of the jeep and waited for Pappy Stagg to calm Tiger. Tiger was sniffing furiously, taking in all the new smells. His tail was curled up against his belly and his ears lay flat against his head. He'd never smelled so many gooks together, and it was all Pappy Stagg could manage to keep him from twisting free and racing back toward the camp gate.

"Calm down, boy. Calm down." Pappy tied a length of nylon cord to Tiger's collar and put him on the ground. "Calm down, boy. You're too damn ugly for these people to eat. You'll be all right if you calm down."

As soon as Pappy put him down, Tiger slipped his collar and crawled under the jeep.

"Fucking contrary little mutt!" Wolverine muttered. He went down on his knees in the mud and pulled Tiger out from between the front wheels.

"You'd think he was born in Kansas or some goddamn place, Top, the way the smell of a few indigenous personnel spooks him." Tiger twisted and squirmed and tried to push Wolverine away with his back feet. "Come on, Tiger! Stop fighting me, goddamn it! No one's gonna let any of these Strikers eat you, for chrissake! Relax!"

Tiger was trembling so violently Wolverine had to pick him up and carry him into the team house.

The Special Forces team house had once been a tax office, and before that it had been a French schoolhouse. It still had most of its original roofing tiles, and where the tiles had cracked or crumbled, they had been replaced by sheets of perforated steel planking and mounds of gray sandbags that blended surprisingly well with the faded orange tiles. The windows had long been sealed, and there were sandbags chest high and five feet thick around the outside walls, but the words *Liberté, Egalité, Fraternité* were still visible, mossy, weathered, and nowhere near as inspiring as they once might have been, in stone relief above the entrance.

Pappy Stagg and Wolverine pushed open the screen door and stepped inside. Immediately Tiger began to sneeze as the odor of cigarette smoke and bug spray hit his nose. Wolverine put him down on the cool concrete floor but kept a tight grip on his leash.

Just inside the door were two rows of cots and a folding card table behind which sat a short, barrel-chested master sergeant with a flat-top haircut and a most unmilitary paunch. When he heard the screen door slam shut he looked up, grumpy as a troll, but when he recognized Pappy Stagg he leapt to his feet and almost knocked over the card table.

"I'll be double damned and shot from a cannon! I couldn't believe it when the radio watch said you was coming, but here you are, ugly as ever, you old buzzard! Tom Stagg! Sit down and take a load off your mind, you sorry old straphanger, you!"

Pappy Stagg and Wolverine pulled up a couple of chairs and sat down, and while Pappy's old buddy rummaged around in a footlocker for something to drink, Wolverine tied Tiger's leash to the leg of his chair.

"Who's your sidekick there?" The team sergeant put a fifth of Jim Beam and three canteen cups down on the card table. "Not the staff sergeant—I've seen him around somewhere. I mean your other sidekick, the four-legged troop in the dirty tiger fatigues. He one of your Airborne hippies from that Lurp platoon?"

Pappy Stagg nodded. "Sure is." He bent down to scratch Tiger's ear. "This here is our number-one relief pointman, Tiger the Lurp Dog. Tiger, this overweight ape here is Cubby Cardiff."

Somewhat relieved to be surrounded by the familiar American scents of the team house, Tiger was no longer trembling. The tip of his tail twitched slightly at mention of his name, and he snuggled up close to Wolverine's boot. He peered up suspiciously at the team sergeant, then sneezed indignantly and looked away.

The team sergeant passed around the canteen cups and the fifth of Jim Beam.

"Go on, pour yourself a man-sized drink. It's the captain's bottle, but he's out on patrol, so we may as well kill it for him."

Pappy Stagg shook his head fondly and poured himself a stiff shot, then passed the bottle on to Wolverine. Cubby Cardiff always had been a larcenous ape, and it was good to know he was still up to his old ways, being generous with someone else's whiskey and bragging about it to show there was no harm meant.

Cubby Cardiff raised his canteen cup and proposed a toast. "To Vietnam!" he said. "It ain't much of a war, but it'll do till something better breaks out."

All three men drained their cups and the bottle went around again. Pappy Stagg poured himself a good three or four ounces. Now that the first drink was out of the way, he'd be able to sip at his leisure.

Wolverine, on the other hand, only wet the bottom of his cup. He was beginning to feel a little uncomfortable about leaving Tiger in a camp full of dog-eating Yards, Cambodes, Viets, and Nungs. And on top of that, he could remember hearing a few bad things about this Cubby Cardiff character's eating habits. Jake LaGrange used to swear he'd seen Cardiff dig the liver out of a freshly killed VC and take a bite out of it, just like some goddamn deep-mountain cannibal.

Pappy Stagg and Cubby Cardiff were reminiscing about Panama, playing the old remember-when game.

"Yeah, that was some full-blown asskickin' bitch of a party we had after that trip to wherever the fuck it was we went to train that Ranger battalion. Where the fuck was that, anyway, Stagg? Honduras?"

Pappy Stagg swallowed a respectable slug of Jim Beam. He shook his head. "Naw, Nicaragua maybe. Or—no wait—it was Chile. Damn it, Cubby, you old ape! We're gettin' old if we can't remember that!" Pappy Stagg laughed and ran his hand over his closely cropped gray hair. "Time to buy that plot of land in Florida and invest in some fishin' gear, I guess."

He drained his cup in three big gulps and reached for a refill. It was good whiskey—cheap but good—and if he was drinking too much, too fast, so what? Wolverine was sipping like an old grandma, and he could drive home if it came to that.

"Nice drink you got here. I always said Beam's as good as Daniels, and a damn sight cheaper to boot, eh?"

Cubby Cardiff belched and waved his hand disparagingly and allowed as how he preferred Jack Daniels himself, but couldn't persuade that skinflint young West Point captain commanding the team to spring loose the few extra bucks for it.

"Every time that young captain—or the buck sergeant we got for a junior medic, for that matter—every time one of 'em goes out on patrol for more'n a day or two . . . why hell's bells, Stagg! They ain't got a bit of consideration for an old man's liver. By God, they don't!" He turned a baleful gaze on Wolverine for a few seconds, then belched again and reached for the bottle to refill his canteen cup.

"These young studs comin' up now ain't got enough sense to lock their bottles away. If it weren't for old goats like you'n me, Stagg, why hell, they'd all be a bunch of fuckin' alcoholics, if it wasn't for you'n me an' the likes of us!"

Pappy Stagg chuckled and topped off his canteen cup. "It's a responsibility, for sure," he allowed. "Don't nobody give a damn about them but us," he added with a solemn nod of his head. "That's why I come to see you today. We've been around, you and me, eh? And we've had it pretty good. But these kids now, we gotta watch out for them, 'cause ain't nobody else gonna do it."

Cubby Cardiff looked into his canteen cup as if searching for something—an insect, or perhaps some portent of the future—in the sediment that washed back and forth in the bottom when he tilted the cup and held it in the light. Didn't make any difference how often you scrubbed a canteen cup, the damn things never came clean. Finally he found whatever it was he was looking for—or gave up the search—and put his cup down on the card table and reached over to pick up a cigarette that Wolverine had left smoldering in the ashtray. He took a drag on the cigarette then stubbed it out and sighed.

"Stagg," he said, exhaling a thin stream of smoke from the corner of his mouth, "Just what're you gettin' at? Speak clear, man, so I know what the fuck you're tryin' to say."

Pappy Stagg lit a cigarette of his own and looked down at Tiger, curled up and sleeping with his head on the instep of Wolverine's boot. Poor little dude looked so trusting and peaceful, it was a shame to have to leave him here with all these strangers and dogeating indigenous personnel.

"I want you to take in old Tiger here for a couple of weeks. We got a rabies scare back in the base camp and the general's got the MPs shooting all the pets.

If you just put him up till the heat dies down . . . He won't be any trouble. He don't eat much. . . ."

"Eat much?" Cubby Cardiff stood up and slapped the side of his head in amazement. "Hell's bells, Stagg! You know what I got in this camp? I got forty-two hungry Nungs. Couple hundred Cambodes and Yards, and more dog-eatin' Viets than you can shake a snake at. I seen how that dog come in here—all shakin' and tremblin' from smelling them indigenous personnel out there. Problem ain't gonna be what he eats—it's what eats him."

It was already the middle of December, and dog meat was a prime winter treat.

"Aw, come off it now." Pappy Stagg wasn't about to let him get away this easily. "I known you how long? Eighteen years? If you can't keep one little pup outa the soup pot, you sure ain't the same Cubby Cardiff I used to know."

"I don't know . . ." Cubby Cardiff looked down at Tiger and shook his head. "He don't look too smart to me. I got me an 'A' Camp to run here. And a whole passel of hungry Strikers. You know how they get when there's a chill in the air; a taste of pup thickens the blood, they say. Like as not, I believe it myself."

Pappy Stagg was drunker than he'd been in months. He stood up slowly, moving like a man with a bad back and a hundred years of hard living behind him. He smiled sadly and put his hand on Cubby Cardiff's shoulder.

"I guess we all get cautious in our old age." He sighed and shook his head. "Just never thought I'd live long enough to see it happen to you."

Tiger lifted his head for a second and growled softly at something moving by outside the team house—a gook perhaps, or a chicken or pig. Wolverine dropped his hand to calm the dog, but he kept his eyes on the two master sergeants, shocked at how old they'd both sounded with all their talk of past adventures and dead or retired friends. And now they were talking about now, talking about themselves, and they sounded even older.

Cubby Cardiff hadn't noticed Tiger's growl. He was thinking about the Ashau Valley, remembering the worst day of his life. He turned his palms up and rolled his eyes toward Heaven, begging Mars or Odin—whoever was the deity in charge of old soldiers—to witness his travails. He took a deep breath and let it out slowly. And then he gave in, for the sake of old times.

"Awright, awright damn it. I'll hide your dog and try to keep him outa the soup pot. I ain't promising nothin', but I'll give it my best shot."

"That's all I want," said Pappy Stagg. He reached down to strike Tiger's back, then stood up and grinned. He looked down and then bent over to give the dog a final pat on the head.

"He's a good dog, that Tiger. He might not look like much, but he's a good dog even so."

At the sound of his name, Tiger's ears perked, and he thumped his tail against the ground. He accepted Pappy Stagg's goodbye pat with a haughty tolerance, blinking his eyes because the hand was heavier than usual, and when Wolverine stood up and followed Pappy to the door, he scrambled to his feet to go with them. He almost made it to the door, but the leash suddenly brought him up short. He yipped in surprise, then whirled, took the leash in his mouth, and threw his weight forward, upsetting the chair to which he was tied and dragging it across the floor until he got as far as the doorway. But the screen door slammed shut in his face. He could hear Pappy Stagg telling Wolverine to ride shotgun and let him drive, and though he yanked once more at his leash, the chair was hung up between a footlocker and the legs of the card table, and wouldn't budge. Frantically, he clawed at his collar and tried to slip it over his head, but before he was able to free himself, Cubby Cardiff had him by the tail and pulled him back from the door. The squat old master sergeant gathered Tiger up in his arms and sat down on his bunk.

"C'mon, my little friend," he said with a gentleness he usually reserved for severely wounded soldiers. "There ain't no use cryin' about things you can't control. They ain't nobody doin' nothin' but what has to be done. He'll be back for you. That old buzzard Tom Stagg came back to carry me out of the Ashau that time—I know he'll be back for you."

Tiger whimpered softly and curled his tail up against his belly, but even when Cubby Cardiff put him down to pour himself another drink, he didn't try to get away. The important thing now was to stay close to the team house, close to familiar American smells, to eat enough to drive away the loneliness. There was no sense in escaping on an empty stomach.

# CHAPTER 16

FOR FIVE DAYS RUNNING THE STORM CLOUDS ROLLED off the ocean, lashing the scrublands and rice fields with sweeping curtains of rain and turning the Louc Ma road into a river of mud. In the town of Louc Ma the sewers overflowed into the shops and houses, and outside the town the farmers shivered under their leaf hats and plastic rain capes as they watched their fields flood and their crops wash away.

The storm swept over the coastal flatlands and lost none of its fury battering the abandoned terraces in the foothills. Far to the west, in the mountains along the Laotian border, Lurp Team Two-Two found itself without communication just after stumbling across a well-guarded high-speed trail. After a brief firefight, Two-Two successfully broke contact with a white phosphorus grenade, then, grateful for the rain that covered their movement, they hit their Escape and Evasion route for Firebase Culculine. All night and all the next day they broke bush, alternately cursing the weather for interfering with their commo and turning the slopes into treacherous mudslides, and thanking that Great Ranger in the Sky for sending the rain and misty darkness that made it easier to evade the NVA patrols that were certainly out for them after the firefight.

They kept moving night and day, pausing only in the thickest of high-ground vegetation to catch an occasional short nap and run up a wire antenna in hopes of raising the relay team. By the seventh day of what should have been a four-day mission, they were so low on food and so exhausted that the team leader broke out his pill kit and passed around the dextroamphetamines.

On the morning of the eighth day they heard signal shots on a ridgeline to their southwest and answering shots very close—a hundred meters at the most—to their northeast. Alarmed to discover the enemy moving in on them, they cut due south, crossing three trails and a freshly swollen stream. They plotted the trails and stream on their map overlays, then jogged west along the contour of a defoliated hillside.

Here, they surprised and killed three NVA couriers. The couriers were carrying oilcloth pouches full of papers. The ATL stuffed the pouches into his rucksack, and the team leader decided to take one of the dead men's weapons—just in case they might have cause to fire again and couldn't risk giving themselves away with the distinctive sound of their own CAR-15s.

Shortly before noon of the ninth day the weather broke, and Two-Two made its way back to its prearranged Escape and Evasion route. The team was still a long way from Culculine, but now the clouds were lifting, and with a little luck and the help of a wire antenna they ought to be able to get the relay on the horn. They had the wire, but they didn't have any luck in raising the relay team. They pushed on to the northeast, over one ridgeline, down a steep draw, and up another ridge.

By now the men of Two-Two were thoroughly exhausted. The skin between their fingers and toes was cracked and bleeding. Their hands, forearms, and cheeks were crisscrossed with thorn scratches and bramble cuts. The leech bites on their legs and necks and waists were beginning to fester. They now had one beef and rice Lurp ration and four cornflake bars to go around, and all of them except the ATL—who never touched the stuff—were coming down hard from the pills. Ever since killing the three NVA, they had seen and heard no sign of the enemy—no trails, no signal shots coming from the flanks—and now they were too tired to do anything but pull themselves up by vines and saplings and bushes, climbing hand over hand for the high ground where they could run out a wire and try once more to raise the relay team.

They were halfway up the slope when they heard a helicopter circling slowly, three or four kilometers to the west. Every man stopped in place to listen, and the team leader unhooked his headset from the loop on his rucksack strap where he'd been carrying it ever since losing commo days before. He put the headset next to his ear and reached back for the pole antenna.

Suddenly there was a crackle of static and then, very softly, Pappy Stagg's voice came over the horn.

"Tacky Blinker Two-Two, Tacky Blinker Two-Two . . . This is Tacky Blinker Eight, over."

Two-Two's team leader grinned and handed the headset to his ATL.

"What did I tell you, huh?" he whispered. "I bet that old bastard had to hold a gun to the pilot's head to get him to fly through this soup. But there he is. You gotta have faith."

The ATL was grinning even wider than the team leader. They weren't out yet—they still had to make it to an LZ, because even if the ship was rigged to drop McQuire harnesses and pull them up through a gap in the canopy, one ship could only carry three rigs, and it wouldn't do to split the team with the weather likely to close in again before Pappy could get back for a second run. And for all anyone knew the NVA was still on their trail. But with Pappy Stagg up there helping them out, it shouldn't be too hard to find some sort of LZ.

"Fuck a bunch of faith," the ATL said aloud. He shook the tangles out of the headset cord and started to acknowledge Pappy's transmission, then paused and handed the headset back to the team leader. "Let's just let him collect some flight time. Now that we've come this far, I feel like humping all the way to Culculine."

He didn't mean a word of it. It just seemed like the right thing to say at the time. With Pappy Stagg up there looking out for them, they were as good as home.

# CHAPTER 17

MASTER SERGEANT CARDIFF WAS WHEEZING AND snoring his way through a dream about a forest of carnivorous trees. A raspy tentacle of vine had just begun to creep up his back when the young medic shook his shoulder. Cardiff woke with a start, sputtering and grabbing for his weapon, then realized that he was in his bunk in the team house, not in the carnivorous forest, and that his weapon was hanging on the wall, not lying at his side.

He sat up and rubbed his eyes. "What is it?" He glanced at the gold Rolex watch for which he'd blown six months' base pay and frowned. "It's 0420 hours, for God's sake! What's up?"

"Tiger. He's out in the wire. He just set off a trip flare."

140

Cubby Cardiff was instantly alert. He kicked off his jungle blanket and leapt out of bed. He grabbed his weapon, then, barefoot and dressed only in his green Army shorts, raced for the door. "Which sector?" he bellowed. "Goddamnit! Which fuckin' sector?"

"West. Just north of the gate." The medic was already falling behind in the rush out of the team house. He barely had time to spin around and dodge the card table before Cubby Cardiff burst through the door, yelling for someone to turn off the current in the wire grid, screaming in Vietnamese that he'd castrate the first man to open fire.

Halfway to the gate the young medic slipped in a tire track and rolled in a mud puddle. He came up running, but Cubby Cardiff was already far ahead, clambering up the ladder to the watchtower with all the grace of an outraged honey bear.

"Outa my way! Outa my way!" He elbowed aside the Nung at the machine gun and grabbed the Starlight scope from the Vietnamese lieutenant who'd been holding it cradled against his chest.

"Give me that scope!" He jammed the Starlight to his eye without taking the normal precaution of turning it off first so that the faint green light wouldn't fall on his face. It wasn't necessary to waste time with dumb precautions when any fool knew there were no snipers out there—and no sappers—just that old buzzard Stagg's scroungy little ragged-eared mutt.

The flare Tiger'd set off was still smoldering in the mud. It wasn't putting out much light now, nothing but an ember's glow reflecting weakly off the ground water, but it was enough to give Cubby Cardiff a reference point. He scanned left and right, looking for movement. His eyes were still adjusting to the strange, washed-out, colorless landscape in the scope, and he couldn't pick up much detail. He fiddled with the focus and suddenly he could make out a Claymore mine attached to a gut-high wooden pole.

There was a trip wire attached to the firing device screwed into the top of the Claymore. The detail had been there all along, and now that he could recognize what he was seeing, Cubby Cardiff felt like a fool. Even if he hadn't grown up in front of the picture tube like most of these kids, he still ought to be able to spot a trip-wired Claymore as soon as his eyes swept over it. After all these years, he should've been able to spot a trip-wired Claymore through a black rubber blindfold.

Muttering and cursing under his breath, he steadied his elbows on one of the sandbags next to the tower's M-60 machine gun. He took a deep breath and let it halfway out, just like he was firing on the record range. Then he slowly followed the wire to Tiger the Lurp Dog.

"Holy Mother of God!" He exhaled and handed the Starlight scope back to the young medic. This was worse than he'd imagined.

The young medic was supposed to be back at the aid station, organizing his stretcher crews, racking up his bottles of serum albumin, and laying out his surgical gear. That was his duty whenever there was a perimeter alert. But this was different. He took the Starlight scope, bent his head to its eyepiece, and brought it up without greening his face. Having grown up with television, he had no trouble finding Tiger on the first sweep.

"Jesus H. Christ!" the medic said very softly. He handed the scope to Lieutenant Hoang, the Vietnamese team's executive officer.

Lieutenant Hoang took the Starlight and held it a delicate two inches from his eye. He had long, gentlemanly nails on his pinkies, and because he was determined to protect this relic of his status in the Confucian world of civilized people, he held the scope

142

with all the stiff propriety of an English matron examining a fine piece of crystal. He never found Tiger, but he handed the Starlight scope back to Cubby Cardiff and shook his head with an absolutely reverent display of sadness. He'd been the first team member—Vietnamese or American—to get to the tower when the trip flare popped, and it was he who had hollered "Ting Ho!" in Chinese to stop the Nungs from firing. He knew the Americans were very touchy about that fat little beggar dog. But he couldn't figure out why.

He was nothing but a mongrel—a dust dog—a scavenging camp follower. His tongue was always hanging out of his mouth, dripping on things. He bit the Dai Uy—the Vietnamese team commander—on the ankle. And worst of all, he lifted his leg against the camp flagpole—he pissed against the flag of the Republic of Vietnam!

He was certainly a local dog. The Americans had poodles and St. Bernards and big, mean, guard-dog Alsatians. They would never have brought an ugly, brown and black, half-wild dust dog with them from America. He was a Vietnamese dog, all right—he even looked like a Striker's cast-off fatigues—and he was only alive today because his ancestors were too thin and mangy for the pot. But now this dust dog, this Tiger, was too fat and too sassy for his own good. He was sassy enough to steal two baby chickens from the Vietnamese team—sassy enough to snap at the Dai Uy and piss on the camp flagpole. He'd had it soft for a while, this dust dog Tiger, but now he was standing in the mud with his tail up against a trip wire, and Lieutenant Hoang secretly prayed to see him hit the wire with his full rump and blow his ass away.

"Very terrible, I think, E-8 Cardiff." The lieutenant had majored in French and English in college, then picked up some Chinese on his own in Cholon,

143

and he could lie like a champ in four languages. "Very terrible, I think," he sympathized. "Very terrible for this nice pet. Very too bad," he said with a sad shrug of regret, thinking at the same time how much more gracefully he could've said it if the Americans only spoke better French.

The Nung tower guard smiled to himself and turned aloofly away from the others. He didn't need a Starlight to see what was going on. The Americans were crazy—all of them. It would be easy to calm the dog down with a bullet and save the cost of a Claymore. A well-placed bullet's impact would throw the dog away from the trip wire and keep the Claymore from going off and blowing a gap in the wire grid and the innermost roll of concertina wire. The Nung had a morbid fear of mines, and he didn't like the thought of repairing that perimeter.

Even Master Sergeant Cardiff had a fear of his own riding on Tiger. "Tom Stagg is gonna skin me alive if that dog just wags his fuckin' tail!" he whispered to the young medic. "I'll give you three to one on your jump pay he blows his ass away." It was always good policy to bet against sentiment and self-interest. That way, you were protected whatever happened.

Cubby Cardiff was a sharp old schemer, but the young medic wasn't impressed. He had a B.S. in psychology in a premed concentration, and he'd been in the Army long enough to see through sour old master sergeants and their pessimistic bet hedging. He also knew enough to up the ante. "Throw in a month's combat pay," he said, "and I'll take you up on it."

Cubby Cardiff nodded in hasty assent and lifted the Starlight.

Out in the perimeter, Tiger was still growling at the sizzling stub of the trip flare. He bristled his ruff and cocked his ears to the front. He lifted his right forepaw, then put it down and lifted his left, and put it down in its original spot next to the right. He lowered his head and sniffed against the taut, unmoving wire. He tasted the ground water with his tongue, then lifted his head and pointed his nose straight into the air to sniff the last whiff of acrid smoke coming off the trip flare. For just a second he looked like he was going to throw his head back even further and give voice to a lonely wolf howl, and Cubby Cardiff shrank back behind the sandbagged tower walls to avoid the mud and dog flesh that would surely be thrown back by the Claymore's backblast. Tiger was standing less than two meters to the side of the Claymore and would probably be blown at least three ways if it went off.

Tiger didn't howl, but his tail moved. It slipped under the wire and stopped less than an inch from the other side. Still taut, the trip wire was now resting on the top of his tail. Cubby Cardiff peeked over the sandbags, then rose and passed the Starlight back to the young medic. He didn't want to see things in all that unnatural, colorless, video detail anymore. A man should be able to count on his night vision.

"Poor dog's situation ain't no better," whispered the young medic. He wished he'd bet base pay instead of jump and combat pay. The difference between E-5 and E-8 would really count for something that way. Jump pay was the same for all enlisted personnel, and combat pay the same for everyone. Right now it didn't look good, and the young medic consoled himself by adding up his jump pay and combat pay, then subtracting the sum from his base pay and discovering that he'd still have enough to save for R&R. With his tail brushing that close to the trip wire, Tiger was certain to blow himself away.

Lieutenant Hoang took the Starlight scope from the medic. This time he scrunched the rubber eyepiece up against his eye and took a long, careful look.

He was secretly delighted. That dust dog of the Americans sure had himself in a fix. His right rear hip was too close to the trip wire for there to be a shadow, and his tail was touching it. His tail was curving up under the wire now, and as fat and undisciplined as that tail was, any second now it was certain to blow the Claymore.

"Pitiful, I think," he said. He handed the Starlight scope on to the American team sergeant and stepped back to stand next to the young medic, where he was less likely to end up with a mud-splattered uniform. He was wet already, but if the backblast of the Claymore happened to hit the earthen ramparts at the wrong angle he didn't want to end up with a faceful of mud and dog blood.

Cubby Cardiff took the Starlight scope from Lieutenant Hoang and shut it off. All this modern technology was well and good, and there was no question but that it could help a good man fight a war. But it was the height of arrogant stupidity to grow dependent on it. He capped the end of the Starlight scope and put it back in its cushioned case.

"From now on," he announced aloud, "we will watch with our own eyes."

He hoped the medic wouldn't try to weasel out of the bet, now that things had gone from bad to worse. That tail curling up under the trip wire didn't bode too well for Tiger's survival.

Suddenly there was a flash of light and a crack of thunder as the Claymore exploded. As soon as the last mud droplet from the backblast splattered against the sandbags at the tower's base, Cubby Cardiff was up again with the Starlight scope.

He could see a huge gash in the ground where the Claymore had exploded. A swath of furrowed mud and twisted wire had been blown through the grid, but there was no sign of Tiger. For just an instant, Cubby Cardiff wondered how he was going to explain this to Pappy Stagg. Then he thought of his wager and forced himself to smile. He handed the Starlight back to the young medic.

"That'll be a hundred-twenty dollars come payday," he said. "There ain't nothin' left of old Stagg's dog now. The poor fucker's probably strewn all over the perimeter."

The young medic had excellent night vision. "You better put away the Starlight scope, boss. Why don't you turn on the searchlight, shine it on the concertina, and start kissing your payday goodbye."

Grumbling about snipers and smartass E-5s, Cubby Cardiff switched on the searchlight and bathed the first roll of concertina wire in a harsh white light.

There was Tiger. He froze for a second, then looked over his shoulder. Hearing one of the Americans call his name, he wagged his tail once or twice, then continued picking his way through the tangles of jagged wire. His coat was caked with mud, and he was carrying his head and tail low, like a skulking coyote. But he moved easily, and there was no sign of wounds or other damage. Halfway through the wire he sat down to scratch his ear with his right rear foot.

Lieutenant Hoang tapped Cubby Cardiff on the shoulder. "Twenty dollars U.S. money," he said, flashing a smile full of gold teeth. "I bet twenty dollars U.S. he go through punji stakes O.K."

Cubby Cardiff nodded unhappily. The punji stakes were the easiest obstacle in the whole perimeter, but after watching Tiger use the Claymore to blow himself a path through the grid, then romp through the inner minefield and pick his way through the gap in the concertina, it would be cowardly to refuse the bet.

"You're on, sir," he growled from the side of his mouth. "He gets through all those sticks and the next rolls of wire, you got your twenty bucks. But I lay you both four to one he don't make the road."

"You're on!" cried the young medic with an excess of enthusiasm.

"Not be easy, I think," said Lieutenant Hoang. "But I think so. O.K.!" He was making good money now, with his share of the whorehouse profits, and he could afford the gamble. It would have been a loss of face to back down after becoming involved in the betting.

The Nuang had only a few phrases of English, but he knew what was going on. Nobody ever got upset if he shot a rabbit in the perimeter, and he dearly wanted to show the American team sergeant how well he could shoot. But now that there was money riding on the dog, he too wanted to get into the game.

"Lao San!" He hollered down to one of the other Nungs lined up along the wall to watch the show. He held up five fingers. His friend, Lao San, looked up and nodded, then drew his forefinger across his throat and the bet was on.

By now, Tiger was used to the glare of the searchlight. The flare had spooked him, and then the sudden explosion of the Claymore had knocked him off his feet and sent him tumbling over a mound of mud. But except for a ringing in his ears, he hadn't been hurt. Very cautiously, he sniffed the ground around the first cluster of punji stakes, then sniffed the tip of each stake separately. They'd been dipped in shit to ensure that any nonfatal wounds they caused would become infected, but too much rain and too much sun had washed away most of the scent. Tiger lifted his leg and pissed on first one stake, then another. He kicked a little wet soil through his rear legs, then squeezed between two stakes and paused to shake some rainwater and mud from his coat.

"That dog ain't gonna make it another two meters!" declared Cubby Cardiff. "Them stakes was easy. They caught some of the blast, but if he makes it through the next roll of wire without settin' nothin' off, he's gonna find himself hemmed in so tight he won't be able to turn around."

It was true. The punji stakes in the next rank were much closer together. But first Tiger had to get through the concertina wire, and this roll was intact.

He approached the closest loop of wire warily and nudged it with his nose, then backed off, spooked when a cluster of beer cans three loops down began to bounce and rattle and the wire itself sprang back and almost rapped him on the snout. He cocked his head from side to side, sizing things up, then reached out with his paw and gave the wire another tentative nudge. Again the cans rattled and bounced, and once again the wire itself jumped and shivered as if it were alive. With a patient sign, Tiger sat down to scratch his other ear and wait for the wire to stop jiggling.

"What did I tell you?" Cubby Cardiff gloated. "He's stumped now. If he tries backtrackin', like as not he'll blow his ass away on one of them mines. You jokers feel like paying up now?"

Both the young medic and Lieutenant Hoang shook their heads.

"C'mon, boss," grinned the young medic, "you ain't getting off that easy."

By now, almost the entire population of the camp was lined up along the wall to watch. The Nungs who weren't on duty were cracking melon seeds between their teeth and making bets among themselves. All of them were wearing web gear and carrying their weapons, and though they were enjoying the show, they were still a little disappointed that there wasn't going to be any shooting. The members of the Vietnamese Special Forces team—all of them except Lieutenant Hoang, who was following Cubby Cardiff's lead and betting against sentiment—hated Tiger and wanted to see him blown all over the perimeter. The Vietnamese in the Strike Force, however, remembered Tiger nipping the Dai Uy's ankle, so they were rooting him on and wishing him the best, while the Cambodes and Yards looked on silently, content to let him work out his own fate. The Americans were almost to a man on Tiger's side. But Tiger had his pride. He ignored them one and all.

Scratching and digging with his nose and forepaws, he cleared a space around him, then went down on his belly and crawled right up to the concertina wire. He rose halfway and touched the bottom of one loop, then jerked his paw back, yipping with surprise and pain. He'd made it through that first blasted-out roll without discovering the barbs on the wire. But now he knew, and now he was leery.

"Barbed wire," said Cubby Cardiff with grim satisfaction, "barbed wire makes believers out of 'em every time."

Tiger licked his forepaw and stood up. The rain had been light all night and now it had stopped completely. The clouds were still thick and dark and low, and there was almost no breeze. The camp odors were trapped in the humid air, and without lifting his nose, Tiger could smell the people gathered along the wall and in the towers to watch his progress through the perimeter. He could smell their cigarettes and sweat, the insect repellent on their skin, and the stench of Nouc Mam sauce, tobacco, liquor, and onions on their breath. He could hear them talking and laughing and moving around, and he could feel their eyes on him. But he didn't care. He didn't like them, he didn't trust them, and he wouldn't let them stop him from going home. He yawned and stretched, his forelegs flat on the muddy ground, his tail high and curled proudly, and his rear end pointing directly at the tower where Cubby Cardiff was manning the searchlight.

"I think he's trying to tell you to kiss his ass, boss," laughed the young medic.

Before Cubby Cardiff could reply, Tiger stood up. He stepped delicately between two loops of the wire and kept on going. He seemed to know just where to put his feet, just how high he could hold his head and tail to avoid snagging the barbs. Without having to think about it, he knew just how much to draw in his shoulders to keep from brushing against the loops and sending the whole roll oscillating on down the line, slapping loops together and bouncing them apart with enough dance to set off every booby-trap for ten meters in either direction.

Tiger was a smart little sapper, and a patient, lucky one at that. There was almost nothing in the world that Cubby Cardiff respected more than a patient, lucky sapper. Now, there was nothing too shameful about being a drunken, tough, old potbellied fireplug of a cockhound master sergeant. And a lot of men smart enough not to try probably daydreamed of seeing the exotic, disease-ridden places where he'd spent a third of his life. A lot of men dreamed of doing the sort of things he, Master Sergeant Cardiff of the United States Army Special Forces, had been doing since he was seventeen. But the one thing he never wanted to find himself doing was crawling through a knock-up mantrap of a perimeter like this one. And the one thing sure to impress him, to raise the goosebumps and bristle his forearm hairs, was the sight of a patient, lucky, wire-dodging sapper going methodically about his job.

"Flaunt it while you got it, 'cause you won't have it long," he whispered very softly so there wouldn't be any chance of distracting or influencing Tiger, out there picking his way through the wire.

The tower and the wall were suddenly silent. Even

the Viets from the strike force cut off their grabass chattering and peered expectantly and nervously over the sandbags.

Stiff, still, bristling, and alert, Tiger the Lurp Dog was standing frozen in the middle of the roll of wire. His ears were cocked forward, and his eyes and nose focused downward on the next step. There, on his chest, tight as the winner's tape at a track meet, was a strand of thick black commo wire that had somehow tangled itself around a loop of concertina wire so thickly strung with fishline trip wires that it looked in the glare of the searchlight like some horrible barbed ring of spider web.

Tiger seemed to cower a little. He flattened his ears against his head, and Cubby Cardiff was sure he saw him lick his chops nervously before squinting and turning his head away. He kept his feet in place but pushed his chest forward, testing the wire, caring nothing for the white phosphorus grenade that was nested at the junction of the web of trip wires. He was only testing for barbs and feeling out the slack. Suddenly he stepped back, took the wire in his mouth, and yanked it free. A thunderous roar of applause and cheering came welling up behind him, but Tiger wasn't impressed. He squirmed on out of the concertina and pranced, head high and tail bouncing like a fat antenna, into the next line of punji stakes.

After a brief, sniffing investigation he had the measure of the stakes. Their foundations had turned to mud, and they'd been arranged in close clusters, rather than banks and lines, so it was easy to wind among them. He was through in fifteen seconds, and after scent marking the last cluster with a jet of urine, he disappeared into the next roll of concertina wire.

Now the only part of him visible from the tower

was his tail. Every few seconds it appeared, bobbing and bouncing beyond another roll of wire.

"You want to toss a month's base pay into this operation, boss?" asked the young medic smugly.

"Sure as hell do!" Cubby Cardiff tossed him an evil smile. "I'm the only swinging dick in the camp that's seen old Nick Hogg's mine chart, and I tell you this: Ain't nothing but God's own angels or a skinny fruit fly can cross through that next twenty-meter minefield and stand up alive on the other side of the fence." He shook his head. "No way, Buck Sergeant. I been in this man's army long enough to know when there's a way, an' I tell you this, goddamn it, there ain't no motherfucking way!

"Will I throw in my base pay against your E-5? You're goddamn right I will! I'll even throw in my pro pay and rations allowance, you wet-nose rookie Buck Sergeant E-5. There just ain't no way he's gonna make it!"

By this time, Tiger was halfway through the last and outermost row of concertina. He was about to enter the minefield—the big minefield—and Cubby Cardiff looked down in astonishment. He regretted having made his bet against sentiment. It wouldn't shorten the odds a bit, but he wished he could hold his breath and silently cheer the poor mutt on. The crazy little sapper was gonna need all the help he could get if he pranced on into that minefield. Cubby Cardiff didn't want to watch.

"Fuck it," he said. He turned control of the searchlight over to Lieutenant Hoang and started down the ladder. "I'm gonna get me a drink. Figure I can hear a mine go off in the team house as well as I can here, so I might as well listen in comfort." He climbed down the ladder and started back to the team house, his respect for old Nick Hogg's perimeter sorely depleted and his faith in the wisdom of betting against sentiment shaken. He walked slowly, skirting the puddles and the mud, his shoulders hunched slightly in anticipation of the blast he was sure would come any second. When he got to the door of the team house he paused to listen to the sound coming from the west wall. At first it sounded like a fight had broken out among the spectators. Men were yelling and shouting, and then came the sound of applause and cheers. Someone, one of the Cambodes most likely, discharged a whole magazine of tracers into the air.

"Goddamn!" He spun around and began to race back to the perimeter. "Goddamn I don't fuckin' believe it!"

He ran, panting, cursing, and splashing through mud puddles, all the way to the gate. He got there just in time to see Tiger the Lurp Dog crawl out from beneath the bottom strand of the barbed-wire fence, step up onto the muddy Louc Ma Road, shake the water from his dripping coat, and lift his leg against the closest fencepost. He shook himself again, then tossed a disdainful glance back at the perimeter and trotted off into the darkness.

"Goddamn, I don't believe it!" Cubby Cardiff rubbed his eyes and pulled on his earlobes and let out a deep breath. "That's one sharp little sapper, that Tiger the Lurp Dog!"

# CHAPTER 18

THE NEXT MORNING, WHEN THE NEWS OF TIGER'S
escape hit the Lurp compound, Wolverine was down
in the operations bunker planning a class on Escape
and Evasion techniques. He was sitting at the
commo desk scribbling on a yellow pad when Cubby
Cardiff came slinking in, all wet and miserable looking, to break the news to Pappy Stagg with first a
philosophical shrug, then an admission of defeat.

"I get the feeling you was testing me somehow,
Stagg," he said. "Ever since that time in the Ashau,
I just don't feel natural around you no more. I know
it's all my imagination, but I still got this feeling
that you planted that dog on me just to see if I could
outsmart him and keep him from getting away.
Well, damn your gawky strap-hangin' ass, Stagg!

155

That Tiger done up and got away, and now you got even further in your debt. Goddamnit."

Wolverine dropped his pencil and pushed his chair back away from the commo desk, but a warning look from Pappy Stagg was enough to silence him.

Cubby Cardiff shook his head in admiration. "Damn your hide, Stagg, you old buzzard! I swear you should have been there to see it! That little dog cost me a month's base pay and made old Nick Hogg's perimeter look like some sort of a goddamn pansy patch. Where in hell did you get him from anyway? I swear his daddy must of been a VC sapper who couldn't keep his dick outa the kennel. He went through all that wire and stake like a pro, Stagg—like a real pro."

"He's a Lurp dog," said Pappy evenly. He puffed on his pipe and leaned back in his chair. "Sergeant Wolverine's pointman trained him. I don't let anybody sack out in my compound unless I know he can cut the mustard—not even a dog. We got some standards around here. Sergeant Wolverine will tell you. We got some standards around here."

"That's right, Top!" Wolverine didn't know whether or not Pappy was down on this Cardiff character for letting Tiger get away, but it was beginning to look that way. He was puffing on his pipe now, a great smile of contentment on his face, as though nothing on earth amused him more than listening to his old buddy's embarrassed bluster. Sometimes it seemed like the calmer Pappy got, the more he made you wish he'd lose his temper and start chewing ass like a normal master sergeant.

"So you met your match, did you? Here I give you a simple job—just keep a pup out of the soup for a couple of weeks, and what happens? I get you drag-assing into my operations bunker at eight hundred hours in the morning, weeping and moaning about how I'm testing you. Damn it, man, have you no pride? I got better things to do than to go around training dogs to break an old buddy's perimeter."

Wolverine wasn't sure whether the "old buddy" was supposed to be old Nick Hogg, who'd designed and laid out the perimeter, or Cubby Cardiff, who was supposed to have kept it invulnerable. But he couldn't help feeling a little sorry for Cubby Cardiff. He was a shifty character—or so people said—but he probably really had tried to keep Tiger tied up safe and secure, and Pappy should have cut him some slack.

"Aw, what the hell," Pappy seemed to relent, "I don't know why I'm being so hard on you, Cardiff. You did the best you could, and you must be feeling a touch down on yourself already, seeing as how your best just wasn't good enough."

Cubby Cardiff had no choice but to laugh.

"You should have been there to see it, Stagg. It was the funniest damn thing I ever saw. That dog had his tail hooked up under more'n one trip wire, and all our glorious Vietnamese counterparts—lousy little dirty buggers, one and all—they were all whooping and giggling and clapping each other on the ass, hoping to see Tiger blow himself away. But it never happened. Ol' Tiger done pissed on the camp flagpole. He nipped the Dai Uy on the ankle—or at least the Dai Uy says he did—and then he up and disappoints all our glorious South Vietnamese counterparts by keeping his own self alive. You should have been there to see it, Stagg. The whole camp was betting and figuring the odds, and it was a show to see, Stagg. Funniest damn thing I've seen in more'n a week."

Cubby Cardiff couldn't help stretching things a bit. Tiger's escape had not really been all that much fun to watch. Give it another five or ten years and it'd be a good story to get drunk and tell over Jack Daniels. But for now, he wondered if maybe he'd better back off a pace or two and keep things in perspective. "Well, maybe it weren't that funny, exactly. But anyway, you should of been there, Stagg. It was a hell of a show." He shook his head, "Damn dog."

The last time Pappy Stagg and Cubby Cardiff had been together they'd talked old times. And now Cubby Cardiff was trying his damndest not to talk about old debts. The two master sergeants were quite obviously over the hill. Wolverine spoke up with the brash voice of youth.

"Three to one says he's back before Mopar. Either one of you old coots feels like making any odds of your own, I'm ready to hear them. If not, just shut up and put your money down. Three to one, he'll be back before Mopar."

Cubby Cardiff didn't feel right turning down an honest wager, but first he had to ask who Mopar was.

"Sergeant Wolverine's pointman," explained Pappy Stagg. "He's on extension leave."

"Pointman, you say? Another one of them Spec Four Hippies, I bet." Cubby Cardiff scratched the rash on his throat and thought about the bet. There was just no way of telling. A dog like that—he didn't weigh much, didn't eat much, hardly ever broke out barking, and he didn't trust indigenous personnel—plus, to top it off, he was born with a camouflage suit . . . A dog like that just might have a chance to make it back.

"Three to one, young Staff Sergeant?" Cubby Cardiff was maganimous. "I don't need them long odds. Hell, I'll take you head-on, even! How's that sound? Even odds he makes it back before your pointman."

It was a fair bet for both of them, and they agreed on fifty dollars, held on each man's honor. Both of them being sticklers for prior coordination, there was no argument when Pappy suggested that the winner was to claim his money only on Mopar's return, even if Tiger beat him back. Cubby Cardiff needed the money to make up, in part, for last night's losses. And Wolverine needed to have Tiger back for the sake of his pointman's morale and his own peace of mind. But Pappy Stagg didn't need anything much just then, so he stayed neutral.

"Sorry, troops," he said. "I am not a gambling man." He reached over for his cup and put down his pipe, then leaned back in his chair and took a sip of coffee. "That's one of my Lurps wandering around out there without a radio or a weapon, and I don't think it ought to be a matter of personal gain."

Wolverine knew that Pappy was joking. But old Cubby Cardiff knew Pappy—had known him for almost twenty years—and he held back his smile. Beneath all his slow ways and easy manner, the old buzzard was taking things altogether too seriously, and Cubby Cardiff wondered if Pappy Stagg was finally going soft and losing his edge.

Two days before Christmas an enormous cardboard box full of gospel tracts and Christian comic books arrived in the Lurp platoon. Since the box had been addressed to the entire platoon, Pappy Stagg turned a deaf ear to Wolverine's pleas that the whole mess be taken up to the Two Shop, run through the paper shredder, and burned. Wolverine had been careful to hide his own mail from everyone but Pappy and Sergeant Johnson, and now he was worried that someone would link him to Sister Janice Wolverton, who was head librarian of the Full Gospel Book Club and Tract Society, and whose name and photograph appeared on some of the tracts. He needn't have worried. Except for one especially lurid comic about the Book of Revelation and the rise of the Anti-Christ, all the rest of the propaganda ended up, unread, in the trash barrels. Wolverine's good name and reputation were safe.

Still, for the next four nights, as he sat in ambush

outside the base camp perimeter, guarding against enemy sappers and scouting parties, Wolverine was tempted to pray that someone—anyone, even a lost ARVN or a forgetful farmer—would come strolling through his kill zone and give him the satisfaction of a holiday body count. But nobody came. The local VC had no reason to approach the perimeter, for they had already memorized every foot of it. And the main-force VC and NVA were staying out in the mountains where they belonged, temporarily at peace with everyone but each other, because most of the American troops had been pulled back to firebases and base camps on holiday stand-down, and the South Vietnamese Army wasn't likely to go out looking for trouble on its own.

It was an idiotic way to fight a war, and Wolverine had trouble believing that either side really trusted the other to honor what Pappy Stagg called "an unofficial, limited, annual holiday cease-fire." But there certainly didn't seem to be much going on anywhere in the Louc Ma area. Nothing, that is, but the Lurp platoon's fruitless ambush patrols. All considerations of strategy aside, Wolverine thought it downright chickenshit of the NVA to play along with a Christmas cease-fire. The only real action anywhere in the area was an impromptu midnight sky show of red and green starcluster flares fired up over the bunker line on Christmas Eve, and that was hardly the sort of thing Wolverine had stayed in the Army to see.

The first week of the new year found Wolverine out on a reconnaissance mission with Team Two-Two, carrying second radio in place of Spec Four Schultz, who was on leave in Bangkok visiting his girlfriend, who worked in a bar, but was selective and swore she wasn't really a whore because she couldn't come with anyone she didn't like. After four days on a ridgeline overlooking the Aloe Valley, Wolverine returned to the compound convinced that Two-Two's team leader was a dangerous glory hound. The dude had an unshakable confidence that nothing bad could happen to him as long as he maintained commo with the relay team and kept faith in himself as an American fighting man, because American fighting men—even non-Airborne Legs— were "more than the equal of any two-bit gook guerillas." He was crazy. It was only Wolverine's restraining presence that had kept him from opening up on a full platoon of NVA that came slogging past their position the third morning on the mission, and it was easy to imagine him taking on a whole regiment if he stumbled across one.

Wolverine was determined to lure a couple of men from Two-Two to his own team. They seemed to be good men—all of them but the TL—and it was a shame to think they'd probably get themselves killed before their team leader rotated back to the States.

When the postmission debriefing was finished, Wolverine hung around to talk to Pappy Stagg, and after a few minutes of discussion, Pappy agreed to let Wolverine have Schultz when he returned from leave.

# CHAPTER 19

ON THE SEVENTH DAY OF THE NEW YEAR, MARVEL Kim returned from Recondo School wearing spotted Korean Army camouflage fatigues, rubber-soled batta boots, and a flat-top Korean Army soft cap with two little tabs of luminous tape, like captain's bars, on the back. His cheeks and forearms were criss-crossed with thorn cuts, he'd lost weight, and there, in plain sight, lashed haft down to his left web-gear strap, was a slim new Gerber Mark II commando dagger.

Gonzales was out on radio relay, Tiger was still on his Escape and Evasion route from the Special Forces camp, and Mopar was still on leave, so it fell to Wolverine to formally welcome Marvel back to the team. Marvel was already down in the bunker in his spotted cammies, blushing because Pappy Stagg had

162

just told him that he had been put in for a medal of some sort. When Marvel saw Wolverine he blushed even deeper, glanced down at his boots, then broke into a sheepish grin and greeted him with a polite nod, but didn't say a word, for Pappy was still talking and Marvel never interrupted anyone who outranked him.

"You did me proud, Spec Four Kim, and I'm damn glad you were there when Sergeant Stabo needed you. Stabo's as tough as a fireplug, and I'm sure he'll come through all right, but according to the sergeant major, he'd have gone under for sure if you hadn't had your shit in order. You did good work, Kim—both in training and on the graduation mission, when Stabo got hit. I reckon we'll be getting you and your partner Mopar some sergeant's stripes any day now. Go on, help yourself to some coffee."

Wolverine felt like an intruder. Pappy had mentioned something about Marvel running into a little contact on his Recondo School graduation mission, but he'd said nothing about a medal, nor about Sergeant Stabo, whoever he was. And Pappy hadn't said anything to Wolverine about Marvel winning the Recondo dagger, although the sergeant major of the Recondo School surely must have told him about that, too.

"Get me a cup too, why don't you, Kim," said Wolverine. "I wasn't expecting you until tomorrow, but it's good to have you back." Wolverine glanced at Pappy, then nodded in Marvel's direction. "See you got yourself a Gerber toothpick there, Kim. Nice knife, huh? You gonna send it home to mother, or just keep it here and hide it from Mopar?"

Marvel shook his head and touched the haft of his dagger for luck. "Neither one, Sarge. You see, it turns out I'm immune to the curse because I'm Korean, so I don't have anything to hide. The dagger stays on my web gear. It's my field knife now. It'd be dangerous to leave it back in the rear when I go out in the field, don't you think?"

Pappy Stagg had little tolerance for superstitious talk of this sort. A soldier had a right to his jinxes and good luck charms, but they weren't a fit subject of conversation in a combat zone. He frowned slightly, gave Wolverine a warning look, and motioned for Marvel to pull up a chair close to the operations desk.

"Sit down, Kim," he said. "I've got some bad news for you."

Marvel handed Wolverine his cup, and holding his own carefully to keep from spilling any coffee on his Korean fatigues, pulled up a chair and sat down.

Pappy Stagg sighed. "Tiger's gone," he said. "I reckon it was my fault, and I don't mind you telling Mopar it was. Figure it's best to have you break the news to him. I know him and that pup was close. Poor kid probably never had a dog of his own when he was growing up. But this is a war, Kim, and it just isn't proper for a man to be moping around over a dog when there's men getting killed. I'll tell you everything I know about the situation, but it's probably best to let you talk to Mopar when he gets back. I don't want none of this affecting his morale, and you can see to that better than anyone."

Wolverine sipped his coffee and listened in angry silence as Pappy told of taking Tiger to the Special Forces camp and repeated Cubby Cardiff's version of his subsequent escape through Old Nick Hogg's perimeter. It just wasn't right for a platoon sergeant—and an E-8 platoon sergeat at that!—to elbow in on a team leader's job this way. If Pappy Stagg was so damned concerned about Mopar's morale, why didn't he wait and break the news himself? Wolverine decided that the old buzzard must be getting senile to jump the chain of command this way. And he was getting soft, too, caring so much about a camp-following mutt and some young Spec Four's morale. The old Pappy Stagg, the Pappy Stagg Wolverine remembered from his first tour in Vietnam, wouldn't have cared two farts in a shitstorm about either one. And if he had cared, he'd ever have let on that he did.

Wolverine finished his coffee and left the operations bunker feeling low and useless. Hell, *he* was team leader—Pappy should have let him talk to Marvel first.

Marvel Kim had always been a model son. Or at least his mother thought he was a model son—but then, there's a lot that mothers never know. She didn't know that before his father's death Marvel had planned to become a gynecologist so that he could charge people outrageous fees to examine the private parts of their wives and daughters. She knew that he'd wanted to become a doctor, but that was all.

She had always been proud of his honor-roll grades, proud of his devotion to the high school science club, and though it saddened her to see his grades plummet after his father's death, she was almost as proud of the way he took over his father's place in the little Oriental grocery—working before and after school each day with never a complaint—as she had been of his good grades. He had always been a good boy, and she was very sad when it became clear that he would never be a doctor, for she knew he would have been a good one. But times were hard. People were losing their taste for the good food of their ancestral lands, and even with Marvel's help the grocery wasn't doing well. There would be no money for college and medical school.

Marvel didn't seem to mind. He told his mother he was content to work in the store, and for the first couple of years it was true. He hadn't really wanted to be a doctor. He'd only wanted to be paid to look at women's private parts. And as he had gathered a collection of pornographic Swedish magazines, which he kept hidden under his mattress, gynecology was no longer as tempting a trade as it once had seemed, for he knew he could look at cunts and clits and labes and hair without the hassle of college and medical school. Of course, his mother knew nothing of the magazines, and so she continued to believe that Marvel was heartbroken losing his chance to become a doctor.

If he hadn't been drafted a few months out of high school, Marvel might have stayed at home forever, running the grocery by day, pumping gas at night, and jealously guarding the virtue of his cute little sisters from the healthy lusts of the neighborhood Samoans. But the draft notice called him away from that battle by pulling him out of the neighborhood and off the island. The Army offered him a chance to see the American mainland for the first time. But more than that, it offered him an escape from a life of almost unbearable boredom and drudgery, an escape from the dull life of a dutiful son going nowhere. His mother had to wipe away a few tears when she saw him off at the bus station, and Marvel had to struggle to keep a solemn face long enough to get on the bus. But once the bus pulled out, he lost his composure, and rode off to the Army dancing in his seat and grinning like the happiest idiot in the State of Hawaii.

It was only after basic training, when he received orders for Advanced Infantry Training and saw that he'd be going to war, that Marvel decided to volunteer for the Airborne. Jump pay was fifty-five dollars a month—enough for hamburgers, razor blades, toothpaste, and beer—and with that to tide him over, he could afford to send his entire base pay home. That might not have been enough motivation to get a man through Jump School, but it was enough financial justification to ease his conscience about volunteering.

Of course, there was more to going Airborne than jump pay, and Marvel would be the first to admit it. He had grown up with the same World War Two movies as everyone else, and it was obvious to him that paratroopers were the sort of men who made their own luck in this life.

He had never told his mother that he was a paratrooper. She had enough to worry about, what with the store doing poorly, Samoans moving into the neighborhood, and three straight-A daughters determined to go to college whether they could afford it or not. Marvel's letters home were always brief and cheerful, full of assurances that he was gaining weight and working in a harmonious office far from the fighting. And since he always reduced his mailing address to numbers, abbreviations, and acronyms, even his three smart little sisters had no idea what he was really doing.

But now, for the first time since leaving home, he was tempted to write his mother an honest letter. He wanted to tell her about the Koreans he'd met at Recondo School. He wanted to tell her about Big Park and Little Park, about Kim Dong-soo and the Korean Army liaison officer, Lieutenant Choi. She'd be proud to know how well they had accepted him. And she'd be even prouder to know that he'd finally spoken Korean in front of a whole group of black and white buddies without getting embarrassed and feeling like some sort of weird foreigner.

Marvel was tempted to tell his mother how he'd ended up winning the Recondo dagger—how he'd learned to distance himself from the curse of the thing. He wanted to tell her about the runs—about the forty-pound sandbag in his rucksack rubbing a hole in his back, about wanting to fall back and run with the pack, but driving on instead, driving on to prove to the Korean soldiers that he was tough enough and strong enough to keep up with them.

Now, for the first time in his life, Marvel was proud to be Korean, and he wanted his mother to know about his pride. But he didn't dare write her. For once he started the story, he'd have to finish it. And that would mean writing about the graduation mission, when Sergeant Stabo, the cadre advisor, got shot. That would mean writing about how he and Big Park had closed Stabo's sucking chest wound with a plastic battery bag while Kim Dong-soo laughed and swore in three languages and rolled grenades down the bank at the VC patrol in the stream bed.

The Koreans were tough and fierce and brave, and Marvel was proud that they had accepted him as one of their own. But he could never write his mother about being a Korean without also writing her about being a Lurp, and that would be inexcusably cruel. Marvel wrote to Mopar instead. Mopar would understand about being a Korean. Once he stopped laughing and swearing, he'd probably understand about winning the Recondo dagger. And once he cooled off and thought about it for an hour or so, he'd probably even understand about Tiger. After all, it hadn't been the fault of anyone in the Lurp platoon. And besides, Tiger was a tough and sneaky little mutt— he'd probably be back in the compound before Mopar.

There were still no lights in the team tent, so Marvel wrote by candlelight. He wrote for two hours, and when he finished his letter he read it over with no small measure of pride, for it was a good letter, full of wisdom and wit, heavy with abbreviations and military jargon. Mopar would understand. He might piss and moan and kick a bit, but in the end he'd understand about the Recondo dagger, and even understand about Tiger.

A week after he wrote to Mopar, Marvel was off on Firebase Alexine with Gonzales, pulling radio relay for a twelve-man heavy team that was checking out a rumored NVA truck park in the Aloe Valley. It was night, and the lieutenant was up at the Two Shop discussing Electronically Derived Intelligence with the major. The new man on Two-Five, Two-Two's former second radioman, Schultz, was off drinking beer with a jeep mechanic from his home town, and Pappy Stagg was down in the operations bunker reminiscing about his earlier tours in Asia. Wolverine was still in the compound, and hoping to loosen Pappy's tongue so he'd get to talking about the old days in Laos, he ran back to the team leader's tent for his bottle. He paused on his way back to the bunker to watch a gunship firing into the dark hills a few kilometers beyond the perimeter. A thin red stream of tracer fire reached down from the gunship and swept back and forth like a lizard's tongue, searching the ground for prey, then flickered hesitantly and receded as the growl of the minigun came, faint and distant, on the still night air. The gunship wasn't as far away as it looked. If it had been, the interval between the firing and the sound would have been greater.

Wolverine took a swig from his bottle, then turned away from the perimeter, bored with the minigun show. He screwed the top back on his bottle, wiped his mouth with the back of his hand, took a deep breath and belched it out again, then started back for the operations bunker. Suddenly he stopped and stood dead still. Someone was coming at him from between the team tents. He spun around, ready to swing with the bottle, then lowered his arm, and shook his head in amazement.

"Holy shit! Mopar! What are you doing here? You still have a few days of leave left, don't you? What the hell—are you crazy? Sneaking up on a man that way, I damn near put this bottle next to your face!"

Mopar had hitched a ride from the airstrip just before last night and had spent the last three hours drinking and getting high with the guys who had given him a lift. He was now very drunk, and he reached out to steady himself against a trash barrel.

"You ain't shit, Sarge," he announced. "If I was a gook I coulda blown your ass away."

Wolverine shook his head again. "You just about scared the living shit out of me, ol' hoss. I didn't even see you standing there."

Mopar had an unlit cigarette in his mouth. He puffed on it—or at least tried to puff on it—then spat it out in disgust.

"Don't you ol' hoss me, you lifer pig! I got a bone to pick with you, and you know it. Fuckin' lifer. I ain't ever gonna trust another fuckin' lifer!"

Wolverine eased over next to the sandbag wall that surrounded the closest tent. He put down his bottle so he'd have both hands free, but Mopar refused to stand up for himself and fight things out like a man. Once again Mopar called him a fuckin' lifer pig, and then to make the insult even more personal, he called him a sissy preacher's kid. Wolverine chuckled and stepped closer to Mopar.

"So you know about that, huh?" He shook his head sadly, then punched Mopar twice in the belly and sent him staggering backward, doubled over at the waist, trying to get his breath back.

"You call *me* a lifer pig?" Wolverine had to laugh. "Sneaking back to the compound with two or three leave days left—and you call *me* a lifer pig? You better get a hold on yourself right quick, young troop! Word is we're going out to plant some Black Boxes in J.D.'s last RZ, and you won't be going if you don't start talking rational. Lifer pig? Hell's bells, Mopar, you're the one who couldn't even last out a thirty-day leave!"

Mopar felt ridiculous. He straightened up and swallowed back the vomit welling up in this throat.

He mumbled an apology, then stooped to pick up his hat. "I'm sorry, Sarge," he said. "I'm just drunk, 'at's all."

"That's better," said Wolverine. "Marvel and Gonzales are out on Alexine. Why don't you just stumble on into the tent and crash. Now go on, get moving. If you can talk rational in the morning, I'm gonna have some work for you. Marvel and Gonzales will be back tomorrow. The lieutenant is up at the Two Shop right now—word is the major wants some sensing devices planted out in RZ Zulme. If you start acting like a soldier again, maybe we'll get the mission." Wolverine shook his head. "If you had a lick of sense, you'd still be home."

"Home? Shit, I was bored, Sarge. Lonely back there . . . snow and all." Mopar lurched to the door of the tent, then paused and leaned drunkenly against the sandbag wall. "RZ Zulme, Sarge? No shit. We'll be going into RZ Zulme soon?" He shook his head and smiled crookedly. "If I'd stayed out my whole leave, I probably woulda missed out on this one, huh Sarge?"

Wolverine shrugged and recovered his bottle. "Maybe so. Now get on in there and sleep it off. I'll tell Pappy you're here."

"I'm sorry, Sarge." Mopar apologized again, then pushed the screen door open and staggered into the tent.

Wolverine shook his head and started back for the operations bunker, thinking how Pappy Stagg was right; these young troopers coming up now were a confused and puzzling lot. Cutting short a leave to get back to the war, then calling someone else a lifer—you couldn't get much more confused and puzzling than that.

# CHAPTER 20

SPRAWLED OUT, FULLY DRESSED, ON HIS COT, MOPAR slept through the night and morning. Helicopters landed and took off from the chopper pad. The screen door banged as men went in and out of the tent on various errands. Forklifts and truck engines growled in the supply depot next to the Lurp compound, and ten meters behind the tent the Slop Shop mess sergeant hollered at his KPs, and the KPs banged pots and pans and played "Sergeant Pepper's Lonely Hearts Club Band," over and over, full volume on a battery-operated cassette player. But Mopar slept on undisturbed. When Marvel and Gonzales returned from Firebase Alexine, he was still asleep and beyond reach of the human voice, so Marvel kicked the legs of his cot to wake him.

"Get up, Mopar, you sorry young lifer! You're back in the Army now, and there's no use trying to pretend it's all a dream!" Marvel kicked the cot again, and Mopar came up swinging then sank back with a sigh and closed his eyes.

"Go away," he muttered. "I still got three days of leave yet."

"Come on, Mopar," Marvel giggled. "Don't go catatonic on us. Get up and tell us about your leave. Did you smash any peacecreeps? How was Sybill Street? I wrote you about Tiger and about Recondo School—the least you can do is get up and tell us about your leave!"

"Yeah," Gonzales nodded. "If you don't get up, Wolverine won't take you on the overflight."

Mopar sat up and rubbed the sand from his eyes. His head ached, his belly hurt, his mouth felt like it was full of cotton, and he had to piss so bad he was afraid he'd spill over if he moved too quickly.

"Overflight? What's this about an overflight?" He was still wearing his boots. He swung them over the edge of the cot, but he didn't dare stand just yet. "I thought I was dreaming all this shit. I thought I was still back home, just dreaming." He rubbed his eyes again and looked around the tent. "Tiger? Tiger's not back yet?" He gave Marvel a dirty look, then rested his head in his hands. "I thought you said he'd be back before me, Marvel, you gooky asshole. And don't give me any crap about my coming back early; I'd still be home on leave if I hadn't got your letter telling me everything was going to hell in a handcart without me."

Marvel glanced over at Gonzales for moral support, but Gonzales only shrugged and retreated to his own cot. "I told you, Mopar, Tiger's fine." Marvel had practiced saying this a dozen times or more—not where anyone could hear, but he'd even practiced aloud a few times—and now when he finally had no

173

choice but to say it, he was surprised at how reasonable and confident he sounded. "There's no sense wasting your time worrying about him. We want to hear about your leave. And then you better get down to the operations bunker to talk to Pappy and Wolverine. We're going to J.D.'s last Recon Zone day after tomorrow, and the overflight's scheduled for sixteen hundred hours today." He paused, then smiled. "That's four o'clock, in case you forgot how to tell time while you were home."

Mopar glowered scornfully. "It's Mr. Recondo, the honor grad himself! He's gonna come on the lifer to me—on my first day back! Get back, Marvel, you lifer dipshit! You already tried to bullshit me in your letter, and I don't want no more of it, not just yet."

He groaned and stood up slowly. He had to get outside and piss. His head was just beginning to clear, but he still didn't dare move too fast. All the way back across the Pacific, and then for a day and a half in the rear while he waited for a flight north, he'd been looking forward to his reunion with Marvel, Gonzales, and the other guys. But now that he was back in the Lurp compound, it felt like he'd never been away.

"I told you, Mopar, I'm immune. The Koreans always score in the nineties on the written tests because the liaison officer cheats for them, and the physical stuff is easy for them. They weren't afraid of the dagger. The Koreans gave it all they had, and one of them even took his tests in English so the cadre would know he wasn't cheating, he wanted the dagger that much. I told you, Koreans are immune to the curse, Mopar. It works the other way for us. I told you before."

"You're the first to win it, you goofy zip. And you don't count as Korean to me. What was it? You were way down in points you said, and then you fucked up and saved some Green Beanie's life and won the dagger by luck and good fortune? I gotta piss too bad to stand and listen to this dorky bullshit, Marvel. You're full of shit and that's it. I gotta go drain the dragon."

Schultz had come into the tent, and since he was now a member of Team Two-Four, he felt it was only appropriate that he say something to welcome Mopar back. "Be careful not to shake it more than once," he said. "The Army frowns on unauthorized fun."

Mopar grimaced and made his way to the door, then paused to turn around and give Schultz the finger.

"Watch yourself, Schultz," he warned, only half in jest. "You ain't on the team for good. You're just filling in until Tiger gets back, so you better show some respect."

Schultz rolled his eyes, shook his head, and laughed. "Can it, Mopar. I don't show respect for nobody dumb enough to cut short his leave to come back to this goddamn place."

Mopar groaned again and pushed through the door with his shoulder. Schultz was a fairly good man in the field, but he was a little too pushy and ambitious for Mopar's peace of mind. Schultz was always bragging about the Silver Star he'd won before joining the Lurp platoon. He was always bugging Mopar to show him a picture of Sybill Street, asking if she swallowed cum, and plying him with other such questions Mopar wouldn't have answered, even if he could. Mopar was sure it was Schultz who stole a picture of Marvel's sisters from his footlocker and taped it to the shit house wall. Marvel was reluctant to blame anyone, but Mopar figured it could only have been Schultz. He didn't have a shred of respect for anything or anybody, and even Tiger had always seemed to regard him with a healthy dose of suspicion. Schultz wasn't bad out in the field, but he was a jerk and a pest and a pain in the ass to be around back in the rear. Mopar hoped he'd only be on the team for this mission, then go back to Two-Two, where he belonged.

The whole team went on the overflight, crowded into the chopper with the lieutenant and Sergeant Johnson, who was to fly bellyman on the insertion and wanted a look at the landing zones. Mopar sat in the right door with Gonzales, Schultz, and the lieutenant looking over his shoulders, but he couldn't see much of RZ Zulme, for the low ground was souped over, and only the two high ridgelines stuck up, like islands in the fog.

Once again, Wolverine selected a high-ground landing zone, but Mopar didn't question his judgment this time. The insertion LZ was on a steep, defoliated hillside on the eastern edge of the Recon Zone, and while it was far from ideal, the air approaches were good, and it didn't look like the sort of place where the enemy would expect anyone to land. Everyone agreed that as long as no one broke a leg or twisted an ankle unassing the insertion ship, it would be a good place to go in. Most of the enemy would probably be in the western part of the Recon Zone anyway, in the valley or next to the river. Some of them were probably on the ridgeline between the valley and the river, for it was there that J.D. had found his last high-speed trail.

A warm rain fell that night, and the next day was drizzly and gray. Wolverine marched the team out to the firing range next to the dump, and all morning they ran through their immediate action drills, practicing fire and movement until they were working as a team. Mopar had been a little rusty at first, clumsy changing magazines and slow in switching from the silenced Swedish K he'd be walking point with on this mission to the CAR-15 he'd have to use for any sustained fighting. But he was still sharp on point contact—good pointmen never forget that one—and it only took him an hour or so of fire and movement to fall back into the natural rhythm of the other drills. He hadn't forgotten any of them—in fact he'd rehearsed them mentally every day of his leave. All he really needed was a little practice to bring him back to his peak form, and Wolverine made sure he got that.

After returning from the firing range, Wolverine and Mopar prepared the premission briefback presentation in which they'd explain their plans for the mission and coordinate them with the Two Shop, the pilots, and the artillery. Mopar asked a few questions, but for once he kept his opinions to himself and didn't quibble with Wolverine's choice of landing zones and rally points.

Wolverine seemed to think it would be an easy mission. The enemy might still have a few men in the area, but they'd be along the high-speed trails or next to the riverbed. There was no way to be sure about such a thing, but he figured the LZ and the swath of grassy lowland they'd have to cross to get to the ridge where J.D. had found his last high-speed trail were probably not under constant observation.

"It's gonna be a piece of cake, Mopar," he said on the way down to the operations bunker to give the briefback. "As long as nobody breaks a leg on the LZ, we'll slide in like a greasy knife. There ain't nothing to crossing lowland, not if you do it at night. And if the major decides at the last minute that he wants us to plant some Black Boxes, well, that's no sweat either. One time, back a year or two ago, I had to plant a series of eighteen relays, with five sensor devices per relay—just me and this young lieutenant, and six Nungs for security. I can't tell you just where it was we planted them damn things, but we sure broke a few immigration laws getting there. This RZ

177

Zulme ain't all everyone's got it psyched up to be since J.D. went under. Now, I'm not one given to extravagant promises, but if there's any sign of Lurp Team Two-One left out there, we'll find it. Then all them mothers and widows can trade in their false hopes for the insurance money due them. A piece of cake, Mopar, it's gonna be a piece of cake."

Mopar wasn't so sure the mission itself would be a piece of cake, but the briefback presentation went smoothly. Wolverine started off with an old joke about Tuffy the Airborne Soldier getting clap, and when he was sure he had everyone's attention, he stepped over next to the large wall-sized copy of the Aloe Valley map-sheet, paused for dramatic effect, then pulled down a transparent overlay sheet and pointed to a red-bordered square in the upper left corner. "This," he announced, "is RZ Zulme. And this," he tapped his finger against a swirl of contour lines near the right border of the RZ, "is our Primary Insertion Landing Zone."

Marvel, Gonzales, and Schultz all sat tall in their folding chairs and tried their best to look like junior lifers, for that was the only sort of pride most of the officers gathered there understood, and they wanted everyone to know how proud they were to be on Wolverine's team. Mopar was just as proud as the others, but he sat slumped in his chair, unwilling to put on the lifer act just to make Wolverine look good.

"Lurp Team Two-Four will insert here at first light tomorrow and conduct a four-day area reconnaissance, with a possible secondary mission of planting sensor devices along this high-speed trail previously reported by Team Two-One of this platoon."

Wolverine glanced over at the Two Shop Major to see if he'd made up his mind whether or not to burden a five-man team with the additional responsibility of planting Black Boxes, but the major's face was without expression, and the Leg artillery captain whose battery would be on call in support of the team didn't seem to know either. If the team did end up planting sensing devices in RZ Zulme, the devices would have a direct radio link to the artillery's Fire Direction Center so that any troop movement they picked up could be disrupted with almost immediate shelling. But the artillery captain just sat there stupidly, as if he were attending the briefback as an Official Presence only and had nothing to do with the work at hand.

Wolverine turned back to his map and continued his briefing. When he was done, he asked for questions, but he'd satisfied the pilots, and the Two Shop major and artillery captain were both so impressed with the way he'd kept backing and turning and stabbing the map with his finger that they didn't feel like speaking up or adding anything. Wolverine hadn't grown up on the Gospel Bus for nothing. He was a good speaker, and he'd made the mission sound like a piece of cake.

It was only when the briefback was over and the pilots and the other men on the team had left the bunker that the major made up his mind and told Wolverine to stop by the Two Shop in an hour to sign for one relay of two sensing devices. This should have been decided earlier, but Wolverine didn't really mind. He'd assumed that the major would finally decide for the boxes, and during his briefback he'd pointed out what he felt was the best place to plant them.

"Right here," he'd said, tapping the map with his finger. "Right here on the trail, by Two-One's last reported position."

Later that night, after preparing his equipment and studying his map until he was sure he'd memorized every contour line, Mopar went off to sit by himself on the roof of the operations bunker. Now more than ever, he missed Tiger.

Maybe J. D. had been right when he said Marvel was more superstitious than a swamp witch and more full of shit than a cholera submarine. It certainly looked that way, now that he'd blown his credibility by winning the Recondo dagger. But Marvel had been right about one thing all along, and Mopar had to admit it. Brushing Tiger had always brought him good luck.

The brush Sybill Street had sent him many months before was in his pocket, but Tiger was gone, and Sybill Street had turned into a snotty college kid, so the brush wasn't worth much anymore. Maybe Marvel was right, maybe a bad-luck talisman like the Recondo dagger could bring the right man good luck. But if that was true, then Mopar figured the reverse must also be true, and a good-luck piece could turn on a man and curse him, so he tossed the brush over his shoulder in the direction of the Slop Shop mess tent, hoping that it would land in the garbage dumpster, or at least near enough to fall sure victim to the morning police call.

The sky was dark and low, but a little breeze was stirring, and it brought the smells of rain and diesel fuel, of smoke, shit, mud, and bug spray. Mopar's nostrils flared, but his throat felt tight and heavy, and it was only his drive-on Airborne spirit that kept the tears from welling up in his eyes.

A trip flare lit up the concertina wire beyond the bunker line and burned very slowly in the wet, misty air, but Mopar couldn't see anything, and neither could the men on watch. He lit a cigarette and watched the flare burn out. Even if there was a gook coming through the wire, he'd be too busy to snipe at the glow of a distant cigarette. But the odds that one lone sapper was trying to sneak into the base camp were very slim indeed. Mopar figured it was probably just a rabbit. Or maybe the wind was kicking up out there on the bunker line and had blown a loose concertina roll into a trip wire. Whatever it was, Mopar knew, it wasn't Tiger the Lurp Dog coming home. But he spent the next two hours sitting on the operations bunker, waiting, just to make sure.

# CHAPTER 21

T HE SKY WAS STILL DARK AND LOW WHEN TEAM TWO-
Four trooped down to the chopper pad, but the smell
of rain was gone, and though the clouds remained,
shapeless and heavy, a warm, dry ground wind was
blowing down the berm and across the pad. It was
an ominous wind, an unseasonal wind, and the
doorgunners and crew chiefs who had been sleeping
with their ships were all up earlier than usual, for it
was not a wind to sleep in. They were huddled between their ships and the berm, boiling water for coffee over heat tabs and bitching about the weather.
Even the pilots had said they were due for a storm,
and there'd be no flying today. Wolverine glowered
at the air crews until they lowered their voices, and

after the Lurps sat down to rest on their rucksacks, only Marvel continued to glance in their direction.

"I don't like that one crew chief, but even more, I don't like the insertion ship." Marvel sounded like he was talking to himself, but the whole team listened anyway. "I'd just as soon walk all the way to the RZ as fly out in that thing."

The pilot of the insertion ship was a captain, not a warrant officer, and he had an aviator moustache, which was a sure sign he was a dipshit. But that wasn't what bothered Marvel. He didn't like the ship itself. "Did you see the design on the pilot's door?" He nodded toward the helicopters. "Did you see that? It's enough to give a man the premission shivers!"

Schultz, as always, was quick with the correction. "It's 'premission jitters,' " he said, " 'Jitters,' Marvel, not 'shivers.' A true Lurp don't even shiver in the freezer."

Marvel didn't mind being corrected, but he didn't like this talk about the freezer. The freezer was far back in the rear, and no man who went there ever returned to his unit. The freezer belonged to the Graves Registration section, and it was unwise to joke about such a place before a mission. Marvel frowned at Schultz and turned to Wolverine, hoping he'd keep the conversation serious. "What do you think, Sarge? Did you see that door design, and the name on the front?"

Wolverine unscrewed the red filter and shone his penlight on the helicopter door, but the beam was thin and weak, and he couldn't see more than a black cat, arching its back in front of a dull orange moon.

"It looks like Halloween, Kim." Growing up on the Gospel Bus, Wolverine had never been allowed to trick or treat, or even to paste bats and black cat cutouts on the bus window. So it was only natural that Halloween was now his favorite holiday. "You must have had Halloween in Hawaii, Kim. You were still a kid when you all got statehood and took on our American holidays. Now, what's so bad about that ship? It's only a Halloween picture, for chrissake."

Marvel shook his head. "But did you see the ship's name, Sarge? You want that thing taking us out to RZ Zulme? A name like that?"

Wolverine knew he'd have to stop encouraging Marvel's maudlin bullshit, but first he had to see what all the fuss was about. He shone his penlight on the nose of the helicopter, and then he had to smile. "Why that's a fine name, Kim! Couldn't be much better if I was naming it myself."

Now Mopar was curious. He sat up and turned his head for a better look, then sank back on his ruck-sack, sighing with exasperation. Marvel could be such a dip sometimes.

"*Bad Moon Rising*—that's a great name, Marvel, you dork!"

Schultz agreed. "As good as *Free Huey!*" he said, referring to another troop slick that sometimes flew for the platoon.

"As good as *Slack Dragon*," said Gonzales, referring to the helicopter that had brought him back from radio relay a few days before.

"I kinda like *Swing Low Chariot*," said Wolverine, but even Marvel protested that choice because *Swing Low Chariot* was a medevac ship, and med-evac ships didn't count. Nobody wanted to ride a medevac ship, not even as a crewman.

The conversation drifted from helicopters to wom-en, to weapons and explosives, then back again to helicopters—to helicopters and weather. It was now obvious that the ceiling wouldn't lift much before noon, but they still stood by, on alert and ready to go.

Since it was already obvious they wouldn't be going out today, Marvel decided to make the disap-pointment more bearable by introducing a new topic of conversation. He asked Gonzales what he planned to do when he got out of the Army, just to find out what he'd say, just to see if he'd say anything at all. Wolverine had never heard Gonzales carry on about the anti-Castro partisans who raided Cuba from Miami, and Marvel figured that if he could get Gonzales going, he could steer him around to talk about the raiders for Wolverine's benefit. But Marvel had figured without Schultz, who just had to cut in and say that he didn't know about anybody else, but *he* was going back to Maryland, where his brother-in-law ran a parts store and speed shop. Mopar scoffed at the thought of Schultz—who claimed his 390 Ford blew the doors off hot Dodges and GTOs—working in a speed shop, but for once Schultz didn't take offense, seeing as how Mopar was probably only jealous. After bragging about his future for five minutes, Schultz asked around to see if anyone else had such splendid plans. No one did. Gonzales and Marvel mumbled something about going to school, buying a car, getting a job, and Wolverine said he was thinking about putting in for a tour in Thailand, or maybe Okinawa. But Mopar said it was all bullshit, said it was a waste of time to talk about anything beyond the mission at hand, and so the conversation died.

When word finally did come down that the mission was being postponed for twenty-four hours, Marvel was as disappointed as everybody else. He still didn't trust the insertion ship, but he always hated to see a mission delayed, and all this idle talk about going back home was beginning to depress him as much as it seemed to depress Mopar.

Feeling weak and let down and sleepy, Marvel trudged off to the ammo bunker with the others, turned in his Claymores, grenades, and C-4 plastic explosive, then went back to the tent to clean his weapon and grab a little sack time. He slept all afternoon, and that evening joined Mopar on top of the operations bunker. Together they sharpened their knives and watched the cloud cover break and scatter. Using Mopar's whetstone, Marvel put a razor edge on the recondo dagger and nodded sympathetically as Mopar told him about his dull and galling leave. It was very sad and depressing. The poor dude hadn't even seen Sybill Street, much less obtained any of her magic brown pubic curls.

"Ah, the hell with her," said Mopar. "I feel kind of bad about my mother crying at the airport, but I don't care that Sybill wasn't there crying along with her." He spat and lit a cigarette. "Wolverine's right, Marvel. A soldier ought to spend his money on whores, and forget about the whole damn civilian world." He shook his head and looked up at the stars and the clearing night sky. There was no moon in sight, but the floating clouds were like puffs of light smoke riding the wind to the west, and he knew they'd be going in for sure in the morning.

"I know it's a lifer cliché, but lifers aren't so dumb, you know. If the Army wanted me to have a girl-friend, they would've issued me one out of supply, just like Wolverine said. From here on, I'm gonna have a professional attitude toward women. If they ain't pros themselves, I don't want nothing more to do with them."

Marvel nodded absently, wondering how long it would be before Mopar got honest with himself and put in to see a career counselor about re-upping. He was clearly headed in that direction. Marvel changed the subject. "You know, this is the kind of night I like best. The weather's clearing up, and we're going in on a mission in the morning. It's good to have you back, Mopar. It really is."

Mopar sighed. He looked out past the bunker line at the dark and abandoned rice paddies and the foot-hills beyond. He couldn't see as far as the mountains, but he knew the sky was clearing out there, too, and the mission would not be postponed for another day.

"Yeah," he nodded, "everything would be perfect if only that fool Tiger would hurry up and come home. I don't mind leaving without him so much, but I sure hope he's here waiting when we get back."

Marvel pricked his finger for luck, then slid the Recondo dagger back in its scabbard and stood up. "I hope so too, Mopar. I really do." He jumped off the bunker, looked up at the sky, then jogged down to the shithouse to ease the churning in his stomach. Premission shivers, premission jitters, and premission shits—for the first time since joining the Lurps, Marvel had all three at once.

Schultz was a jerk sometimes, but he had a lot of Airborne spirit, and he cared about his teammates. Mopar might hate him—and so might Marvel, for that matter, though he would never let on if he did. And then there was Gonzales, who hated everyone the same, and Wolverine, who tried to be hardnosed all the time, dropping people for push-ups when they fucked up the reaction drills. Schultz liked them all, but he knew they didn't like him—or at least it didn't seem that they did. He was sure about Mopar, but it was hard to say about the rest of them.

Still, Schultz had a lot of Airborne spirit, so when he saw Marvel come back to the team tent without Mopar, he decided it was time to visit the top of the operations bunker, just in case Mopar was still sitting there, moping over that girlfriend of his, who had obviously shot the poor dude down something awful. Schultz was part of the team now, and that made Mopar's morale his own concern. So as soon as he had finished taping down his equipment so that it wouldn't rattle in the field, he went off to cheer up Mopar.

At first he tried to sound reassuring, telling Mopar

that he wasn't the first guy to get shot down by some impatient girlfriend back home. "Why, back in my old company there were a lot of guys who got shot down something awful, Mopar. Worse than whatever it was that happened to you."

Mopar groaned and looked away, hoping Schultz would take the hint and leave, but Schultz ignored the hint and went on unabashed.

"Why, there was this platoon sergeant in Third Platoon—a gruff old Orville Snorkle type of lifer. Been married ten years to some girl he knew in high school. And then one day they drop us some mail out of this resupply ship, and ol' Sarge has got himself a letter with a picture inside, a picture of his old lady sixty-nining with some fat dude! So what's he do, Mopar? What do you think that old lifer did?"

Caught up with the story, Mopar could only shrug and hope Schultz would come to the point without too much off-the-wall bullshit.

"Why, that old lifer passed the picture around the whole company, then stuck it in the band of his helmet cover and wore it there until the rain and wet leaves washed it all away. That's what he did, Mopar. That there was the smartest lifer I ever knew."

Mopar resisted the urge to hop off the bunker and knock Schultz on his ass. Schultz was trying to smooth things over the night before a mission. He was just trying to be friendly, but going about it the wrong way.

"Forget it, Schultz. Go back and study your map."

Schultz smiled. Seeing Mopar's sales resistance start to fade, he decided to make his pitch.

"What you need is a plan, Mopar. A plan. Now, it so happens I've been doing a little research, and I've come up with just the answer: Have you ever heard of a disease called granuloma inguinale?" Although he rarely carried his full aid kit on reconnaissance missions, Schultz had trained as a medic and took great pride in his knowledge of sexually transmitted disease.

"What's that? Something like the clap?"

Schultz shook his head. "Worse, much worse! So much worse that it's better by far for your purposes. It's a VD, but one so rare Army medics don't even look for it. You can smuggle it home with you. Then, after you've done what you have to do, you can get yourself cured, and don't ever fuck her again. It's a perfect plan, Mopar. Now that you got a plan, you can forget about what's-her-name for a while and get your mind clear for walking point."

Mopar was disgusted. He hawked and let fly with a real goober, hoping the wind would carry his missile on to Schultz's boot, but not quite daring to aim it there in the first place. He missed by a foot.

"You know, Schultz," Mopar said after a moment of thoughtful silence, "that's just about the sickest thing I've ever heard. If we weren't going out in the field tomorrow, I think I just might rip your fucking throat out for saying something like that about somebody you don't even know. Sybill Street would never do anything like that cunt in your story, and I'd never do anything like your plan—not even to *your* girlfriend, or *your* sister!"

"I'm sorry, Mopar." Schultz was sincerely apologetic. "I didn't mean any offense—I was just trying to cheer you up."

"Fuck off, Schultz!" growled Mopar. "I've had enough of your sicko crap for tonight. I was thinking about the weather when you came along—I damn sure wasn't wringing my heart over Sybill, or anybody else."

"Sorry, man," said Schultz, "I was only trying to cheer you up."

"Go on back to the tent," said Mopar. "I don't need no cheering up."

# CHAPTER 22

W ELL PAST FIRST LIGHT THE NEXT DAY THE INSER-
tion ship *Bad Moon Rising* flared over the Landing
Zone, and the Lurps of Team Two-Four jumped out
onto the defoliated hillside and began beating their
way uphill for the woodline, a hundred meters to the
west. Wolverine and Marvel had to get their commo
checks on the move, for there was no place to lay dog
here in the open.

Mopar, leading out on point, had to bite his lower
lip to keep from cursing as he ducked and wove and
crashed through the chest-high tangles of dead vegetation that had looked so much less formidable from
the air. The pilot had dropped the team too low on
the hillside, too far from the concealment and security of the wooded high ground that the defoliant

planes had neglected to spray, and now there was nothing to do but bust ass and hope that the closest gook was a ridge or two away and unable to see or hear them struggling up the slope.

Mopar tried to set a fast pace, but the going was much slower and much more difficult than he'd imagined it would be when helping Wolverine plan the mission. He'd moved through defoliated areas before, but never one quite this strewn with hazards. Although all of the life had been sapped out of them, a few of the smaller trees were still standing, and when he brushed against their wilted branches, their leaves crumbled into an abrasive powder that worked under his collar and ground into his skin. When he tried to avoid the standing trees, he was forced to step blind over some of the fallen ones, and this was a good way to turn an ankle or trip and fall into the thorny fronds of dead palm that filled the spaces between the branches. Mopar kept his eyes on the ground ahead and tried not to look up at the woodline too often, because it was far too easy to imagine an NVA machine-gun crew hiding there in the leafy darkness. There was no way to move silently, and with almost every step he winced at the cracking of dry bamboo or the rattle of dead leaves. It seemed to him that he was making much more noise than the four men behind him, and once or twice when he glanced back, he could see Wolverine frowning at the racket that everyone was making. But there was no signal to slow down, and so Mopar kept driving on, straight ahead.

Although still low in the sky, the morning sun was fierce and hot, and there was almost no wind. The camouflage paint was beginning to run on Marvel's face, and there was a smear of blood on Wolverine's right cheek where a dry leaf or a thorn had cut him.

Now more than ever, Mopar resented the Air Force "Ranch Hand" crews—the defoliators—who lived in air-conditioned safety back in the rear and only saw the country they were destroying from the cool comfort of their airplanes. Mopar wondered if they thought they were accomplishing something worthwhile with all their spraying. If they'd ever had to hump a defoliated hillside in the sun, they'd know better. The defoliant planes never killed any enemy soldiers, but they killed everything else they sprayed. Everything else, that is, except the leeches. Even here, on this sere and lifeless hillside, there were leeches everywhere—inching along the ground, clinging to boots, and falling off dead leaves onto the passing Lurps. The damn things were almost indestructible. There were only two ways to kill them. It had to be one by one, with a squirt of bug juice or the end of a burning cigarette. But Mopar had no time for either method now. He was too anxious to get into the woodline; he would worry about the leeches later. They were sure to be even worse in the shade.

But at least there didn't seem to be a machine gun waiting in the trees this time, for if there had been, it would have opened up by now. Mopar drove on without stopping, and the men behind followed up the slope and into the woodline.

Ten meters into the trees, Wolverine called a halt. The men formed up in their security wheel, then sat down carefully, rucksacks touching, to listen for sounds of movement. Marvel got a commo check with the artillery on Culculine without having to switch to a pole antenna, and Wolverine radioed the team's position directly back to Pappy Stagg without having to go through the relay.

Mopar wasn't sure, but he thought he could remember Marvel saying that J. D. had had to run up a pole antenna just to reach the relay team for his first position report in RZ Zulme. Of course, J. D. had gone in on the low ground to the north, and the weather hadn't been this clear, but Mopar couldn't help feeling that somehow J. D.'s commo problems had been—at least in part—his own fault. It seemed like half the time he'd been on J. D.'s team, they had stuck to the high ground, hunting commo. Mopar could remember one time when J. D. took out a dead battery for a spare. It was only human to screw up occasionally, but Mopar was sure that Marvel and Wolverine would never do anything *that* stupid.

After laying dog for more than an hour without hearing anything but normal jungle sounds and some very distant artillery fire, the team moved out to search the saddle of the ridge. There was little undergrowth, and movement was easy, but Mopar took his time, stepping and pausing, then stepping again. He swept his security zone cautiously, for he hadn't been in the field for more than a month, and he was worried that his senses had been dulled by soft living and spending his leave indoors. It was reassuring to see Marvel back there on slack, even if he did look naked, now that he'd given his M-79 grenade launcher to Schultz. Still, Marvel hadn't used the damn thing since that day Farley got killed, and it was better to have him give up the M-79 than the radio.

It didn't really make much difference what sort of weapon he carried, Marvel was the best slackman Mopar had ever worked with. Every time he looked back and saw that goofy smile, Mopar knew he'd be safe, no matter what happened. Mopar was walking point with a silenced Swedish K this time, carrying his CAR-15 tied across his chest, and if anyone but Marvel had been walking his slack, the unfamiliar weapon in his hands would have been most uncomfortable.

Shortly after noon Wolverine called a halt. The team sat down in a tight wheel, and after Marvel and Wolverine made their commo checks and called in their situation reports, it was time for chow. Being the new man on the team and still ignorant of some of Wolverine's rules, Schultz immediately pulled a beef and rice Lurp ration out of his thigh pocket and began to eat it dry. Normally the pointman ate first, but this time Mopar didn't object. He exchanged glances with Marvel, and smiled with smug disapproval, for Schultz was really wolfing it down, blissfully unaware that it was bad form to eat more than a cornflake bar for lunch the first day out. The more a man ate, the more he had to shit, and it was unprofessional to shit more than once on a five-day mission. Not only was it unprofessional, but it was also inconvenient and possibly even dangerous. Turds and toilet paper were sure signs of passage, and anyone sloppy enough to gorge in the field would probably be too careless to bury his scat. Wolverine never made a big thing out of it, but both Farley and J. D. had insisted that everyone on their teams swallow a couple of paregoric pills the night before a mission. Although he was glad to see Schultz acting like a rookie, Mopar hoped that he'd at least had the sense to cork up with paregoric the night before. A turd could compromise everyone.

The sun was still strong, and a few clouds, visible through the breaks in the canopy, rode the wind and moved on smartly. But the leaves dripped, and the air was dank and heavy with the smell of rotting vegetation. When it was Mopar's turn to eat—after Schultz had polished off a whole ration and a can of C-ration peaches—he nibbled on a cornflake bar, washed down a couple of salt tablets with a long swig of water, and tried not to think about all the hamburgers and chocolate milk shakes he'd had on leave. Marvel could talk for hours about hot pickled cabbage, marinated beef, shrimp-fried rice, and pizza with pineapple and ham, but Mopar had simpler tastes. Hamburgers, milk shakes, iced Pepsi-Cola, and french fries drenched in catsup were more his speed. He rarely daydreamed about food, but now he sorely regretted not having made more of a pig of himself while on leave. When Wolverine leaned over with his map and pointed out the finger of land he wanted to check out next, Mopar could only nod half-heartedly. It was hard to clear his imagination of double-meat California burgers and chocolate shakes and fill it with terrain features.

But once he was on his feet again, once he was moving among the trees, alert and cautious, his rucksack digging into his trapezius muscles and the silenced Swedish K smooth and cool in his hands, he no longer regretted all the hamburgers he hadn't eaten and all the milk shakes he hadn't drunk. It was good to be back in the field again, good to be back with Marvel and Wolverine and Gonzales, good even to be out in the field with that pushy jerk Schultz, and Mopar wouldn't have traded this mission for all the California burgers and chocolate milk shakes in the whole civilian world. This was the real world—here and now. This was the big time. Everything else was frivolous civilian luxury, and Mopar had had enough of that on leave.

They spent the rest of that afternoon combing the ridgeline for signs of passage. Gonzales found a rusty ham and lima bean C-ration can and a white plastic spoon that everyone else had missed, but that wasn't much of a find. There probably wasn't a ridge or valley anywhere in Vietnam that didn't have a few old ration cans lying around somewhere, so Wolverine didn't waste radio time calling it in. There were no trails on this ridge—no trails, no paths, no tumble-down thatch and bamboo hootches, no fresh caches, no sleeping positions or dug-in bunkers, no discarded equipment (except the plastic spoon and the C-ration can), and no enemy troops lurking in the shadows. The ridge was just too clean, and that made Wolverine uneasy. He had Mopar move the team to what the map said was the highest ground on the ridgeline, and there they formed their security wheel to rest up for the night's movement.

After sitting silently for an hour and hearing nothing unusual or alarming, Wolverine gave Schultz and Mopar permission to nap. While Mopar slept, Marvel got another commo check with the artillery, studied his map, ate two cornflake bars, and examined his antennas for the fifth time since receiving the mission order three days before. Gonzales wet his finger to test the wind, fished a waterproof cigarette pack out of his thigh pocket, glanced at Wolverine for permission to smoke, then lit up with a survival-pack lighter. This was the first time Wolverine had ever let anyone smoke in the field, and Gonzales was surprised that he'd given permission. Though it was fun to touch the burning cigarette to the leeches on his boot and watch them writhe, smoking always made him thirsty, and he was worried that he'd have to cough or clear his throat during the coming night march. So after a few drags, Gonzales passed the cigarette around. He did not light another.

Wolverine was restless. He stood up and moved a few meters away from the others to piss, then returned and woke Mopar. "Park your rucksack and come with me." He pointed through a break in the trees to the west, where they could see the sun sitting above the next ridge as if waiting for official clearance to set.

"This place is all wrong," Wolverine whispered. "I figure they were supposed to defoliate this ridge here, not the hillside we came in on. But look, the trees are thinner to the west, and that damn valley ought to be at least single-canopy jungle. Instead, it looks like some goddamn African savanna. Let's take a little point recon while the light's still good. I want to find a safe and easy way downhill. If we're lucky, we can get another look at that valley before it gets too dark."

While Wolverine moved on to whisper something in Marvel's ear, Mopar rubbed his eyes and wiggled his arms out of his rucksack straps. He untied his CAR-15, placed it carefully on his rucksack, and stood up with the silenced Swedish K in his hands. Now that Wolverine mentioned it, maybe it was a little bit strange that there was much thicker vegetation on the high ground than there was down in the valley. He knew that there had to be a line of trees along the edges of the little stream that ran north-south through the valley, but the valley had been so full of fog he hadn't been able to see it on the overflight. Maybe people used to live down there before the war—if there ever had been a time before the war. Maybe the valley had once been farmland. Or maybe a fire had burned away the jungle. It hadn't seemed so strange a place on the overflight—what he'd seen of it—and on reflection, it didn't seem so strange now. Mopar had seen a lot of places where the high ground was covered with double- or triple-canopy jungle, but the valleys were grassy and open. Maybe it was a little strange for such a narrow valley to be so open, but then Vietnam was a very strange country, and there was no sense in trying to figure it out.

Mopar followed Wolverine southwest for fifty meters or so, ducking occasional low branches and stepping carefully, for the ground here was slick with mud and fallen leaves, and the slope was steeper than the contour lines on the map had indicated. The sun was still hanging, round and red, above the next ridge, but the ridge was darkly ominous. In spite of himself, Mopar couldn't help thinking about J. D. He was probably still on the ridge. He was probably already part of that ridge by now, his flesh given way to mud and mold and insects, his bones lost in the ferns and creepers, or strewn among the leaves and shadows. Maybe Marvel was right, maybe the ridge was haunted. But if Marvel was right about that, then it followed that all of Asia was probably haunted, because there sure wasn't enough land for everyone to have a proper grave. But since only a gook would worry about such a thing, Mopar put it out of his mind. He eased up next to Wolverine and whispered in his ear.

"What do you think, Sarge? It's kind of slick but the two ridges almost come together south of here, so we can probably avoid crossing any open ground if we move down that way."

Wolverine shook his head. "Too thick," he said. "Too steep. Too tight, and maybe too many gooks. They're out there, don't let this cold ridge here deceive you. They're down there, and if they have any idea we're here too, then they've got this valley bottled up at both ends. We'll have to cross near the widest point and—"

He was just about to say "and cut across on a northwest azimuth" when he heard a sound that made him stop and listen. Someone was playing a bamboo flute. The sound was faint, and if the breeze hadn't shifted in his direction, Wolverine wouldn't have heard it. But he had heard it, and he recognized the sound. He'd had another pointman once, a Vietnamese pointman who had played a bamboo flute, and no matter how faint the sound, hearing it now gave him the chills.

"Listen!" he whispered excitedly. "Do you hear it?"

Mopar closed his eyes for a second and tried to concentrate, but he couldn't hear anything except the birds in the treetops and the gentle rustle of the breeze in the foliage. He cupped one hand behind his ear, but still couldn't hear anything. Finally he shrugged and shook his head.

Wolverine forced himself to smile. He ran his tongue over the gap in his teeth. "A flute," he whispered. "Someone is playing a flute, but I can't get an azimuth on it. Turn your ear into the wind and maybe you'll hear it."

Mopar turned his head this way and that, but still he couldn't hear anything unusual. He wrinkled his nose and took a deep breath, hoping to catch a scent of smoke or food. If only he'd had a nose like Tiger's, maybe he could have picked up on a revealing scent. But he'd spent the first nineteen years of his life trying not to smell things, and the last six months hadn't been enough to bring his nose back to what it would have been if he'd been using it all along.

"Sorry." He shook his head again. He hadn't heard anything unusual, and he hadn't been able to smell anything but the jungle and his own sweat and insect repellent. Still, if Wolverine said he'd heard someone playing a flute, then it was certain that there was a musical gook somewhere out in the valley. Wolverine could be a real lifer sometimes, but he was no fool. He couldn't have stayed alive for three tours in Special Forces if he was the sort who imagined things that weren't really there.

"Let's get back to the radios and have Marvel call in some arty," Mopar suggested in an even lower whisper than before. "We can blow that valley to hell, then sneak across before the smoke clears."

Wolverine shook his head. He wasn't stupid enough to fool around with artillery this early in the mission. He was accustomed to working in places that no friendly artillery could reach, so he had never developed an unhealthy dependence on it. And anyway, if the other side suspected that there was a recon team in their midst, the best way to verify their suspicions would be to start calling in artillery.

"Over there." He nodded in the direction of a brake of fresh bamboo. There were few trees growing in front of it, and the leaves were in sunlight, but all behind was shadow. From that brake there would probably be a good view of the widest part of the valley, and across to the dark side of J. D.'s last ridgeline. But the vegetation between the bamboo and where they now stood was so thick and tangled they'd probably have to move uphill to the crest, then work down from above to reach it. They'd have to move quickly, but all the time they'd have to keep a running mental file on any slick places or fallen branches, because they would probably have to cover the same ground at night. The sun was already beginning to edge down behind the far ridgeline, and Wolverine knew they'd have to hurry if they were to get to the bamboo for a last look before the valley got dark.

"You lead out," he whispered. "That's your job, and you're good at it."

Mopar nodded. He knew he was good, and he knew he could get to the bamboo before the sun went much lower. In five minutes they were peeking through the bamboo leaves with Wolverine's binoculars, and in another fifteen minutes they were back with the rest of the team, going over the proposed route of their coming night march on their maps, briefing the other guys on the vegetation they were likely to encounter and the most likely trouble spots they'd have to sneak past. They hadn't seen any sign of enemy, and Mopar hadn't heard any, but both Mopar and Wolverine were sure that there were enemy soldiers in the valley. Mopar was so sure that he lied and told Marvel that he, too, had heard a bamboo flute.

Marvel smiled placidly and nodded at this news. Night was coming down through the treetops and the wind was rustling the leaves. Marvel was wide awake and ready to go, and the knowledge that the other side was relaxed enough for music stoked his confidence. But he knew they couldn't start down just yet. "Ten o'clock," he whispered in Mopar's ear, using the civilian hour because Mopar had just come off leave. "Pappy called while you were gone and said he was laying on a gunship to circle off station and give us an air relay while we're in the low ground, back us up if we step on anyone. Tell Wolverine the call sign is Cola Seven."

Mopar frowned at Marvel for being a dork. Wolverine was sitting eighteen inches from Marvel's right elbow, and Marvel could just as well tell him himself.

"Go on, tell Wolverine," Marvel whispered again, this time loudly enough for Wolverine to hear what he was saying. "Twenty-two hundred hours. Gunship call sign is 'Cola Seven.' You're the ATL, pass the word on."

Wolverine scowled and put a finger to his lips. They were going to need better noise discipline than this to sneak across that valley and up the next ridge undetected, and there was no time like the present to start cracking down. He took out his pad and scribbled a few words on it, then passed it around for the others to read in the deepening gloom.

"Hand signals only. Make noise tonight and I'll have your ass—if the NVA don't get it first."

Marvel read the note and blushed. Mopar read the note and glowered at Marvel. Schultz knew what the note was probably all about and passed it on to Gonzales unread. Gonzales read the note and nodded his approval. Mopar and Marvel were starting their squabbling early this mission, and he was glad to see Wolverine put a stop to it right away.

As soon as it was dark enough to move by the glowing rot on the jungle floor, Wolverine had Mopar lead the team to the edge of the tree line above the bamboo brake. Here they waited for the gunship to come on-station. It was a long wait, and rather than sit up worrying about the valley crossing or wondering where Tiger was and what he was doing that night, Mopar decided to catch a few more hours of sleep. He slipped out of his rucksack straps, laid his Swedish K on the ground next to him, and placed his CAR-15 across his chest where he could grab it instantly if something happened. He touched Marvel on the shoulder and signed his intention to sack out, then rested his head on his rucksack and closed his eyes. Soon he was asleep, dreaming that he and a skinny North Vietnamese girl with crooked teeth were walking hand in hand down a sunny lane between a thorny hedgerow and a line of tall palm trees, heading, he supposed, for some mud-walled house where they would lie together on a wicker mat, looking up at the ceiling beams and smoking cigarettes. It was a pleasant dream, even if it didn't seem to promise any sex, but it was a dangerous dream at the same time, and as soon as he realized that it was, after all, just a dream, Mopar forced himself to wake up and try to forget he'd had it.

He pulled back the knit cover of his watch and checked the time. There was still more than an hour to wait before they could start moving out. To kill the time, he tore off the corner of a cocoa packet, sloshed in a little water, and made himself some Ashau Valley fudge. After he had licked up the last of the gooey mess, he put the empty packet back in his rucksack pocket. He ate a cornflake bar and doused his boots and pant legs with insect repellent. He could see the sky to the west—dark, starless, and ideal for night movement—but he could barely make out Marvel on his right and Gonzales on his left. The wind was rustling in the bamboo, but the treetops were still, and the air was fetid with rot, sweat, and the smell of wet leaves.

Mopar thought about Tiger—pictured him lying whimpering, wounded, and hungry on some lowland paddy dike. That was too depressing, so he forced himself to think of Sybill Street instead. He tried to picture her going to her mailbox and finding the long, plaintive letter he'd written her on the plane back to Vietnam. Maybe she'd throw it away after reading the first page. Or maybe she'd keep it to show to all her snotty peacecreep friends at school. Mopar was sure that they'd get a big kick out of it, probably be surprised that a Vietnam GI could write at all. He didn't have any idea what she'd really do with the letter when she got it, but he was sure she would never even try to understand why he'd written it in the first place. Mopar didn't understand that himself, but he didn't regret having sent it. Maybe someday he'd see Sybill Street again, but he wasn't going to waste his time writing her anymore.

It was safer to dream about enemy women than it was to think about a cold-hearted peacecreep like Sybill Street. She was smart, but she wasn't smart enough to understand about the war. She didn't understand anything that wasn't part of her comfortable civilian world. So the hell with her! She could throw the letter away, or she could keep it to amuse her friends. But that was about all she could do. She damn sure couldn't help anyone get across a valley full of sleeping gooks and up to J. D.'s last ridgeline. So there was no use in thinking about her anymore.

# CHAPTER 23

**W**OLVERINE HUNKERED DOWN WITH HIS HEADSET
and tried to get Pappy Stagg on the horn, but after
whispering his call sign and waiting for the normal
five count, he heard the relay team come on the air
instead. After checking back with the rear, they
came up with word that the gunship that would be
flying air relay for the valley crossing would arrive
on station in five minutes. Wolverine had always
marveled at how civilian radio stations came in so
much more clearly at night, while military transmissions often seemed to get lost between the pushes.
He knew that Pappy was down in the operations
bunker—as he was every night there was a team in
the field—and he had to smile when the relay team
warned him not to step in any slit trenches on his

crossing. That was Pappy's message—a private joke, passed on to lighten the tension. Once, two years before, Wolverine had jumped into a field latrine full of green shit and diseased scum. He'd done it for the best of reasons—to avoid being spotted by an NVA sentry—and the story had followed him everywhere in Special Forces. Now the story would probably catch up with him in the Lurp platoon, but Wolverine didn't really mind. It wasn't the sort of thing to hurt a man's reputation—at least not in a reconnaissance unit. Hiding in a field latrine was a hardcore thing to do. And since the NVA sentry had walked right past without seeing him, it had also been the smart thing to do.

After terminating the transmission, Wolverine dug his pill kit and a roll of luminous tape out of his shirt pocket. He shook out five tablets of dex, took one, and passed the others around. He got two of them back, but didn't try to guess who hadn't taken them. Next he shook out five codeine pills and passed them around. He got all of these back because no one was bothered by a cough, and it was believed that codeine would dull a man's senses and make him sleepy. He passed around the tape and made sure that every man put two little tabs of it on the back of his hat, so that the men behind him could see to follow in the dark. The tape wouldn't be visible at more than a few meters, so the enemy wasn't likely to spot it, and it was a good thing to have for night movement, when a man always had to worry about losing contact with the rest of the team.

Now they could hear the gunship. It was far away on the other side of the river, circling wide and lazily over the dark hills and cloudy draws along the Laotian border. It could barely be heard over the wind in the trees, but Wolverine and Marvel both got clear commo checks with it off their whip antennas, so it wasn't too far away. Wolverine hoped the pilot had enough sense to fly high and never circle any one ridge too long. It would be a shame to lose the relay halfway across the valley.

It was time to move out at last. Mopar stood up and shrugged to shift the weight of his rucksack. He ran his thumb over the safety switch of his weapon—just to be sure—then glanced back at Marvel, took a step forward, slipped on a muddy patch of leaves, and had to grab a bush to keep from falling *kerbang* on his ass.

Marvel smothered a giggle, but Schultz snickered out loud. Mopar glowered back at them, then shrugged again and moved out. Anybody could slip at night in the jungle, but only a fool would laugh aloud when it happened, or almost happened, to someone on his own team. Besides, if a man had to slip, now was the time to do it.

Digging in with the edge of his boots to minimize the danger of sliding or pitching forward, Mopar led the team around the bamboo and down the slope. The clouds were growing steadily darker, and the wind was blowing enough to sway the branches and cover the sound of their movement, but Mopar was very careful not to shake the leaves. Every time he brushed up against a low sapling branch he paused to let Marvel come up close, so that he could take the branch with his free hand and avoid having it swing back to slap him in the face.

The high bush and trees slowly gave way to ferns and tall grass, and though the slope was leveling out now and footing was easier to find, the farther into the valley the team went, the harder it was to stay in shadow. Mopar looked up at the sky and sniffed the wind. The clouds were thick and dark and low, but there was no scent of rain.

A lizard croaked off to the right, and someone—Schultz or Gonzales, from the sound of it—snapped a dry bamboo stalk underfoot, but Mopar knew the sound wouldn't carry far in the grass, so he drove on without stopping.

Thirty meters into the valley, they paused for Wolverine and Marvel to get commo checks with the gunship, and then moved on again. Crouching to keep his eyes level with the top of the grass, and sighting on a crest of ridgeline that loomed up ahead, Mopar led the team northwest, toward the stream that ran through the center of the valley. It was easy movement. The wind had combed the tall grass free of tangles and clumps so that it parted smoothly and fell back in place after each man had passed. Marvel closed up behind Mopar, and Schultz closed up on Wolverine—so close that he trod on his heel—for the grass was high enough to swallow a man and it was safer to bunch up than to risk separating the team. Schultz was walking tall and the two little tabs on the back of his hat were easy to follow. Gonzales was having a fine time on rear security. He was delighted at how the grass closed up behind him and left no visible wake. It was almost like wading through water.

Suddenly Mopar held up his hand and went down on one knee. He could hear voices to his right front, and he glanced back to see if Marvel had heard them too. Marvel had heard them, but he couldn't understand what was being said. He shrugged and turned up one hand, then looked back at Wolverine. Gonzales and Schultz were hidden in the grass, but Wolverine was still standing. His face was turned toward the sound of the voices, and he appeared to be listening intently.

There were only two men talking, and they were speaking in normal voices—sure sign that they were at ease and unaware that anyone was close enough to hear them. Wolverine took a grenade out of his pouch and straightened the pin, but he didn't think he'd have to use it. The two enemy soldiers were complaining about their new squad leader, bitching about how he'd sent them out here in the grass away from the stream, just because they'd dozed off in the afternoon's political lecture. Wolverine had to smile. Troop indoctrination was the same boring bullshit in every army.

For more than an hour the five Lurps waited, watching for fireflies, resisting the impulse to slap mosquitoes, and listening to the crickets chirp and the frogs croak and *rib-it*. The conversation on their right front continued, but only Wolverine could understand it. The enemy soldiers were complaining about their food. The rice was gritty and full of pebbles. Little Phoung had broken a tooth that very morning, and someone else hadn't been able to shit for five days. This was the sort of thing Wolverine was glad to hear. Soldiers were always bitching about their chow, but it sounded like these two had a legitimate gripe. Wolverine wondered how long it had been since they'd had a good piece of meat or some fresh vegetables that hadn't been picked in the wild.

Finally, while the two soldiers were talking about home, the wind shifted. Wolverine bent back the pin of his grenade and motioned for Mopar to stay down and crawl off to the left—to the southwest, away, he hoped, from the main enemy encampment. Twenty minutes of miserable crawling and many grass cuts later, the team paused while Wolverine sent in a report. When they moved out again, they felt safe enough to walk. But now even Schultz stayed bent over and kept his head almost level with the top of the grass.

Step by step the grass grew shorter and the bushes and trees more numerous. Mopar slowed the pace and began moving from bush to bush to stay in the darkest shadows. Water began to ooze up through the grass roots, and the grass finally gave way to ferns and creepers and broadleaf plants. Mopar motioned for Marvel to come forward and cover him, then darted across an open space into a dark line of low trees and thorny bushes. As soon as he was safely in the shadows, he turned to cover Marvel's crossing. Soon the whole team was in the bush line. Mopar and Wolverine huddled together over a compass, and then the team moved out again.

Ten meters on they halted. They could all hear the stream now, but they could hear no voices, could hear no snoring, and so it seemed that they might be able to cross here, where the water was likely to be deeper and faster than it was to the north. But first Wolverine sent Mopar and Marvel on a point reconnaissance.

They found a brake of thick bamboo to the south, and beyond that a maze of vines and black palm and elephant-ear plants. Marvel spotted three bamboo fish traps among the rocks in the stream, but there didn't seem to be anyone in the area to tend them. To the north, there were many trees with exposed roots, another thicket of vines, ferns, and leaves, and at least ten million leeches. But there were also trees on the far bank, and their boughs overhung the stream and kept it in the darkest of shadows. Marvel wanted to find a small rock and toss it into the water to see if that got any reaction, but Mopar overruled him with a shake of his head. This was, he'd already decided, the best place to cross, and when he and Marvel returned to where the others were waiting, he pointed out the direction to Wolverine, put on his rucksack, and immediately started back to the ford. Five minutes later the whole team was across the stream —wet and leech ridden, but safe enough to set out Claymores and lay dog while the gunship returned to the rear to refuel. When the gunship came back over the horn, they moved out again, and three hours later they were well up the slope of J. D.'s last ridgeline, set up for the rest of the night in the thickest vegetation they could find, with Claymores out in all directions. They had good commo with the relay team on Culculine, and when Marvel slung up a wire, he could talk directly to Pappy Stagg back in the Lurp compound.

Now Wolverine knew who had refused the dex. No sooner were the Claymores in place than Mopar and Gonzales let him know that they wanted to crash for a few hours. Wolverine nodded and let them sleep. He was surprised that they were tired. Crossing the valley had been a piece of cake.

All that next morning Mopar led the team along the slope of the ridge. The five Lurps stayed close together as they moved. Beneath the tall canopy the trees were like pillars in some gloomy hall and the mulch of dead leaves was like a soft carpet on the ground. They crossed washes full of mossy rocks and slipped through tangles of saplings and vines, where the sun shone through and thorns ripped their hands and cheeks. They paused from time to time to rest and listen to the sounds around them, but they always paused in place, staying in order of march and not forming the security wheel. Once Schultz thought he heard someone chopping wood on the crest of the ridgeline, but it was only a woodpecker in a nearby tree.

Once they did hear voices—loud voices, coming from the valley they'd crossed the night before. But even Wolverine couldn't make out what was being said, and by the time he'd taken out his compass, the voices were gone, so he didn't bother to report them back to the rear. It would be a waste of radio time to call in voices without also giving an estimated location, and Wolverine was in no mood to waste radio time. By now, everybody on the relay team and back in the Lurp compound knew that there were gooks in Recon Zone Zulme, and there was no use exciting them with something as vague as voices in the valley.

By midmorning the team was only thirty meters from the high-speed trail. Here, at last, Wolverine signaled for the men to form up in a wheel, with security all around, and put out a couple of Claymores—just in case someone stumbled along uninvited while they were laying dog.

After sitting long enough for each man to eat a ration, and for Marvel and Schultz—who were both coming down rather hard from the dex they'd taken the night before—to catch a short nap, Wolverine sent out a point recon to scout the high-speed trail, a back approach to J. D.'s last position, and—if safe to do so—to the other trail farther on to the north, J. D.'s "upper trail," where he'd heard troops moving whenever there was a lull in the noise of the motorcycles.

Since Mopar and Marvel worked so well together, they were naturally chosen to conduct the point recon. After huddling over a map and compass, they touched up the camouflage paint on their arms and faces, parked their rucksacks, nodded to Wolverine, and slipped away from the others. They returned less than an hour later, stepping out silently from behind the enormous, mossy tree where they said they'd reappear, their chests and thighs muddy from crawling and their face-paint streaked from heavy sweating.

Wolverine listened silently as Mopar gave him a rundown on the situation. The high-speed trail was every bit as wide as J. D. had reported, and although the many weeks of intermittent rain had destroyed any motorcycle tracks, there were a few fresh bootprints in the mud. The other trail, the "upper trail," was little more than an overgrown path through the trees, and it was at least ten meters farther away from the other trail than J. D. had re-

211

ported. Wolverine nodded sagely at this good news. It wasn't surprising that J. D. had reported it as a high-speed trail. Any path with people moving on it would seem like a high-speed trail at night in the jungle. But Wolverine was glad to know that it wouldn't be necessary to have someone standing guard there while he planted the sensing devices. Security would be thin enough anyway.

"What about the site itself?" Wolverine asked. He was whispering more often now, and Mopar couldn't decide whether that meant he was getting slack and lazy, or just being practical. It was a pain in the ass to be always scribbling and passing field notes around. Besides, if one or two of the notes fell out of someone's pocket onto the ground they could compromise the whole team.

"Approaches are easy, right across the trail and up around from behind. There's a lot of ferns at the side of the trail, so we can't be seen."

"The site? What did you find there?"

Mopar shrugged uneasily. "Good concealment. Carpet of dead leaves, a few bushes. That's it. Marvel thinks the place is spooky."

Wolverine didn't much care what Marvel thought about the place. He wanted to know if they'd found the bodies.

Again Mopar shrugged. "Nothing. No brass. No bones. No equipment. No bullet holes or shrapnel scars on the tree trunks. Marvel's right, Sarge. The place *is* spooky. It's like J. D. was never even there."

Wolverine ran his tongue over the gap in his teeth. He dismissed Mopar with a nod, then reached back for his headset and called the radio relay with a situation report. As soon as he finished his report, he gestured for everyone to saddle up and get ready to move out. Maybe they'd find some sign of Two-One farther down the ridgeline. And maybe they wouldn't. But at least it wouldn't be necessary to plant the Black Boxes in the middle of a stinking bone pile, and Wolverine found some consolation in that.

While Marvel moved off a few meters into the bushes behind Wolverine to stand rear security, Mopar, Schultz, and Gonzales put out their Claymores and took up security positions just off the trail. They had rehearsed this at the firing range before the mission, and now they all moved into place without a whisper. Wolverine was left with the Black Boxes and both radios, and as soon as he'd called in his location, he began to dig.

He'd planted sensing devices of all kinds in all sorts of places, but he didn't believe any of them were worth the money they cost or the trouble of putting them in. He'd planted Black Boxes much like these along infiltration routes in Cambodia and next to two-lane dirt roads in Laos. He'd tied automatic cameras to trees on the mountains east of the Ashau. And once he and three Vietnamese Strikers had rigged cleverly camouflaged microphones in the ceiling beams of a temporarily deserted VC command bunker in the Mekong Delta. The microphones hadn't worked, and as far as he knew, neither had any of the other sensing devices. Maybe the automatic cameras would have worked all right, but before anybody could sneak back into the area to recover the film, someone in Higher targeted the place for an Arc Light—a B-52 strike—and reduced the slope where they were hung to a smoking wasteland.

Wolverine didn't have too high an opinion of Electronically Derived Intelligence, but he was an old hand at planting sensing devices. He dug two holes a few feet apart, just behind the thickest trailside foliage, then worked the plastic boxes down in the holes and moved them around until the bubbles in the monovial windows showed that they were level. He arranged the ferns to conceal the two thin antennas, removed the safety wires from the self-destruct mechanisms, then gently covered the boxes with loose soil and dead leaves.

After calling back to the artillery battery on Firebase Culculine to make sure the devices were transmitting properly, he signaled for Marvel and the others to bring in their Claymores and get ready to move out. The artillery was under orders not to fire on the boxes until after the team was extracted from the Recon Zone, but Wolverine didn't completely trust them to remember those orders and abide by them. One of the boxes was supposed to be sensitive to ground vibrations and the other to human sweat and uric acid. If they didn't work any better than most of the other devices Wolverine had planted, some poor gook would have to step on one of the boxes and piss on the other to bring a fire mission down on his head.

But Wolverine wasn't going to take any chances. If the team stuck around to monitor the trail, maybe—just maybe—the boxes would start sending because of *them,* and some trigger-happy hotshot in the Fire Direction Center might forget it was his own people out there and call a world of shit and shrapnel down on them. And besides, it was bad patrol procedure to stay in one place any longer than necessary.

Originally, Wolverine had planned to move back to the south after planting the boxes. There was a bluff overlooking the river in the southwest, and he'd planned to set up there and watch for water traffic. But there was another bluff to the northeast, overlooking the valley, and since J. D. had probably been moving in that direction—headed back toward his insertion LZ for an emergency extraction—it seemed best to continue north along the ridgeline in hopes of finding some sign of Team Two-One. Wolverine radioed his change of plans back to Pappy Stagg on a wire antenna, then brought down the wire, switched over to a whip, and gave Mopar the high sign to lead out.

They had been moving slowly all morning, but now they moved even more carefully. Every four or five paces Mopar paused, and the men behind him stopped to listen for sounds of movement. Every hour or so Wolverine called a halt and had the team move into a tight wheel, to lay dog and listen some more, for they could hear occasional shouted commands down in the valley.

It was impossible to see what was going on, and Wolverine and Marvel could only hear a few of the shouts distinctly enough even to guess at their meaning, but it seemed like the gooks were having a training session of some sort because one of the most persistent commands—the only one the Lurps could hear clearly—was "Faster! Faster!" That wasn't the sort of thing an officer would have to shout if his troops were just resting or going about their daily chores.

So far, it seemed that the troops in the valley had no idea that an enemy reconnaissance team was in the area. Wolverine wanted to keep things that way, at least until the next morning. Then, if the bluff offered both concealment of some kind and a decent view of the valley, it might be time to stir things up a tad, to give those poor hungry troops down there in the grass a little live fire training.

For the rest of that afternoon Wolverine insisted on strict noise discipline. There was no whispering and no crashing through the bush. The team stayed under the thick canopy, where there was little undergrowth. They used hand signals and field pads, and except for an occasional location report, all radio communication was conducted in squelch code rather than voice.

Shortly before dusk, Wolverine called a halt and had the team form up in a security wheel. It was time for the late afternoon hush to descend on the jungle, and he wanted to take advantage of it to listen for the sounds of enemy troops. There were probably some on the ridgeline now, perhaps moving along the high-speed trail toward the river or coming up from the river to cross into the valley. Even though they had heard nothing on the ridgeline all day, the river was wide enough and deep enough for boats, and Wolverine figured the poor dudes in the valley would be looking for a resupply to come in. Even the North Vietnamese Army couldn't function forever on a diet of gritty rice and wild vegetables, and they'd have to cross the ridge to get to the river. The day before, when he and Mopar had been looking down on the valley from the other ridge, the wind was blowing in the treetops, but now the air was still, and Wolverine was confident that he could hear enough to get a compass azimuth on any sound.

The five Lurps sat back and waited. The birds stopped singing, and the mice and snakes and frogs stopped moving in the undergrowth. Soon the only sound was that of water dripping from the top of the canopy to the leaves below. Mopar scratched an insect bite on his cheek while Marvel daydreamed, but Wolverine's brows knitted as he strained to hear. Here and there a lone cicada rubbed its legs together, and before long, ten thousand others joined in and the buzzing became a roar. The buzzing diminished, then welled louder and stopped, much more suddenly than it had begun. Mopar cupped his hand behind his ear, hoping to hear the bamboo flute he'd failed to hear the evening before, but almost immediately the silence was broken by another chorus of insect songs, and then, as if by command, the canopy came alive with the clamorous chirping of bats. Night birds screamed and tittered in the upper branches, and the raucous lizards on the ground and tree trunks barked *fuckyou fuckyou* at the deepening gloom and shadow.

Wolverine tapped Mopar on the shoulder and gestured off to the north. It was time to start looking for some thick bush in which to spend the night. They'd have to be moving out early if they wanted to be on the bluff overlooking the valley when the sun came up.

Halfway through their shared watch that night, Gonzales tapped Mopar on the shoulder and leaned over to whisper in his ear. "Remember J. D. that time in the Aloe Valley?"

Mopar nodded, surprised that Gonzales was breaking his noise discipline just to reminisce. "Yeah, he wasn't like that all the time, but that once was enough. That's why I joined Two-Four. J. D. was nuts."

Gonzales grunted softly and fell back into his customary silence, leaving Mopar to wonder, once again, just what it was that a glum and straightlaced spic like Gonzales could so admire in a rash and colorful soul like J. D.

Mopar had been J. D.'s pointman on six or seven missions, while Gonzales had only been out with him once, that time in the Aloe Valley. And that was one mission Mopar wished he could forget. He'd never been so nervous for so long a time. The mission had been a steady progression from bad to worse. They'd been shot out of their primary insertion LZ and so had to go in on a highly visible but unguarded secondary landing zone, and from the time they hit the ground until they were pulled out under fire two days later, they'd had constant movement around them. The tension had been almost unbearable.

Even before boarding the chopper, Mopar'd felt uneasy about the mission. J. D. had just come back from a Hong Kong R&R, and even though the Aloe Valley was full of tall yellow grass at that time of year, he'd insisted on wearing the new green and black leaf-pattern camouflage suit he'd had custom tailored on Nathan Road. Everybody else was wearing faded tiger stripes because they blended well with any sort of vegetation, particularly tall grass. But J. D. insisted on wearing his tailored cammies, saying they made him look like the baddest African in the French Foreign Legion or some sort of savage Congolese mercenary out to kill himself a few Simbas and rape a few nuns. Thinking back on it now, Mopar could clearly see that J. D. was nuts.

They'd moved off the secondary LZ into the bushes and elephant grass and had immediately found themselves in a maze of paths and trails. They were forced to spend most of their time hiding in the grass, listening to gooks, and watching them pass, sometimes so close Mopar could've reached out and touched them. Heavy rains hit them early the first night, messing up their commo with the relay on Firebase Alexine, but the rain covered the sound of their movement and gave them a chance to start edging toward an extraction LZ while most of the gooks were covered up and trying to sleep. Early the next morning the team set up in a patch of raspy grass and cactus, less than a hundred meters from an LZ and only ten meters from a trail. They'd hardly had a chance to get a couple of Claymores next to the trail when three NVA officers, all of them carrying clipboards and wearing holstered pistols, came strolling casually down the trail in front of them.

Mopar could remember holding his breath and watching the gooks approach in the grass. He remembered wishing they'd hurry on by and not look to their left. But as soon as they drew abreast of the team, J. D. rose up suddenly like an avenging angel of death, a Claymore charging handle in one hand and his CAR-15 jumping and spitting and barking in the other. He was grinning, and Mopar would swear he'd heard him yell, "You snooze, you lose, Chuck!" just before he squeezed the Claymore handle and blew the gooks away.

There was hardly time to strip the bodies of weapons and papers before the whole place was swarming with angry gooks. Bullets cracked and clipped the grass like steel-jacket hornets, and Mopar threw out more than a few rounds of his own, just spraying the flanks. After a wild, running firefight and a quick, dangerous extraction by Pappy Stagg in the Command and Control Ship, the team was out. Mopar was still trying to catch his breath and start coming down from his adrenaline rush when J. D. went back to playing the role. He fired up a Kool, shook his head with philosophical sadness, and apologized to one and all for having caused so much trouble.

"It's just I can't help it, you dig? I mean, I just *got* to ice somebody when I'm looking this good!"

Mopar took a sip of water from his canteen and leaned over to whisper to Gonzales, to ask him if he thought J. D. had done something that dumb out here in RZ Zulme. Gonzales shook his head, but didn't bother to whisper any reply.

Mopar just didn't understand. Maybe J. D. had let himself get carried away, just that one time. But that didn't mean he was dumb, or nuts. That didn't mean he wasn't a hardcore dude and a badass Airborne Ranger. Gonzales knew that J. D. wasn't the least bit afraid of these gook *comunistas*, for he'd seen the proof that morning in the Aloe Valley. J. D. was a bad nigger and a very crafty dude, and Gonzales had a hard time believing he was really dead.

# CHAPTER 24

FROM MIDNIGHT ON, THE WHOLE TEAM WAS UP ON hundred percent alert, sitting in the darkness, invisible even to each other, grenade pouches open and Claymore handles in their laps, as what sounded like the whole North Vietnamese Army moved into the valley from the passes to the northeast of the ridgeline.

Before dawn the team abandoned its night position and began picking its way very slowly through the jungle. Sweating even in the chill mist, his gloved left hand extended in front of him to protect his face from hidden branches and vines, Mopar led the team toward the bluff, and the men behind him followed very closely, guiding on the luminous tape on the back of his Lurp hat and listening to the new arrivals shouting back and forth to their comrades, sounding relaxed and confident, as if they were moving into a bivouac site outside Hanoi instead of a narrow valley within artillery range of Firebase Culculine.

The sun was just peeking over the opposite ridgeline and the valley was still in mist and shadow when Gonzales and Schultz set up rear security in the treeline behind the bluff while Mopar, Marvel, and Wolverine crept forward on hands and knees to part the ferns and get a look at the enemy. The valley was full of soldiers, and even in the faint light and gray morning haze, Mopar could see them stacking crates and rice bags, fetching water from the stream, cleaning weapons, sipping from canteens, stretching, resting, and standing around dug-in fires in idle groups, waiting for breakfast. The enemy resupply had come—not from the river and across the ridge, but overland, through the valleys and draws and passes—and with the resupply had come reinforcements. Mopar had never seen so many gooks bunched up like that before, and the sight was awesome and exciting.

He tapped Wolverine on the arm and reached for the binoculars, but Wolverine pushed his hand away and shook his head, unwilling to risk giving the team's presence away with lens glare. The gooks were close—some of them no more than fifty meters away at the foot of the bluff—and were easy to see without binoculars.

Most of them, at least most of them that Wolverine could see, were in sweaty green uniforms and either brown boonie hats or gray pith helmets. Judging from the way they looked around in the light of daybreak, they'd moved in during the night and were now getting their first look at the valley. Wolverine motioned for Mopar and Marvel to ease back away from the bluff, and then, after one more look, he pulled back with them. After hunkering down over his headset to send in a report, he scribbled on his field pad, tore off the top sheet, and passed it around to the others.

"Shame to pass up a clusterfuck target like this. Let's show them some arty."

Marvel was the first to read the note, but the last to nod his approval of a fire mission. He wanted to be on the other side of the ridgeline when the rounds started coming in, but Wolverine seemed determined to stick around long enough to observe and adjust for effective fire, and Marvel had no choice, finally, but to grin and nod, and go along.

Wolverine glanced at his map, then gestured for Marvel's headset. He took the headset, folded his Lurp hat and sweat towel around it, and called the artillery. He warned the Leg in the Fire Detection Center to whisper his readback, then he sent in his fire mission: "Troops in the open, two rounds white phosphorus on preplotted concentration Bravo Six-Nine, will adjust."

Bravo Six-Nine was a hundred-fifty meters away, in the darkness on the far side of the valley. Wolverine and Marvel crept forward and hugged the ground, waiting for the crash, waiting to adjust to the flash and white smoke of the WP rounds. The whole team waited and listened for the distant guns, listened for the shells to come ripping through the air, but they heard neither, for the shells didn't pass overhead and the guns were too far away. But the gun crews were fast and accurate. Seconds apart, the two shells hit right on the preplot, bursting white and throwing up a gentle-looking rain of burning phosphorus that pattered down like sizzling water all around. The shells had been deceptively quiet, hitting and exploding with more of a *crack* than a *boom*, but the screams and curses that followed them were loud and horrible, and very, very satisfying.

Wolverine was on the horn as soon as he saw the

first flash on target. He adjusted up fifty for the stream bed, lined up another gun or two, then called in HE—high explosive—to sling a little shrapnel around. The gun crews were on their toes today. For more than a week they'd been firing nothing but random harassment and interdiction on unobserved targets. Now they were delighted at the thought of racking up some body count. Even the Leg in the Fire Direction Center began to get into the spirit of things, whispering on the horn and giving Wolverine a perfect readback every time he called in an adjustment.

"Ten confirmed. Thirty-five probable." Wolverine could only guesstimate the body count, but he felt he had to give the gun crews some sort of encouragement, so he gave them some numbers.

The high-explosive rounds began to come in fast and tight—*boom! boom! boom!*—shaking the ground, tossing off storms of shrapnel, blowing dirt, branches, grass, rice sacks, and men into the air. Dirt, debris, and spent shrapnel spattered on the face of the bluff, and Marvel covered his ears so he wouldn't hear anything flying past his head and get spooked. Surviving artillery was pure luck, and he figured a man could be just as lucky with his ears protected.

Impatiently, Mopar crawled forward to peek out through the ferns, but Wolverine grabbed his rucksack and pulled him back, then hunkered down with his headset and brought in a second and a third gun. The valley was swarming now with angry gooks, screaming gooks, shouting gooks, crying gooks, and dying gooks.

The crashes, the explosions, the pandemonium and panic in the valley, were incredible. Once more Mopar crawled forward to peek out through the ferns, and this time Wolverine didn't stop him. All the gooks were down now, except for one wounded man who jumped up and down in the stream, waving the stump of his left arm in the air, screaming and cursing, firing back at the sky with his good hand until he exhausted his magazine and fell back into the bloody, muddy water to die.

The headset in his hand and Marvel tagging behind, Wolverine joined Mopar in the ferns. He peeked out and grinned. He felt like Jehovah Himself, sitting on the bluff, calling down fear, death, and destruction on the poor dudes in the valley. Whispering into his headset, he methodically walked the 155s up one side of the stream and down the other, then blasted the feet of both ridgelines with the smaller 105s. Between explosions he could hear the poor dumb fuckers on the other side going nuts, calling for their mothers, pleading for medics, cursing and shouting and trying to get their shit together. But they didn't have a chance. The rounds kept coming in, falling right and left, up and down, north and south and east and west. Wolverine was having a high old time. Just to ensure a uniform pattern of destruction, he brought the 105s in on the bottom of the bluff, scaring the other Lurps, forcing them to shrink back and make like turtles, cringing against the noise and falling twigs, half-expecting a rain of hot metal.

"Got to keep the whole place jumping!" he whispered to himself as he rose up on his knees to watch three rounds of white phosphorus burst in the tall grass and set it on fire.

"Die, you pissants! Die!" he chuckled, loud enough for Marvel to hear him over the screams and noise in the valley. "You fuck around, you lay around!" he exulted. "You snooze, you lose! Back to hell, you little pissants! I got you now!"

He leaned closer to Marvel and cupped his hand next to his mouth. "I love it!" he half-shouted over the crash of incoming shells. "Artillery is a beautiful thing once you learn to appreciate it!"

Marvel gave him a quick and nervous smile, then ducked and covered his ears as two more rounds hit the foot of the ridge. Wolverine was flipping out. He was bringing up the 105s too close to the team now. Worst of all, he was sticking around to enjoy the show. A shell hit halfway up the slope, jolting the team and bringing a shower of twigs and dirt and broken branches down on them. At the next lull in firing, Marvel peeked out apprehensively from the concealment of the ferns.

Wounded men were everywhere, thrashing and moaning and screaming. Some of them were on their feet, staggering around in confusion; others crawled up on the mounds of loose dirt the shells had thrown up, as if hoping the soft, warm soil would make their pain go away. One man had been flung into the branches of a tree, and his intestines hung down from the branches like shiny yellow hose. But most of the dead were harder to spot than the wounded because they looked like piles of dirty laundry, not men. Marvel wasn't about to count them just so the artillery could have its body count.

The damage was terrible, but not all of the men were dead or seriously wounded. Marvel watched, fascinated, as they began standing up and looking around, policing up their weapons and forming into tight little clusters—men again, but no longer soldiers, as they huddled together instead of spreading out the way they should have.

Wolverine wasn't through with them yet. Another volley came screaming in, and Marvel ducked back, horrified at what he'd seen, angry at Wolverine, and very anxious to get the hell as far away from that valley as he could.

But first he had to take one more look, just to be sure he'd never forget what he'd seen. A shell had just hit in the middle of the stream, and other shells were still coming in, exploding on the slope of the opposite ridge. Yet already men were spreading out in an assault line on the near side of the valley. An officer in a gray pith helmet leaped up on a mound of dirt, ignoring the wounded men clawing at his pant legs, ignoring the shells exploding on all sides, and began waving a little blue flag on a bamboo pole over his head. Marvel could see that he was shouting, but he couldn't hear him. Suddenly the enemy officer pointed the pole right at the bluff where the Lurps were hiding and dipped it once, twice, three times. Marvel and Wolverine ducked into the ferns together, pulled Mopar with them, and scrambled back to the others. Somehow the gooks had spotted them, and now there was no time to lose.

The whole team was up in an instant, falling back into the treeline and getting away from the bluff. Without waiting for them to reply, Wolverine ordered the relay to have Pappy crank up the gunships, then hung his headset on his rucksack strap to free his hands. But Marvel ran with his headset in hand, bouncing against his cheek, as he panted over the horn, begging the artillery, "Keep it coming! Fire for effect on the goddamn slope, but don't bring it down on top of us!"

Mopar was flat bookin'! Vines, bushes, saplings, thorns—they were all in his way, but none of them slowed him down. Marvel's fire mission came crashing in behind them with a jolt, spewing shrapnel and branches and dirt up the slope and into the treeline, but the team kept running. Mopar glanced back to make sure no one was hit, then continued to plunge into the jungle, heading for the tall trees and the dark canopy, his Swedish K on automatic and his CAR-15 loose, banging against his chest. He could hear gooks yelling behind him, and it sounded like a thousand men were swarming up the slope now. Mopar had to get the team to high ground, where they could hide or hold out until the gunships came to save them, and he had to do it fast.

Shells were still falling in the valley, but even over their crashing and booming and wham-bam impact, Gonzales could hear gooks shouting back and forth, hacking through the thick stuff with machetes, beating the bush like tiger hunters. Gonzales didn't want to be hit from the rear, so he tried running sideways to cover his security zone, but he tripped and fell in the thorns, then scrambled to his feet with blood running down his forearm. He looked back once at the team's clear wake of bent branches and broken vines, then, swearing to himself in Spanish, he turned his head to the front just in time to see Schultz lose his footing and go down on the slippery rocks of a wash.

"My fuckin' ankle!" Schultz whispered, trying to keep the fear from his voice. "Twisted it." He grimaced when Gonzales pulled him to his feet, but with Gonzales pushing from behind he managed to grab some vines and pull himself out of the wash. Gonzales heard a rifle bolt crash home off to his left rear. He paused just long enough to whip a grenade out of his pouch and pull the pin, then let fly the handle and tossed the grenade in the direction of the sound. He scrambled madly up the bank and almost knocked Schultz on his face trying to get away.

The grenade went off with a dull boom in the wash. A burst of automatic fire clipped the twigs over his head, but Gonzales was ready. He lobbed another grenade toward the wash, but it hit a branch, bounced off to the side, and went off so close a piece of shrapnel whizzed by his ear.

"Cut it out!" Schultz yelled over his shoulder. "You'll blow us all away!" He stumbled again, and would have gone down if Gonzales hadn't been there to catch him.

"Fuck the ankle, man! Drive on! Airborne! Run!" Gonzales panted as he shoved Schultz ahead of him. A sudden burst of fire clipped the leaves a foot from his head. Gonzales forgot about Schultz, spun around, got off a longer burst of his own, then ducked to the left and got off two more short bursts, firing by instinct, firing blindly, without a target. He didn't stick around to see if he'd hit anything. Changing magazines on the run, he caught up with Schultz and urged him on. They were under the canopy now, but he could hear gooks jabbering and shouting behind them, and more gooks struggling upslope on the left flank. Gonzales tossed another grenade behind him, then pitched one more down the slope between the trees. He now had only three grenades left, and he hoped they'd be enough to slow the *comunistas* down when they got to the high ground.

There was another burst of firing to the rear, but the trees took the rounds and the Lurps just kept on running. The gooks were making noise on purpose now, crashing in the bushes, shouting and firing blindly in hopes of scaring the Lurps into firing back, but the Lurps knew better than to fire now, and continued to run until they made the crest of the ridge. Here, they slowed down and began picking their way cautiously through the trees. The gooks weren't as close as they sounded, but Wolverine couldn't raise the relay on the horn when he called again for gunships, and he was getting a little worried.

Schultz was barely keeping up. He passed the sawed-off grenade launcher and a bandolier of anti-personnel rounds up to Marvel, then tripped over a tree root and would have fallen against Wolverine if Gonzales hadn't grabbed him.

Marvel hung the bandolier across his chest and slung the grenade launcher under his arm where he could swing it up quickly. He touched the heft of his dagger for luck and turned to sweep to the right, where—so far—there had been no sounds of flank movement. He was sweeping his security zone out of force of habit now, out of good training, out of caution and curiosity, out of a fine sense of responsibility, but he didn't expect to see anything. Suddenly his radio headset crackled with static, and the Fire Direction Center came calling across, as clear, relaxed, and loud as an AM hillbilly disc jockey.

"Two-Four, this here is Redleg. Y'all got any more traffic for me? Over . . ."

Marvel winced and twisted around to turn down the volume, but something caught his eye and he froze, his stomach tight, his thumb paralyzed on the safety switch of his rifle. He didn't know what he'd seen, but he knew he'd seen something moving in the gloom to his right. Forgetting about the radio, he forced his thumb to ease his selector switch from safe to full automatic, then, just as the shadows broke around a muzzle flash, he dropped and rolled, and emptied a magazine into the shadows. He swung up the grenade launcher and blasted the bushes, then dropped the M-79, slapped a fresh magazine into his rifle, squeezed off a three-round burst, rolled into Wolverine, and kept firing.

Wolverine was dead. Marvel knew it immediately, knew it even as he got off his last burst with the new magazine and saw Mopar join in with a line of tracers. Wolverine was dead. Marvel could feel the warm, sticky blood and something horrible and pulpy up against his forearm, but he reloaded and kept firing, squeezing off three-round bursts, aiming at darkness and leaves, hoping he was hitting something other than plant life. He popped another anti-personnel round into his grenade launcher and blasted the bushes again, then drained another magazine, reloaded, and got off one more short burst before remembering the drill and forcing himself to look at Wolverine.

Wolverine was lying on his back, his knees drawn up to his stomach and his weapon clutched at port-arms across his chest. His Lurp hat was gone, and the top of his head was dark and misshapen. Marvel gagged and shook a clump of sticky hair off his hands, then crawled closer. He tried to peel Wolverine's fingers away from the trigger guard, but the fingers wouldn't move. Cursing and sobbing, he yanked the rifle's front handguard, but he couldn't break Wolverine's death grip. Marvel knew he had to get the weapon. He had to get the weapon out of the way so he could get to the radio. He had to get the radio, and he had to get to the codebook and mor-phine in Wolverine's breast pocket. But it was no use. He yanked again, but Wolverine would not let go.

"Gonzales!" Mopar shouted. "Time-fuse Clay-more! Downslope—to the right! Quick! Just toss the fucker and yell! We got to bust out!"

"I'm hit," sobbed Schultz as he fired sporadic bursts into the trees to the right. "Goddamn them! Don't they know I'm hit?"

But nobody knew, and nobody cared until Gon-zales darted forward with his time-fuse Claymore and tripped over him on his return. "Up!" Gonzales scrambled to his feet, even though bullets crackled around him and clipped the branches overhead. "Get up!" He grabbed Schultz by the rucksack strap and jerked him to his feet. "Run, man! You can still run!"

Schultz stumbled, got his footing, and staggered after Mopar, his twisted ankle forgotten, the pain in his side sharp and alarming.

"Leave him, Marvel! Break contact! Run!" Gon-zales cried as he sprinted past Wolverine's body. The Claymore would be blowing any second.

Marvel hesitated, wiped a smear of blood from Wolverine's lips, tried to pull the radio out from un-der him, then gave up, lobbed a grenade into the bushes, and shot to his feet just as Gonzales's Claymore boomed and swept through the trees. The backblast almost flattened him, but he managed to keep his feet and run, firing blindly to his right, sobbing angry tears for Wolverine.

He was the only one firing now, and as soon as he realized that he stopped. A strange, unnatural quiet came over the ridge. The birds were silent in the treetops. The artillery was no longer falling in the valley. The gooks were no longer calling to each other and beating the bush. The only sounds were the rustle of vegetation, the heavy breathing and muffled sobs of the fleeing Lurps, and the cries of the wounded on the slope and in the valley.

Mopar slowed to a walk, but this was still too fast for Schultz. He stopped and stood still for a second, then swayed, and collapsed. Cursing softly in Spanish, Gonzales lifted him by the armpits and dragged him on.

"I can walk," Schultz protested feebly. "Please, man, let me go!" He was still sobbing, still breathing in short, shallow gasps because of the pain in his side, but he was determined to walk, determined to get out of RZ Zulme alive. His head was swimming, his mouth was very dry, and his side hurt more with each step, but he didn't want to stay, he didn't want to die.

The trees were tall and straight, and Schultz tried to imagine them zipping past like roadside telephone poles. But instead, they seemed to crowd in around him. There was a flash behind them, and in a panic he broke free from Gonzales and lurched forward, trying to get away from the sudden noise and confusion and fear. The air buzzed and cracked. Everyone was shooting now—everyone everywhere. Schultz didn't know where to run. He slipped and fell and lay there on his stomach, trying to remember whether or not he'd changed magazines. His side hurt something awful. Nothing had ever hurt this awful before. It hurt too much to breathe.

Schultz was tempted to close his eyes, but he knew there were gooks all over the ridge, and he didn't want to die. He wanted to go home. But his side hurt something awful, and he probably would have just stayed there, with his nose in the rotting leaves, if Mopar hadn't come sliding in next to him with his arms full of weapons.

"Take one!" Mopar threw an M-16 down next to Schultz and made him take it in hand. "Now listen up, you cocksucker! Gonzales is dead. There's only three of us now, so grab onto my rucksack and don't let go. Now, ready—all right now— go!"

The two of them came up together, Mopar in the lead and Schultz hanging on to his rucksack, crying and gasping, swearing that he'd kill Mopar when they got back to the compound. "I'm hit, Mopar! I'll kill you, Mopar!" he babbled, but Mopar paid no attention.

Somehow Marvel had reeled a Claymore out next to Gonzales's body. As soon as Mopar and Schultz ran past, he squeezed the charging handle and was out of the bushes, running, before the dirt and twigs could reach him. The enemy was getting altogether too close. Marvel wondered what in the hell was taking the gunships so long. They should have been coming on station by now. He cursed the gunships, he cursed the relay team, and he cursed Pappy Stagg. But then he remembered Wolverine lying dead on his radio, and he cursed himself for not having been able to recover it. All of the firing had stopped when the Claymore blew, but now Marvel had a new and terrible worry. If the gooks had Wolverine's radio and codebook, maybe they could get control of the gunships.

Marvel had to do something. He paused and slung his rucksack around to the front long enough to change to the command net, then slung it back and worked his free arm back into the strap. Whispering frantically into the headset, he tried to get the gunships on the line, tried to get Pappy Stagg, but he couldn't even raise the relay team on Firebase Culculine. He hooked the headset onto his rucksack strap and stepped up his pace to close in on Mopar and Schultz. At least he wouldn't have to worry about having his own helicopters called in on him: If he couldn't raise the relay, then neither could the gooks. He touched the haft of his dagger and tried to put Wolverine and Gonzales out of his mind.

It wasn't hard to catch up with Mopar and Schultz. Schultz was just about done. He clung to Mopar's rucksack, trying to move his own feet, but stumbling and barely managing to keep from going down and pulling Mopar with him. The whole side of his tiger suit was dark and sticky with blood, and he couldn't hold up his head. Marvel could hear Mopar panting and cursing with soft venom as he tried to keep Schultz from giving up.

"Why don't you die, motherfucker? You sumpthin' better than Gonzales and Wolverine, asshole? Candyass! I ain't dying for you, and neither is Marvel. Keep up, candyass! Keep up, or I'll leave you, and I won't even shoot you first! Sumpthin' better'n Wolverine and Gonzales? Shit! Drive on, candyass! Hold on and run, motherfucker!"

Schultz tried to keep up. He hated Mopar more than he'd ever hated anyone, and he was determined to show him he could make it. He was trying to keep up, trying not to drag the team down, but his side hurt worse than something awful now, and his ankle wouldn't support him. It was just so goddamn unfair! Everything was just so damn unfair! Didn't they know that he was hit? Schultz was sure he could hear the gooks pulsing in the trees, pulsing like some sort of fever music. He let go of Mopar's rucksack, stumbled a few drunken steps to the side, and sank down on his knees. His cheeks bulged, and he swallowed hard, then toppled sideway, and was still.

Mopar dragged his body into the deep bushes where the gooks wouldn't find it right off. Hurriedly, he stripped Schultz of his dogtags, his ammo, grenades, map, and canteens. There was no way he and Marvel could carry any more weapons, so he broke open the two that Schultz had been carrying, stuffed the bolts in his rucksack, and left the rest of them with the body. There wasn't time to go through Schultz's pockets for morphine, or to unlace the strobe light from his web gear suspender. Since the gooks already had Wolverine's codebook, that no longer made any difference.

The gooks weren't firing or tossing grenades anymore, but they were still out there, still making noise, and still getting closer. They were making noise on purpose now, trying to scare whoever was left into firing and giving his position away, but neither Mopar nor Marvel was dumb enough to take the bait. If the gooks were smart they would have been silent, they would have been listening, and moving slowly and cautiously. But they were angry. They had the scent of blood and revenge in their noses, and they didn't think that the racket they were making in the bush would work to their prey's advantage.

Mopar crawled out of the bushes and sat on his haunches next to Marvel. He was breathing hard, too scared to keep a catch out of his whisper. "Wh-what now, Marvel? If . . . if it comes to that, I won't leave you, man. I promise—if it comes to that, I'll stay. Wh-what do you think? We getting any gunships?"

Marvel frowned and held up his hand. While Mopar was hiding Schultz, he'd slung up a wire antenna, and now the gooks were making so much noise he figured it was safe to transmit. He could hear Pappy Stagg and the relay team, and even the drawling loudmouth from the Fire Direction Center, cutting in on each other, trying to find out if anybody knew what was going on in Recon Zone Zulme. The gooks were coming closer now, making even more noise then before, so Marvel broke in with a last report.

"This is Tacky Blinker Two-Four. Everybody's dead but me and the pointman." Suddenly Marvel couldn't remember the simplest CAR code, but it didn't matter anymore. "About to commence E&E. Be advised: This net is compromised. Say again: This net is compromised—they even got an SOI. This is it. We're going off the air to commence E&E." Marvel realized he was talking too much, talking too loudly. "Wish us luck, and get them gunships up. This is Two-Four. Out."

He turned off his radio, yanked out the wire antenna and let it hang. He knew he'd been too dramatic with that final "Two-Four. Out," but the chances were he wouldn't live long enough for the embarrassment to set in. The gooks were firing again, fifty meters or so to the rear. Marvel hoped they'd shoot each other, but he knew there were more of them on the slope and still more in the valley. It was their country, they were everywhere. He forced himself to smile his sappiest smile.

"Well, Mopar," he whispered, "You're a good pointman. Can you get us out of this mess?"

Mopar swallowed hard and unsnapped the flaps of his grenade pouch. "No sweat, Marvel. The two of us can slip past anybody." He sighed and straightened a grenade pin. This was no time for sentimental, defeatist, peacecreep bullshit and Mopar knew it. "We'll make it, Marvel," he whispered, trying his Airborne best to sound like he believed what he was saying. "It'll be a piece of cake!" There was nothing to it but to do it, to give it their all now, just for the cameras—just in case . . .

The gooks kept moving in.

# CHAPTER 25

TIGER THE LURP DOG CHOSE A DRIZZLY EVENING
when there were no teams out for his return to the
compound. He paused to sign in with a jet of urine
against the compound gate, then trotted down the
muddy drive and up to the operations bunker, his
left ear hanging in shreds, his right eye swollen
shut, his ribs showing, and his coat patchy with
mange and mud and grease. Any other dog would
have looked terrible, but not Tiger. He looked splendid and proud. His head was high and his tail waved
behind him like a flag.

Within minutes, almost the whole platoon had
crowded into the bunker to celebrate his return.
They slapped each other's hands and laughed and
carried on, trying to pat him or scratch his good ear,

but Tiger just moved on from one man to the next, sniffing their boots, wagging his tail, and after he had exchanged greetings with everyone he crawled off under the commo desk to get away from all the hands.

"Run get a chili Lurp ration," someone suggested. "He looks hungry, and that's his favorite."

Sure enough, someone immediately ran off for a ration. But even when it was mixed with hot water and put in front of his nose, Tiger wasn't interested. He far preferred beef stew rations or beef and rice, and since he could still taste his last meal of carrion rat, he turned up his nose at the bland packet of freeze-dried chili.

Even without Marvel Kim around to spell it out for them, everyone agreed that it would be lucky to pat a sneaky little dude like Tiger. It was also agreed that no real Lurp would let a little mange, a little mud, or a little grease stay his hand. But no matter how they tried to coax him, Tiger wouldn't come out from under the commo desk. There were just too many boots out there, too many hands, and he felt much more comfortable and much safer looking out from behind Pappy Stagg's protective knees.

Sergeant Johnson muttered something glum about Tiger missing his main man, Mopar. The lieutenant didn't want to hear such talk. He decided to lighten the mood, and at the same time to let the troops know he was still one of the guys, even though the major didn't let him go out in the field with the teams anymore.

"Naw, bullshit! He's just clamming up on us, that's all." He shook his head in admiration. "That's one crafty little mutt, that Tiger the Lurp Dog. His agent's probably got the book and movie rights all tied up, and he's just keeping quiet, hoping we'll pay to see his adventures. Smart little fucker, ain't he? Hardcore little fucker, too. He didn't let a few sores and a swollen eye or a shredded ear slow him down. Foul little dude. He's the only real Lurp in this whole platoon!"

Tiger didn't let this extravagant praise go to his head. He stayed under the commo desk, calmly licking the sores on his legs and only occasionally lifting his nose to check for a smell he might have missed. Finally Pappy Stagg got fed up with the grabass and bullshit and chased everyone but the lieutenant out of the bunker, then talked Tiger out from under the commo desk and lifted him up onto his lap for a look at his legs and eye and shredded ear. There wasn't anything he could do about the mange—he'd have to consult the vet down at the Scout Dog platoon about that—but the sores didn't look too bad, and on close examination, neither did the swollen eye or the shredded ear.

Pappy Stagg was a good medic, and Tiger didn't resist or try to get away, even when the old lifer rubbed medicinal cream into his sores and dabbed around his eye with a cotton swab dipped in peroxide. Tiger was a tough little mutt, but he was very tired, and as soon as Pappy Stagg was done with him, he jumped down and scurried back under the commo desk. After pacing a tight circle to make sure he'd have enough space to turn around and stretch out if the mood struck him, he sank down, rested his head on his forepaws, and went to sleep, leaving Pappy Stagg and the lieutenant more or less alone in the bunker for the first time since Two-Four went under out in RZ Zulme.

Lieutenant Longman didn't really count for much in the Lurp platoon. Before the Two Shop major put a stop to his filling in on short teams, he'd proved himself to be a skilled soldier who enjoyed carrying the second radio and never showed any great desire to interfere with the team leaders. Back in the rear, he knew when to turn away blind. The troops considered him harmless, and most of them actually liked him. He kept a reasonably correct distance from the Spec Fours, and he tried to listen to his NCOs. But he was still a commissioned officer, still the platoon leader, and from time to time he had to assert himself, just to keep in practice. He'd been in a jolly mood with all the men gathered to welcome Tiger home, but now the bunker was almost deserted; Tiger was curled up asleep under the commo desk, and Pappy Stagg was once again back to his hopeless radio watch, listening to Two-Four's compromised push, unwilling to give up on Mopar and Marvel. If anything, Tiger's return had encouraged him, and the lieutenant was worried that the old bird was losing his professional objectivity.

"Why don't you turn that damn thing off, Top?" he said. "Go get some sleep. You look like death warmed over."

Pappy Stagg turned away from the bank of radios and cupped a hand behind his ear. "Speak up a little, would you sir? I can't hear you over the rushing noise of this radio."

Lieutenant Longman frowned. He stepped over to the commo desk and killed the radio. "Go on, Top. Why don't you go get some sack time? For the last eight days you've been up in a spotter plane or helicopter every day, and then sitting down here at the commo desk all night, listening to that compromised push. Face it, Top. You're wasting your time. Even if one of them's still alive, even if both of them's still alive—they either got their radio turned off, or else the battery's dead by now. We don't have any teams out, so you can relax and take a night off. Roust a couple of the Spec Fours to come down for radio watch, if it makes you feel any better. Or I can stay down here all night, if you want to go crash. I still got to write all those next-of-kin letters, so I can listen for you, and if we get any traffic on that compromised push, I'll let you know."

Lieutenant Longman was a little worried about Pappy Stagg. He really did look terrible. The lines on his forehead were deeper and more numerous than they'd been a week or so before, and his eyes were tired and bloodshot. The wrinkles around his eyes looked deeper too, and he was smoking too much. He was still a strong old bird, but now he was beginning to look more old than strong.

"Go on, Top. Go on down to the tent and sack out. You need the sleep." It was a suggestion, not an order, and to show that he wasn't trying to be a prick, the lieutenant reached over and turned the radio back on, but kept the volume down so low that only Tiger could hear it, and Tiger was too busy dreaming about dead rats and wounded birds to listen with his good ear.

Pappy Stagg put down his Nick Carter spy novel and pushed his chair away from the commo desk. Rubbing his big hawk nose and the weary place between his eyes, he looked the lieutenant up and down, then requested permission to speak off the record, man to man and soldier to soldier, with no rank involved.

Lieutenant Longman nodded, and as Tiger stirred in his sleep, Pappy Stagg stood up to take unfair advantage of his height.

"All right, sir," he began with normal military courtesy, to cover his ass if the lieutenant took things the wrong way. "Now forgive me if I get to talking out of hand, but I want you to listen up, and listen up good, sir. I'm forty-seven years old, and I've been in this man's army damn near thirty years. I'm a master sergeant, E-8, and I been up and down the ladder twice—earned my stripes, lost 'em, and earned 'em again the honest way each time, through hard work and kicking ass."

The lieutenant nodded again, for he'd heard all this before, and of course it was true. He wasn't too sure what Pappy had been busted for—that was many years in the past—but if anyone in the Army had come by his stripes honestly, it was Pappy Stagg.

"Now, I don't mean no offense, sir, but I been on jump status for twenty-five years, and I probably got more time in the prop-blast of a C-119 than half the officers in this brigade got in the chowline. I've faced planes, I've faced tanks, and I've faced suicide attacks. And let me tell you, sir, I shit my pants the same for them all. I've been in three and a half wars and a hundred deadly hassles in places you ain't never heard of, sir. I've got the scars to prove it."

Lieutenant Longman nodded once more. He'd seen Pappy without his shirt, and the zipper-like scars on his belly were even more impressive than his huge and faded Airborne tatoo.

"Talk about shrapnel? Hell, sir, I've got enough metal in me to where I don't trust my own compass. I've been shot, and stabbed, and hit over the head with chairs and bottles and high-heeled shoes. I've been froze in blizzards, broiled in the sun, steamed in jungles worse than what they got here, and damn near crippled in a shot-down helicopter or two."

Pappy paused to make sure the lieutenant was taking it all in without getting his feathers ruffled.

"I'm always horny, usually hungry, and drunk more often than I should be. I've had dysentery three times, scurvy once, blood fever twice, and at least eight doses of the clap. And I don't need no young lieutenant looking out for my goddamn health, telling me when I need some sleep! Have I made myself clear . . . sir?"

Lieutenant Longman shrugged. "All right, Top. It's up to you." There wasn't much else he could say without puffing up and acting on his military dignity, and he knew that his dignity wouldn't be worth much without Pappy Stagg's respect—at least not in the Lurp platoon, it wouldn't be. "You and Tiger can hold down the fort all night if you want. I'm gonna try and scare me up some late chow."

The lieutenant started for the bunker exit. He had one foot on the sandbagged ramp when he paused and turned around to get in the last word—as was only proper, seeing as how he was an officer, and a gentleman to boot.

"Two-Two's going out in the morning, Top. This is the last night we can waste a radio monitoring a compromised frequency. Tomorrow things will be back to normal, back to the proper codebook, Top. You stay here if you insist, but I'm sending a runner down in case you want to catch a nap. We're gonna need you on your toes in the morning."

Lieutenant Longman sighed and shook his head. He looked down at Tiger, sleeping peacefully, his head now resting on one of Pappy's boots. "It ain't easy sometimes, but you gotta remember, you gotta be hard. People die, but life goes on, Top. Hell, you oughta know that better than anyone."

Pappy Stagg grunted something along the lines of "Goodnight, sir." Tiger whined softly in his sleep. And the lieutenant left the operations bunker, satisfied that he'd made his point without pissing the old bird off any more than necessary. There was no doubt about it, Pappy Stagg was getting a touch grouchy in his old age.

With the lieutenant gone, and Tiger sleeping under the commo desk, the operations bunker seemed almost normal again. Pappy eased his foot out from under Tiger's head and walked across the bunker to the coffee urn. As he waited for the coffee to heat up, he tried to figure out just what was missing from the bunker, what it needed to seem like a home. It needed a couple of sharp Spec Fours, nosing around the more glamorous field manuals—Ranger, Special Forces Operations, hand-to-hand combat—all full of beatnik bravado, but curious about the profession, ready to start getting serious, ready to take a little grownup pride in becoming soldiers. And it needed some young lifers, a couple of staff sergeants maybe, still full of piss and vinegar and Airborne spirit, still young enough and dumb enough to believe a man could make it on his own. An operations bunker just wasn't a home without a few young lifers hanging around, trying to get the role down to where it was first or second nature.

Stretched out beneath the commo desk, Tiger's sleep was momentarily broken by a crackle of static in one of the speakers above him. The sound was very faint, for the volume was still turned low, but Tiger was alert. His good ear perked and his shredded ear twitched and tried to stand. He sniffed the bunker air, then opened his good eye and lifted his head to look around. Pappy Stagg had taken his coffee cup to the other side of the bunker and was standing with his back turned as he thumbed through the mission files. The bunker seemed very lonely.

The next time he heard the speaker crack and hiss, Tiger didn't even bother to open his one good eye. He trusted his nose more than he trusted his sight or his hearing, and his nose gave him no reason to wake. Still sleeping, he sniffed and squirmed. When Mopar called to him from inside the speaker, called to him from behind the static, he thumped the sandbags with his tail and slept on, dreaming of old friends, familiar scents, and soft voices in the night. It was a short but pleasant dream, and when the speaker fell silent again, Tiger the Lurp Dog woke with a stretch and a yawn, and went off through the drizzle to check out the team tents and sit on the berm looking out over the chopper pad, waiting for Mopar, his main man, waiting for his team to return from wherever it was they had gone. It promised to be a very long wait, and finally, at dawn, when the rains returned in earnest, sweeping the compound and sending rivulets of water streaming down the berm, Tiger rose and trotted off to the bunker between the first and second team tents, crawled inside, and went to sleep with his nose next to one of Mopar's socks and his tail resting, fat and still and lazy, on what was left of poor J. D.'s pearl gray pickpocket hat.

## ABOUT THE AUTHOR

From late 1967 through 1969, Kenn Miller served in Vietnam, where he did "just about every job on a Lurp team, from team leader on down." He is a native of Ann Arbor, Michigan, and he currently resides in Taiwan, where he is an English teacher. TIGER THE LURP DOG is his first book.